READY TO TAKE FLIGHT?

Join the fight against the Raptors and
send your own dragons into battle!
Play now by visiting

scholastic.com/riseofthedragons

RISE OF THE

DRAGONS

Book 1

ANGIE SAGE

- SCHOLASTIC INC. -

ISBN 978-1-338-35413-3

10 9 8 7 6 5 4 3 2 1   19 20 21 22 23

Book design by Abby Dening

First edition, March 2019

Printed in China   62

Scholastic US: 557 Broadway · New York, NY 10012
Scholastic Canada: 604 King Street West · Toronto, ON M5V 1E1
Scholastic New Zealand Limited: Private Bag 94407 · Greenmount, Manukau 2141
Scholastic UK Ltd.: Euston House · 24 Eversholt Street · London NW1 1DB

1

Sirin Sharma

Night was falling on London. Thick gray clouds were tumbling in from the east, bringing with them the smell of the distant sea. At the top of the oldest, scruffiest tower block south of the river, Sirin Sharma switched on the light in the tiny apartment that she shared with her mother and their cat, Sammi.

There was a plaintive mew at her feet, and Sirin scooped up the small black-and-white cat. "Hey, Sammi," she whispered as she peered out into the gathering darkness. Sirin held Sammi close as she looked down at the long lines of roofs far below, snaking away into the misty gloom. She saw streetlights glimmering a dull yellow, and pairs of car lights moving slowly, winking like little demon eyes. She looked up at the sky and watched the drizzle coming down, and, pressing her nose against the cold glass, she squinted and thought she could pick out the distant dark line of the sea.

A sudden wild gust of wind rattled the window, and Sammi twisted out of Sirin's grasp and jumped down. Sirin pulled the thin curtains closed and turned back to reality, to the chilly little room where her mother was sitting on the scruffy sofa, wrapped in a quilt on which Sammi was now making herself comfortable.

"What would you like to do, sweetheart?" her mother asked. The unspoken *on our last evening together* hung in the air, heavy but unsaid.

Sirin had already decided. "Tell me about dragons," she said at once. "And our stone."

Her mother smiled. "I thought you might say that." Her hand—delicate and fine like the foot of a bird, so thin that Sirin could see every bone—reached into her pocket, and she drew out a small soft leather pouch, from which she took a beautiful round stone encircled by a thick silver band with a loop on it. The blue-green metallic sheen on the stone seemed to move like oil on water. "Here you are, sweetheart," her mother said, and placed it in Sirin's outstretched palm.

Sirin closed her fingers around the stone. She loved how it grew hot in her hand. She imagined she could still feel the heat of ancient dragon fire, and she was always surprised by its weight, which was, her mother said, heavier than gold—"because this is what happens to any stone caught in a plume of dragon fire."

Together Sirin and Sammi snuggled under the quilt and settled down to listen to their dragon story.

"Once there were dragons." Her mother spoke the familiar words and then stopped to take a breath. Sirin heard the wheeze deep in her mother's lungs and felt a chill of dread settle in her stomach. She squeezed the dragonstone harder and tried to concentrate on her mother's voice as she continued: "A long, long time ago, so long ago that most people have forgotten, humans and dragons lived in harmony together. There were forest dragons, sea dragons, mountain dragons, and dragons from the great rolling plains, and as time went on, even city dragons."

Her mother began to cough. Sirin ran to find a glass of water, and as the coughing subsided, her mother said weakly, "You tell me the next part, sweetheart."

And so Sirin wriggled back beneath the quilt, pulled Sammi onto her lap, and tried to continue the story she loved and knew so well. "The dragons were wise and ancient creatures who had great patience with us young and quarrelsome humans. Some people were lucky enough to become so close to a dragon that they stayed together for life. They even understood each other's thoughts. When this happened, people said they were 'Locked.'" Sirin stopped and looked at her mother. "Wouldn't that be amazing, to Lock with a dragon?"

Her mother looked at Sirin's dark green eyes, shining with excitement. She ruffled her daughter's short brown curls and said, "It would indeed. But I'm not sure Sammi would like it. Cats and dragons do not get along."

As if to confirm this, Sammi jumped off the quilt and stalked out of the room, her tail held high in disdain.

Now that she was eleven, Sirin understood that, however much she wished for it, she would never see a dragon. Dragons were long gone and were not coming back. Indeed, most people thought they had never existed at all. Sirin smiled wistfully. "Well, Sammi won't ever need to worry about that," she said.

"I don't suppose she will," her mother agreed. "Now, where were we?"

And so Sirin's mother took up the story once again. And as night descended and the room grew dark, leaving only a pool of light around the sofa, Sirin allowed herself to forget her worries and be transported to a place where dragons and humans lived as equals, side by side. She listened to her mother's familiar tale of the beautiful world that the dragons and humans built together and then, more sadly, how it fell apart. She heard how a group of dragons and humans became drunk on power and began to prey on others. How the dragons called themselves Raptors and, encouraged by their human Locks, developed a taste for human flesh, and the world became a fearful place with danger in the skies.

Sirin snuggled close to her mother and watched the shifting colors of the dragonstone glinting in the lamplight. "Do you think it was Raptor fire that made this?" she whispered.

"Who knows?" said her mother. "I like to think it belonged to one of our ancestors caught up in a dragon battle, and that they survived to tell the tale. There were a lot of battles in the last dragon days."

"The last dragon days . . ." Sirin murmured sleepily.

In a soft, low voice, Sirin's mother finished the story. "In the last dragon days, they say a silver dragon came through the clouds: bright as sunlight upon water, fast as quicksilver. And the Silver saved us. It led the Raptors up into the sky and took them away forever. They even say a Silver will come again someday . . ."

As if pleased the dragons had gone, Sammi reappeared. The little cat jumped up and snuggled into the quilt, purring softly. Sirin's mother thought of the hospital, so bright, so loud and full—and yet so empty—waiting to take her in just a few hours' time, and she knew there was something she must say. "Sirin, you know that while I'm in the hospital, you and Sammi are going to stay with Ellie, don't you?"

Sirin nodded. She had been looking forward to staying with her friend Ellie, but now, as the time drew near, she didn't want to go anymore. She just wanted to be with Mum.

Mum coughed and continued. "And I know you'll have a lovely time. But, sweetheart, I just want to say that whatever happens, I will always be with you. You know that, don't you? Because mums are like dragons. They are forever."

Not daring to speak, Sirin nodded.

They sat together quietly, listening to the distant sounds of the traffic in the streets far below, and at last Sirin fell asleep. Her mother looked down at Sirin, curled under the quilt, her eyes fluttering beneath their lids as she dreamed, and she decided to let her daughter stay sleeping where she lay, held close and quiet beside her.

They would spend their last night together, secure and warm in a circle of soft lamplight—for who knew what the future would bring?

2

A Flight of Raptors

A world away, at the top of Fortress Lennix, high on a mountain, a tall, thin figure in close-fitting tunic and trousers, a bright blue sash around her waist and her long cloak flapping around her heels, strode across a wide and windswept arena. Heading toward a small group of dragons—each and every one of them a fearsome Raptor—D'Mara Lennix, clan chief, watched the final rays of the setting sun send a rainbow of color glinting from the mix of Green, Red, Yellow, and Blue dragons.

D'Mara watched with approval as the sun disappeared behind the vast bulk of Mount Lennix, which reared up behind the fortress, and a deep shadow fell across the dragons. This was the First Flight, the elite force of Fortress Lennix, and D'Mara disliked seeing sunlight on their scales, making them sparkle like jewels. For D'Mara Lennix, dragons were serious creatures of power and darkness. She glanced up at the mountain peaks surrounding the fortress and noted with satisfaction the stillness of the air and the clear sky. It was a good night for a raid.

D'Mara's pointy, steel-tipped boots clicked their way rapidly across the landing yard, which occupied the entire top of Fortress Lennix: a massive square edifice of granite with its roots sunk into the bedrock of the mountain pass many hundreds of feet below. It was here, in a warren of chambers connected by a maze of passageways, that the dragons of Fortress Lennix lived.

Many had been hatched and raised at Fortress Lennix from eggs raided from their once tranquil homelands, their peaceful dragon natures warped by their Raptor upbringing. Others, in search of power and excitement, had defected from their tribes, and some of them had ancestors who had Locked with members of the Lennix family way back in the mists of time.

Like any band of ambitious, aggressive creatures living in close proximity, factions had emerged among the Raptors. Until recently these had been finely balanced and of no threat to the Lennixes themselves, but lately D'Mara had become aware of a group of younger and more impatient Raptors who were growing dangerously restless. Now, for the very first time, she felt a flicker of anxiety as she walked across the wide, windswept courtyard toward the raiding party, uncomfortably aware that a young Red named Valkea, surrounded by her cronies, was watching her every step.

Among the First Flight was one human: Edward Lennix, D'Mara's husband, and leader of the raid that night. Edward—a foxy-looking man, square-set with slightly bandy legs, wearing his dragon riding leathers and a red sash—watched D'Mara's progress with impatience, tapping his spurred raiding boots impatiently upon the cobbles, anxious to be off. "I don't see what she's fussing about, Decimus," he remarked to the powerful, battle-scarred Red who was his Lock. "Wish she'd let us get going. I reckon we're in for a good night's hunting."

Decimus looked down at the man he knew better than any creature—dragon or human. Like all dragons, Decimus spoke his species' own language, a lilting melody of sounds known as dragon-song, but Edward had never gotten the hang of it. The only words Edward could understand were *kill*, *fire*, and—oddly—*kitten*. And so, in the way that only Locks could, Decimus sent a message straight into Edward's mind: *All in good time, Lennix. Savor the moment. Those Greens are worth the wait.* And then he sent a blast of hot, pig-scented breath down onto Edward's bristly mustache.

"You're right, as ever," Edward agreed. "Permission to come aboard?" It was exceedingly bad form to climb onto a dragon—even one's Lock—without asking first, and Edward Lennix was a stickler for good form.

Permission granted, Lennix was his answer, and Edward swung himself up into the dip at the base of the dragon's neck. He leaned back and settled himself against Decimus's broad shoulder blades, pleased that by the time D'Mara reached him, he was no longer at his usual height disadvantage.

"Good evening, D'Mara," he said, raising his left arm from the elbow in a Lennix salute. In deference to family, he did not clench his fist but kept his palm open outward.

"Good evening, Edward. Good evening, Decimus," D'Mara replied, returning the salute. Prudently, she stopped at a safe distance from Decimus, who, unlike Edward, was not afraid of her. Decimus enjoyed occasionally stepping on D'Mara's foot accidentally-on-purpose in retaliation for the insults D'Mara regularly hurled at his Lock.

D'Mara surveyed the impressive group of dragons lined up behind Edward and Decimus. Impatient to take flight, they were striking sparks off the cobbles with their talons, their hot breath sending clouds of steam into the air. Pleased as she was with the array of power before her, D'Mara was not entirely satisfied. "Edward. Where are the other riders?" she demanded.

"I'm running this raid, not you, D'Mara," Edward replied with confidence born from being seated on Decimus. "Once we're away, I don't want any orders given but my own."

D'Mara was edgy: Edward seemed unaware of how important their mission was. "Edward, Decimus, listen to me," she said urgently. "You *do* both know what you are looking for, don't you?"

Decimus did not deign to reply, but Edward was affronted. "Eggs," he snapped.

"Very funny, Edward," D'Mara snapped back in return. She took a few steps forward, and for one heady moment, Edward thought she might kiss him good-bye. "Just remember what I said about the affinity between Greens and Silvers; I am utterly convinced the Greens are harboring a Silver egg. A *Silver*!" D'Mara told him. "You *must* clear this nest. Get to the very dirt at the bottom of it. Scoop it all out. Take *everything*. Have you told the flight that?"

"The flight is under orders to raid the nest and scrape it clean. And that is what the flight will do," Edward replied coldly. He leaned down, and in a low, angry voice, he added, "I will *not* be questioned in public in this manner, D'Mara. Especially about this obsession of yours."

D'Mara's steely dark eyes glittered angrily beneath their hooded lids, and her intricately twisted braids seemed to coil themselves even tighter, like little black snakes getting ready to strike. "I will question you as I see fit, Edward Lennix. Get me that Silver. It has to be there. It *has* to be."

D'Mara ground her teeth with frustration. She would have led the raid herself, but her own dragon, Krane, was recovering from the dreaded scale fever, and she would fly no other.

Edward sat back and stared stonily out into the distance. "D'Mara," he said coldly, "I have told you that if the Silver egg that matters so much to you really is there, we will get it. We will get it and we will bring it back here. That is my word. And my word is my bond."

D'Mara glanced back to see Valkea and her crew eyeballing her. "It might be a matter of life or death. For us. For our whole *family*, Edward."

Edward gave a snort of laughter. "Oh really, D'Mara, don't be so melodramatic. I know you just want another trinket." Edward saw a fearsome look of thunder cross D'Mara's features and he backtracked fast. "We'll get you your Silver," he promised.

"See that you do," D'Mara said curtly. And then she turned on her metallic little heel and strode away.

From deep in the shadows a massive, although somewhat faded, green dragon watched D'Mara go. Bellacrux, the Lennix Grand and most ancient of all Lennix dragons, made a point of knowing all the business of Fortress Lennix. Bellacrux's acute hearing had caught every word that had passed between D'Mara and Edward, and now her mind was whirling with the exciting possibilities a Silver egg would present. A Silver! She had waited countless years for this.

Bellacrux watched D'Mara push open the doors to the Lennix quarters and disappear inside. The old dragon's keen eyes followed D'Mara's rapid progress up the stair turret, her slender form silhouetted against the warm yellow lamplight, and as D'Mara appeared in the darkened window of her room at the top of the watchtower, Bellacrux methodically sharpened her talons upon the grinding stones placed at the feet of every arch—a Silver was something one needed to prepare for.

It was time for the First Flight to leave. They took off in the traditional way, along the wide, cantilevered runway of stone that stuck out like an enormous diving board from the ramparts of the landing yard. The first to go was, naturally, Decimus. The heavy-footed dragon thundered along the runway, and at the very last second—when even Edward had begun to wonder if this would be the time Decimus plunged over the edge like a rock—the dragon rose slowly into the air and then circled above, watching as one by one, the rest of the flight took to the air.

Bellacrux sharpened her last talon and looked up at the wheeling dragons as they jockeyed for position behind Decimus, taking up the distinctive arrow formation, their white underbellies each proudly bearing the three-pronged Raptor tattoo. Bellacrux's keen gaze followed the arrow of the First Flight as it headed off down the long, narrow pass that would take the flight out of the mountains and set it on its way to the Greens' secret valley, which was—alas for the Greens—secret no more.

Bellacrux watched until the dragons were distant specks in the night, and then she took the wide, winding walkway down to her chamber in the top floor—Level One—of the Raptor Roost. She walked slowly across the Grand Atrium, and when she reached the huge, ornately decorated double doors that led into her chamber, she aimed a quick burst of hot air at the boots of her old servant, Harry, who was taking a nap. He leapt up and began to pull the huge doors open while Bellacrux waited, impatiently tapping her sharpened talons on the shining marble floor. The doors swung open, Harry gave a bow, and Bellacrux walked into her magnificent green-and-gold chamber, freshly cleaned, strewn with soft rugs and huge embroidered cushions, with a low table of fruit and lean meats awaiting her attention—as befitted the Lennix Grand.

Bellacrux settled onto the cushions, hooked a delicate talon around a lamb's tongue, and dropped it into her mouth, while excited thoughts went spinning through her mind: *A Silver! A Silver would change everything . . .*

3

Joss

Joss Moran woke with a start. He lay on his narrow plank bed in his shepherd's hut and stared, terrified, up at the roof. A synchronized *swish-oosh, swish-oosh, swish-oosh* of wingbeats was making his wheeled hut rock like a boat at sea.

There were dragons overhead.

With his heartbeat thudding in his ears, Joss lay stone still, afraid that any movement he made might somehow attract the dragons' attention—and the dragons flying above were not the kind you wanted any attention from, *ever*. For Joss knew from the rhythmic, military timing of their wingbeats that this was a flight of Raptors.

Joss thought of the sheep he had corralled at twilight and hoped they didn't panic and break out of their camouflaged pen. A flight of Raptors could destroy a flock in minutes—and take their shepherd with them. Although Joss figured that if the Raptors got his sheep, it would be best if they got him too: He didn't care to think what would happen to him if he lost Seigneur and Madam Zoll's precious sheep.

To Joss's relief, the Raptors passed quickly overhead, and soon the air was still and quiet once more. He pulled his scratchy blanket around him and thought of happier days, when not all dragons he encountered were vicious Raptors. When his parents were alive, he had known many gentle dragons who had actually liked humans. There had been a young Yellow, a delicate sand dragon, who had taught him the basics of dragonsong, but on the very day that the Yellow had offered to give him his first dragon flight—something Joss had longed for—a flight of Raptors had killed his parents, the sand dragon, and all her baby siblings.

Joss pushed down his longing for the old, happy times and closed his eyes—but as soon as he did, a terrifying image came into his mind: the three-pronged tattoo on the white underbellies of the Raptors as they dived onto his mother and father, and the shine of their sharpened talons as, curved and lethal, they emerged from their sheaths for the kill. Joss wriggled down beneath the blanket and began to chant the soothing sounds of dragonsong to himself. Soon the lullaby that the sand dragon had once crooned to her baby sisters sent him tumbling into a deep, and happily dreamless, sleep.

It felt like only seconds later when the light of the rising sun pouring in through the gaps in the hut's planks woke him. Joss tumbled blearily out of bed, splashed some icy water over his face to shock himself awake, and pulled his fingers through his tangled dark curls. Then he opened the flimsy door to his hut and looked out onto a beautiful morning.

The hut sat in the center of an ancient stone circle. Joss had pushed it there himself, because he had felt safe there, as if the great standing stones were guardians watching over him—although when he thought about it, that made no sense at all. But not a lot in Joss's world did make sense when he thought about it, and he generally made a point of *not* thinking if he could possibly help it. And in particular, Joss did not think about the nineteen years of indentures that both he and his sister, Allie, had still to serve the Zolls.

Joss smiled at the scene before him. The air was clear and crisp and there was a dusting of frost on the ground. Five great standing stones rose up some twenty yards in front of him, catching the first rays of the sun, the tiny crystals trapped within them glittering like diamonds. Beyond his sparkling guardians a series of gentle hills rose up, sprinkled white with frost, their tops tinged with the pink of the sunrise. Joss shivered; he was skinny and felt the cold badly, and his threadbare jerkin and trousers were no match for the morning's icy chill. He grabbed his blanket and tied it around his neck as a makeshift cloak and hurried down the steps, touching his worn circular doorstep for luck. Then he set off toward the sheep pen.

Joss was walking across the open ground when, to his horror, he saw dark in the pale morning sky the telltale arrow of the Raptor flight returning. He hurled himself onto the short, springy grass and curled up beneath his blanket, shaking with fear.

The air began to shudder with the vibrations of synchronized wingbeats. The flight was so low that Joss could hear the wheeze of dragon breath and the creaking of the wings and he braced himself, convinced that the next thing he would feel would be the stab of the razor-sharp claws—he knew only too well that no Raptor would pass up the chance of easy human prey. But Joss was lucky; the Raptors had their claws full. If he had dared look up, he would have seen that each dragon carried an iridescent green egg—except for the youngest dragon, a Blue, at the rear of the flight. His egg was a delicate silvery gray.

At the head of the flight, Edward Lennix felt triumphant. "Well, Decimus," he said. "That was a grand night. We cleared that nest right out."

Winged a few Greens too, Lennix, his Lock replied.

"The flight must have their fun," Edward replied. "And I do believe we got D'Mara's Silver trinket. I saw that young Blue pick it up along with a pile of dragon dirt."

Ha! Dragon dirt, came his Lock's chuckle. *That will teach him to be so timid. You raid a nest, you go in fast and focused. It's no good hopping around the edge like a constipated chicken.*

Edward smiled. Decimus had a fine turn of phrase that always amused him. He glanced back at the old shepherd's hut rocking on its chassis and the terrified shepherd boy cowering under his cloak pretending to be a rock, and Edward Lennix laughed out loud— on a morning like this, it felt good to be a Lennix.

As the flight cleared the hills beyond the stone circle, the young Blue, whose name was Ramon, looked down at the spoils clutched in his talons. It had been dark when the Raptors had raided the nest, and Ramon had not noticed the difference in egg color. But now the rising sun revealed the awful truth—he had made a terrible mistake. He had picked up a *rock*. He thought of the ridicule that returning with a rock would attract and, deciding that he would rather be thought slippery-taloned than stupid, he decided to get rid of it. And so, as Ramon flew over the hill that rose up behind the sheepfold, he let go of his burden and flew on, hoping no one had noticed.

From beneath his blanket, Joss felt a distant *thud* upon the ground. He froze. Had a Raptor landed? Was it now thundering down the hill, wings outstretched, teeth shining with dragon spit at the thought of its breakfast waiting for it on the grass? Joss felt weak with fear. He knew he should get up and run, but where could he go? There was nowhere. He was alone and defenseless and there was nothing he could do about it. He lay waiting for the terrifying roar of a Raptor about to feed, but after a little bit Joss grew brave enough to warily raise the edge of the blanket and peer out. He gave a sigh of relief: There was no slavering Raptor waiting to eat him. Indeed, the flight was miles away now, no more than a distant V-shaped speck in the sky heading toward the dark, jagged line of mountains on the horizon.

Joss stumbled to his feet and, shielding his eyes against the slanting rays of the sun, he saw to his astonishment a large rock hurtling down the hillside toward him. Spurred on by the steep slope, the rock was gathering momentum, bouncing its way rapidly down the slope, somersaulting as it went. Fascinated, Joss stared, and it was only when the rock hit an outcrop and launched itself into the air that it occurred to him that he ought to get out of its way. And so, with the rock winging toward him like an ancient cannonball, Joss at last sprinted out of its path. There was a heavy *thump*, and the rock landed in the grass and came to a halt.

Intrigued, Joss hurried over and knelt down to get a closer look. The rock was shaped like a huge egg but was rough and pitted, with a deep crack running across its middle, caused, Joss guessed, by the fall. He looked more closely and saw that it was not just a boring gray, but was covered with small silvery speckles that glinted when the sun caught them. *Allie would love it*, he thought. Joss was stroking one of the speckles, thinking how smooth it felt, when he snatched his hand away as if stung and leapt to his feet. Something inside was *moving*. As Joss hung back, staring at the rock, he heard a sound from deep within: *tap-tap-tap . . . tappity tap tap . . . tap tappy tap . . .*

Fascinated—but also just a little bit scared—Joss watched the deep crack begin to widen and saw within its shadows a flash of brilliant silver. Then, shockingly, a sharp blade like a dagger was thrust out into the sunlight. Joss jumped backward, lost his balance, and sat down hard on the ground, but not once did he take his eyes off the rock. Rapt, he watched the dagger saw its way along the crack, up and down, up and down, slowly opening up the space. The sensible part of Joss told him to run, to get out of the way fast before whoever or whatever was holding the dagger jumped out of the rock, but something held him there, enthralled. And then, when the silver dagger pushed its way out and revealed itself to be a sharp egg tooth on the tip of a tiny silver dragon snout, Joss knew exactly why he hadn't run—the battered gray rock was a dragon egg.

Now the smooth head of a silver dragon began to push its way out. Joss knelt down, cradling the surprisingly heavy head and supporting the infant dragon as it struggled to push the thick shell of the egg apart with its two short front legs helped by its shockingly long, curved silver claws. And then, in a sudden, slippery rush, the silver dragon was free and Joss was right there, catching the tiny damp, shiny creature before it hit the ground. Feeling happier than he could ever remember, he gazed into the silver dragon's deep green eyes. "Hello," he whispered. "My name's Joss."

Joss. Like an echo, his name came back into his thoughts. It felt, Joss thought, as though the dragon was saying it. But he told himself that was not possible. *Joss,* the voice came again. And then, more excited, *Joss, Joss! Hello.*

Joss smiled at the little dragon in his arms. "Hey, is that you?" he asked.

Yes, yes, it's me! The voice came, fast and squeaky, tumbling into his thoughts. *Joss, it's me—Lysander!*

4

Coffee

Just before dawn Sirin woke, cold and uncomfortable on the sofa. And alone. She leapt up, suddenly fearful that Mum had already gone. "Mum . . . *Mum*. Are you there, Mum?" she called out, hurtling down the corridor.

"Sirin?" Her mother's voice came faintly from the tiny kitchen. Sirin pushed the door open to find Mum sitting at the rickety little table with Sammi ensconced happily on her lap. "Hello, sweetheart," her mother said. "What are you doing up so early?"

"I woke up and you weren't there," Sirin said. She saw her mother's eyes tear up and she hurriedly added, "So I came to find you. Shall I make us a coffee—a *real* one? The kind you used to have back home when you were little?"

Her mother smiled wistfully. "That would be lovely, sweetie," she said, "but I don't think we have any."

"We do!" Sirin said triumphantly. "I got some yesterday. Specially for you."

Sirin reached into the back of the food cupboard and took out a small brown paper packet. She peeled back its dark blue sticker and opened it up. With the rich smell of ground coffee filling her senses, Sirin took the packet over to her mother. Mum's sense of smell was almost gone now, but Sirin knew she could still smell coffee if she breathed in very deeply. Sirin watched her mother lift the open packet to her face and inhale luxuriantly. A smile spread over her face. "Ah, Sirin. It's a lovely blend you've got there. It smells of . . . *mmm* . . . sweet things and sunshine."

Sirin glanced up at the window at the gray dawn light trying to filter through the grime. They needed all the sunshine they could get, she thought.

Sirin set about making coffee just how she and Mum liked it. Confidently, she put the finely ground coffee and three spoons of sugar into their tiny copper pot with its long handle and topped it up with water. And then, just as Mum had taught her, she held the pot carefully over the gas flame and watched the thick mixture bubble up, taking it away just before it overflowed. Three times Sirin did this, contentedly aware of her mother's approving gaze following her every movement.

And then, with Sammi purring quietly, Sirin and her mother sat together in the little kitchen—warm now from making the coffee—sipping the thick, sweet liquid from a pair of delicate cups that had once belonged to Mum's own mother.

If Sirin could have frozen time right then, she would have done so. But coffee grows cold and time moves relentlessly on and Sirin knew that every second was taking them closer to the buzz on the door phone and the ambulance men coming up in the elevator, bringing their chair to take Mum away.

5

Allie

Joss's sister, Allie, was also up before dawn. She slept in the kitchen outhouse in the backyard of the Zolls' compound, and if she did not get up to give the yard geese their grain, they began honking at sunrise—and there was nothing Madam Zoll hated more than to be woken from the depths of her feather bed by disagreeable geese.

Allie fed the geese and then began on her mountain of tasks for the day. She lit the range, fetched water from the well, set and lit the big fire in the great hall, and then began the only task she looked forward to: preparing the shepherd's basket. Allie had strict instructions about what was to go in the basket: no meat, no bread less than three days old, no butter, no fresh milk, and absolutely nothing sweet. Scared as she was of Madam Zoll, this was the one time Allie defied her. Whatever good things she could find for Joss, he would have. This morning the basket was an especially good one: a thick slice of ham, two pickled onions, three bread rolls only a day old, a huge slab of cheese, two small apples, and the end of a fruit loaf.

Smiling, Allie wrapped up the treasures in a cloth, fixed the top onto the basket, and hurried out of the kitchen only to run straight back in again—she had heard the unmistakable sound of an approaching flight of Raptors. Allie cowered in the shadows of the doorway as memories flooded her. Fiercely, she rubbed her eyes, telling herself that it was the dust swirling from the down-draft from the wings as the flight swept overhead that was making the tears prickle against her eyes, and she forced herself to look upward. She saw the trident tattoos on the white bellies of the dragons and the glint of stolen dragon eggs. *I hate you, I hate you!* Allie thought, with some difficulty pushing down the urge to scream it out loud, sending it up into the sky.

Allie watched the flight until they were safely past Joss and his sheep and clearly heading home, then she took a deep breath and hurried across the wide, deserted compound in which the farm-house sat within its high, metal-spiked walls. She glanced up at the watchtower, which Seigneur Zoll had built the previous year so he could shoot wolves—and anything else that annoyed him—from the comfort of his own armchair. To Allie's relief, the tower was empty. She hated it when the seigneur followed her every step with his beady little black eyes.

It was just over a mile across undulating open grassland to the stone circle, and Allie walked fast, watching the treacherous skies. But it was, despite the Raptors, a beautiful morning. The light frost crunched beneath her feet and the last of the stars were fad-ing, leaving the sky pale and clear apart from a few pink clouds on the brightening horizon. The air smelled fresh and Allie's spirits rose at the thought of seeing Joss. As soon as she rounded the foot of the hill that hid Joss from the prying eyes of the Zoll watch-tower, she stopped and gazed down at the mysterious stone circle with Joss's ramshackle old hut parked incongruously in the mid-dle. A low shaft of light from the rising sun shone suddenly through a gap in the surrounding hills, illuminating the magnificent tall stones, making the crystals within sparkle. Allie was fascinated by the ancient stones, some of which were linked together like giant doorways, which she sometimes imagined as gateways to another world. And today, Allie thought as she breathed in the stillness, the place felt even more magical. It was, however, deserted. Usually Joss would be running to meet her, starving hungry and anxious for a fellow human being to talk to.

A wave of fear washed over Allie as she headed down the path. *Where was Joss?*

Allie broke into a run. *Maybe*, she told herself, *just maybe he's overslept*. Her heart beating fast, she raced across the stone circle, her eyes locked on the hut. As she drew near, she saw the hut rock slightly upon its wheels. Relief flooded through her: Joss was in there—no doubt in a panic over waking late. Allie ran up the steps and threw open the door. "Hey!" she laughed. "You lazybones, you . . ." She stopped dead, her mouth fell open, and not another word came out.

Joss looked up and grinned. At first, all Allie noticed was how happy her brother looked, as happy as when their parents were still alive. He was kneeling beside the pile of straw that served for his bed, and on the straw was a . . . a *thing*. All she could see was a brilliant silver metallic glint of smooth interlocking surfaces, which formed the shape of a creature. *Maybe*, Allie thought, *Joss had found a suit of silver armor made for some kind of animal*. She loved the brilliant green emeralds set in its little headpiece; they seemed so bright and natural that she could almost believe they were real eyes . . . Allie screamed. The eyes *were* real. They were looking straight at her.

"It's a dragon," Joss whispered. "A silver dragon." The glittering emerald eyes turned from their brief inspection of Allie back to the person they were really interested in: Joss. "He's called Lysander," Joss said.

Allie stared in amazement—a *dragon*. A baby dragon so small it must be just out of its egg. And it was *silver*. Allie had no idea that a dragon could be silver. "But how . . . I mean where . . . where did you find it?" she stammered.

"He was in an egg!" Joss said. "And it came rolling down the hill, straight to me. It was like he came to me specially. And you know what, Allie?" Joss's eyes were shining. "After he hatched, I heard his voice in my mind. I really did. He said, 'Hello, Joss!' And he told me that his name is Lysander."

"Joss!" Allie gasped. "That must mean . . ."

"That we've Locked!" Joss finished her sentence for her. "And now we'll be partners *forever*. And we'll live together and do stuff together and . . ." Joss broke off and looked at his sister properly for the first time. "Allie," he said, suddenly quiet and serious, "it's my dream come true."

Stunned, Allie lowered the breakfast basket and sat down on the steps of the shepherd's hut. Dragons were never good news in their family. "Joss," she said, matching his serious tone, "you do remember what happened to Great Aunt Ettie?"

Joss looked up, puzzled. "Uh?" he said.

"Oh, come on, Joss," Allie said, "you know perfectly well what happened. Ettie got snatched by the Lennixes to serve the Raptors. And then she had the nerve to Lock with their Grand. With *Bellacrux*. And Bellacrux killed her. Joss, *that dragon killed her own Lock*."

Joss was defiant. "What are you saying, Allie? Lysander would never do that. *Never.*"

"I hope not, but you have no idea what Lysander will be like when he grows up. He's not exactly a normal dragon, is he—who knows what Silvers are like? And I suppose you haven't even thought about the Zolls?"

Joss groaned. "Why do you have to spoil everything by mentioning *them*?"

"The Zolls won't go away just because we don't mention them, Joss," Allie told him. "What do you think they're going to do when they find a silver dragon on their land, huh?"

Joss shrugged.

"I'll tell you what they'll do. For a start they'll take him for themselves. And then, because he's silver, I expect Madam Zoll will sell him for a nice bag of money. For *lots* of bags of money."

Joss looked devastated and Allie at once felt guilty. "I'm sorry, Joss," she said. "But this is serious. We have to make a plan about what to do."

Joss wished Allie would let things be. He just wanted to enjoy the magic of having a baby silver dragon here in his hut, right now. "I know we'll have to think of something," he admitted. "But Allie, first come and meet Lysander. Please?"

Allie stepped into the dimness of the shepherd's hut and went over to the curled-up ball of silver lying on the straw. The little dragon, tired after the struggle to get out of his egg, had fallen asleep. "Isn't he beautiful?" Joss whispered, gazing at Lysander with the doting expression of a new mother.

Allie nodded. She looked at the small creature shining so bright that it was hard to believe he was not made of metal. She watched the rise and fall of the dragon's little fat stomach and saw his soft, furled wings. He was utterly beautiful and seemed so very vulnerable. *I've never seen trouble look so sweet*, Allie thought. And then, trying to shrug away her worries, she said, "Hey, Joss. I brought your breakfast basket. It's outside if you want it."

Suddenly Joss realized he was hungry. "Oh, yes, please," he said.

They sat on the steps and while Joss ate, Allie gazed up at the tall stones that encircled them like sentinels protecting them from harm. *Which*, she thought, *Joss and Lysander are surely going to need.* Joss insisted Allie share the precious fruit loaf with him, and when they had finished, he put his arm around his sister's shoulders. "Hey, don't look so worried," he said. "I won't be like Ettie, you know."

Allie looked somberly at Joss. "Jossie, it's the Zolls I'm worried about."

"Well, *don't* worry. We'll think of something."

"I hope so," Allie said. But what it could possibly be, she had no idea.

6

Egg Count

From her watchtower D'Mara Lennix peered through her night spyglass at the returning flight. Her heart beating fast with anticipation, she began to count the Raptors back in. To her delight, she saw that each one carried an egg in its talons, although they were too far away to tell the color. Too excited to wait a moment longer, D'Mara hurried down to the landing yard to direct operations. She was not going to allow anyone to mess up this most momentous of landings.

The yard was buzzing with excitement. Three of her four children were there: fourteen-year-old twins Tamra and Mirra, and their older brother, sixteen-year-old Declan, all stood in the center of the orange landing cross. They were holding a large net between them, waiting to assist the dragons as they landed. Kaan, their younger brother, had not shown up.

Anxiously, D'Mara hurried over. Landing with an egg gripped by the feet was a tricky maneuver for a dragon and required human assistance. The egg had to be dropped to a safe place; otherwise it would be smashed by the weight of the dragon touching down. However, it was important for the dragon to come in as low as possible to avoid what was known as egg-shock, where the embryo sac was ruptured and its occupant often died.

It was a tense moment as the stolen clutch of the Greens approached the landing area in Fortress Lennix. Decimus came in first. He slowed to a hover above the landing yard and Edward leaned out and yelled at his son, "Declan! Get on the blasted cross! Right *now*! We're coming in!"

Declan felt annoyed. He had been waiting on the center of the cross for the last ten minutes until, just as the flight drew in overhead, his stupid sisters had pulled the net away. He knew they had planned it so that, as ever, he got the blame. Irritably, Declan pulled the net and his twin sisters back into position. He looked up and saw the huge white expanse of Decimus's belly and its scarred trident tattoo immediately above. He felt the powerful downdraft from the wings and saw clasped in the dragon's thick yellow, curved talons a large, shimmering green egg. "Hold it *tight*!" he yelled at his sisters, and then he bellowed upward, "Drop! Drop!"

Decimus, an old warhorse of a dragon, did not like being shouted at by a youngster. He would drop the egg when he was ready and not before.

"Drop!" Declan yelled once more. "Drop *now*!"

Lennix, tell that cub of yours to shut it, will you? Decimus's irritable growl snapped into Edward's head.

"Quiet, Declan!" Edward yelled down.

Declan scowled. He was only doing his job.

Decimus let go of the egg. It fell just off center into the net, which to Declan's relief was held at the perfect tension—not so tight that the egg rolled off and not so loose that it hit the ground.

"It's just a green," Declan heard his mother say, disappointed. "Give it to them." She waved her hand to indicate the anxiously waiting Roost assistants, immaculate in their white Roost uniforms. They took the egg and carried it carefully to a long box of straw awaiting the clutch at the edge of the yard.

As Decimus flew off to land elsewhere in the yard, the next Raptor came in for the drop and the siblings prepared themselves once more. D'Mara watched her children with something verging on approval. After the fifth successful drop, she walked over to the egg box to peruse the spoils and to try to quell her anxiety. She noted that the first egg that had come in was by far the largest. *Very probably the next Green Grand*, she reckoned. Normally such a catch would thrill her, but a feeling of unease was creeping over her. *Where was the Silver?* D'Mara became aware of brisk footsteps, and turned to see Edward approaching, his foxy little mustache quivering with excitement. Her heart soared with relief. It was clearly good news.

"We dug them all out," Edward told her excitedly. "Every single one. Cleared out the place. Scraped the nest clean. We're going to get a fine crop of green Raptors, I can tell you." He laughed. "And I think you might also find we got the certain something you were after."

D'Mara seized hold of Edward's hands, her eyes glittering so bright that they made Edward think of shards of black glass. "You found a Silver! I knew it, I *knew* it!"

"It wasn't easy," Edward said. "The Greens put up a fierce fight, but they didn't stand a chance. That's their entire clutch gone, D'Mara. Totally wiped out."

"Oh, who cares about the Greens," D'Mara snapped. "They're nothing more than a pile of namby-pamby mud grubbers." She turned back to the landings and squinted up into the morning brightness. "But what about the Silver? Where *is* it?"

"Be patient, D'Mara," Edward said. "It was right at the bottom of the nest. Funny-looking thing it was, all covered in dragon dirt. That young Blue took it—what's his name now? The fast one . . . Ramon, that's it. He was the last in the flight."

D'Mara's face went white. "Are you telling me that you left the most precious egg of all to the youngest, most inexperienced Raptor?"

"Ramon may be young, D'Mara, but he's a fine Raptor," Edward returned snappily. "Aha, look, he's just coming in now."

D'Mara and Edward watched the last member of the flight swoop down toward the orange landing cross and saw Declan and the twins hurriedly drop the net and get out of the way. Their egg-catching skills were no longer needed—for there was no egg to catch.

D'Mara swore and wheeled around to face Edward. "Where," she demanded, "is my Silver egg?"

Edward stared at the Blue, who had landed and was looking around uncertainly. "I—I don't understand," he stammered. "I saw him take the Silver. I *saw* him."

D'Mara stared at her consort through narrowed eyes. "You saw nothing of the kind, you slick of dragon slime," she hissed. "You spineless little liar."

"But I did, D'Mara. Ramon got it; I swear he did."

D'Mara saw Edward's bafflement and she knew her consort well enough to believe him. "Well then, Edward," she said, drawing her sharp little filleting knife from its sheath, "that Blue of yours will just have to tell us what he did with the egg, won't he?" And with that she marched away across the courtyard, sparks flying from her metal-tipped heels. She stopped in front of Ramon. "Where's the egg?" she yelled.

Silence fell in the landing yard. The Raptors of the First Flight, who were heading toward their quarters, swung around to watch.

Ramon stared at D'Mara and her knife in shock. He tried to speak, but the soft lilt of dragonsong dried in his throat, and he sent a frantic look at Decimus. "You will tell me what you have done with my egg," D'Mara said in a low voice so full of threat that it sent shivers down Edward's spine. "You will tell me now or I will fillet out your scales *one by one*."

The watching Raptors exchanged shocked glances and Decimus huffed a warning at D'Mara: Senior member of the Lennix clan she may be, but this was no way to treat a Raptor, let alone a member of the First Flight.

"Mother, please!" Declan said, with an anxious look at the dragons around him. "You can't do this. Let me talk to Ramon first. You will get no sense from him with a knife."

D'Mara rounded on her son. "You're too soft, Declan. You'll never be respected with that attitude."

Edward put a restraining hand on D'Mara's arm but she shook him off. "Let Declan try first, my love," he insisted. "We'll put the Blue in the dungeon and Declan can talk with him. Then, if he gets nowhere, you can have as much time as you wish down there." He lowered his voice. "The Raptors don't like it, you know."

D'Mara looked around. She saw the glittering yellow and green eyes of the Raptors focused on her like a battery of guns, and only now did she notice the dragons' low and angry hissing. Reluctantly, she stepped away. "Make him tell you everything," she told Declan. "You've got an hour."

Declan led Ramon away before D'Mara had a chance to change her mind. The watching Raptors parted silently to let them through and then trooped back to their chambers, still muttering among themselves. Two of Ramon's friends went to find Valkea: This was something she would want to know.

It wasn't long until Declan ran into his mother's room at the top of the watchtower. "Well?" demanded D'Mara.

"He dropped it on the low hills near the Zoll compound. By the stone circle. He thought the egg was a rock."

D'Mara thumped her fist down onto her ebony desk. "Idiot dragon." She turned to Edward. "I blame you. You did not brief the flight properly. I want that egg back. And I want it *now*."

Edward was furious with himself. He had given D'Mara his word that he would bring back her precious Silver egg and he had not kept it. He knew she was right—Decimus should have been entrusted with it, but Edward was not going to give D'Mara the satisfaction of admitting to that. He answered curtly, "Decimus and I will go at dusk and pick it up."

"Dusk!" D'Mara was aghast. "Why not now?"

"Because I don't want that nosy Zoll man watching us from his tower, that's why," Edward replied.

"What does it matter whether he watches us or not?" D'Mara scoffed. "Zoll's nothing but a mere tenant."

"He may be our tenant but he does have a claim to what falls onto his land," Edward countered. "And I'd rather keep good relations with him, if you don't mind, D'Mara."

D'Mara did mind, but without a dragon to fly, she knew she had little choice in the matter. She must allow Edward to do it his way. "Very well, Edward," she said. "But I expect that Silver egg back here tonight. You do realize how important this is to us, don't you?"

Edward shrugged.

"Edward, the Raptors are getting restless. You very well know that humans are much less easy to source nowadays. As it is, we really don't have enough to give our Raptors the maintenance they require, and how we are going to cope with this new influx of eggs I really do not know. There is trouble brewing, mark my words."

"It doesn't help you threatening to torture one of them!" Edward pointed out.

D'Mara flushed. "I've disciplined Raptors before, Edward."

"Yes, but not like that. And not without consulting the senior Raptors."

"We're walking a tightrope," D'Mara said. "If we look weak they'll turn on us, and we can't let negligence go unpunished. And that idiot Blue lost the *Silver*, Edward. It dropped the very thing that could get our Raptors' loyalty back."

Edward laughed. "Why? Do they like silver trinkets too, D'Mara?"

With great difficulty, D'Mara restrained herself from punching Edward's smug face. She contented herself with leaning toward him and watching him flinch away. "Do I have to spell it out for you?" she hissed. "The Silver will give us access to the Lost Lands—a whole new world. We can take what we want from there. We can give our Raptors everything they require and more. That will seal their loyalty forever."

Shocked, Edward stared at D'Mara. "You don't really believe all that rubbish about the Lost Lands, do you?" he asked.

"It is not rubbish," D'Mara told him angrily. "I'm telling you, Edward, if you don't get that Silver, this time next year there won't be a Lennix family here. Fortress Lennix will be run by Raptors and we'll be a pile of bones in the poop pit." And with that she strode off, leaving her husband scowling after her.

There was no doubt about it, Edward thought; D'Mara was losing her grip on reality. The Raptors were perfectly fine, or would be if she would only show them proper respect and stop pulling idiot stunts like she had tonight. Besides, Decimus would have told him if there was any real trouble stirring. It was just an excuse to get hold of a Silver egg. He wandered over to the edge of the yard and stared gloomily out at the mountains. He wished they'd never found the stupid thing in the first place.

7

Lysander

All day, Joss kept his flock close to the fold so he could be near Lysander. He divided his time between checking on the little dragon—who slept like the baby he was—and collecting every fragment of the egg case and putting it in the hut. Joss knew that a hatchling needed to eat its own egg case to give strength to its bones, and he was determined that Lysander should have the best start in life possible.

It was a wonderfully sunny day and Joss savored every minute. Sitting on the short, springy turf watching the sheep, he took out an apple saved from the breakfast basket. He looked at it longingly, and then decided to keep it for Lysander. To stave off the hunger pangs, Joss lay back and gazed up at the puffy white clouds drifting across the sky. Surrounded by the soporific sound of sheep nibbling the grass, his eyes slowly closed, and as he drifted into a doze, Joss had the strangest sensation that he actually *was* Lysander. He could feel the rough floor of the hut, the curl of his tail tucked under his head, the scratchiness of the sheep-smelling blanket on his soft, smooth scales. The day passed slowly, and at last, as the sun dropped toward its evening horizon, Joss herded his sheep back into their pen. Then, stepping through the lengthening shadows, he made his way across the circle toward the hut.

Inside the hut, Lysander knew his Lock was near. Excited to be close to Joss once again, the dragon sat up and waited for the door to open. But on the other side of the door, Joss stopped. Allie's warning words came back to him and he felt suddenly afraid. Suppose Madam Zoll had come nosing around while he was putting the sheep away? Suppose she had found Lysander and taken him away? But as he stood there a voice came into his head: *Hey, Joss. Can we play now? Please, please can we?*

Joss laughed, pushed open the door, and a small silver ball of energy hurled itself at him. He scooped Lysander up into his arms and then sat with him on the step playing count-my-claws and pull-my-tail. As the sun began to drop down behind the western hills, Joss decided to let Lysander run free—it would be dusk soon, and Madam Zoll never ventured out after dark. He set Lysander down on the grass and watched as the little dragon raced through the stone arches, moving so fast that he seemed to be no more than a flash of silver light. *Like quicksilver*, Joss thought. And that wasn't the only thing about Lysander that was quick—he was growing fast too. Already he was considerably bigger than he had been that morning.

Joss reached into his pocket for the apple he had saved and sent a message over to his Lock. *Hey, Lysander! There's an apple here.*

Lysander came bounding over, took the apple, and ran off with it. A message came through to Joss: *Can't catch me!*

Bet I can! Joss sent, and he was off, running after Lysander as the dragon looped his way in and out of the doorways of the stone circle. After three laps of the circle, Lysander suddenly stopped and sat down. Joss—ever the anxious parent—hurried over to the dragon, afraid he had hurt himself, only to find Lysander fast asleep and the apple, peppered with dragon tooth marks, rolled onto the grass. Joss picked up both dragon and apple and carried them back to the hut.

Joss had just settled Lysander onto the straw bedding when he heard a noise—*someone was outside the hut*. He froze, his heart pounding with fear. Madam Zoll! She must have seen Lysander and now she'd come to take him away. Joss tiptoed over to the door and leaned all his weight against it. He would never let her take Lysander from him. Never, never, *never*.

Joss felt someone push the door. Digging his heels into the floor, he pushed back with all his strength. No one was going to get inside. *No one*. And then he heard a voice, soft and puzzled: "Joss? Joss, are you there? Are you okay?"

Weak with relief, Joss threw the door open. There was Allie, her dark, wispy hair escaping from her plait, her face flushed from her run across the fields, smiling broadly just like she used to when they were still with Mum and Dad.

"Allie! Oh, it's so good to see you!" Joss said. He hadn't realized how much he had missed Allie that day. It felt wrong not to have her sharing such an important event in his life.

"I wanted see you and Lysander," she said, still breathless from her run. "They didn't see me go, but I can't stay long. How is he?"

Proudly, Joss showed Allie the sleeping dragon. "He's grown so much," Allie said anxiously. "He must be twice the size as he was this morning."

"He is," Joss smiled. "They say Silvers grow fast, don't they? He's a real quicksilver."

They tiptoed out of the hut and sat on the steps as the sun began to sink toward the hills. "So, have you thought about what we're going to do with Lysander?" Allie asked anxiously.

Joss turned to his sister, eyes shining with excitement. "Oh yes, *lots*. Oh, it's so exciting."

"Joss! I don't mean the games you're going to play with him. I mean how are we going to feed him? How are we going to keep him from the Zolls? Think about it, Joss. Please, just *think*."

"I *have* been thinking," Joss said, sounding hurt.

"Good," Allie replied.

"I've been thinking that Lysander is our freedom! As soon as he's big enough, we can escape. We can fly away on him and they'll never be able to catch us. Ever!"

Allie sighed with exasperation. "But how are we going to keep Lysander secret until he *is* big enough?"

"We can do it, I know we can," Joss said, his eyes bright. "And then as soon as he's grown you can sneak out one night and we'll fly away and the horrible Zolls will never ever see us again."

"We could go back home," she said wistfully. Allie thought of their small settlement beside the ocean, the school with a handful of children, the games they had played on the beach, the happy evenings they had spent listening to the grown-ups talking late into the night. But then Allie remembered how, one by one, the families had disappeared. Some trekking into the mountains for safety, some taken by Raptors while out fishing, and others who had never come home from foraging trips. And then the terrible day when it had all ended: their parents taken by a flight of Raptors while she and Joss had lain hidden beneath an upturned boat. "Except there's no one left to go back to," she ended sadly.

"But we can find new places," Joss said, "and new people to be with."

Allie shook her head. "There aren't that many people left now, Joss. The Raptors have seen to that."

But Joss refused to be downcast. "Allie, even if that's true, we can still get away from here. We can still find somewhere away from the Zolls, safe from the Raptors and—"

Suddenly Allie gasped and leapt to her feet, pulling him with her. "Inside! Get inside the hut," she hissed.

Joss's fears all came tumbling back. "Why?" he whispered.

"Raptors!" Allie pointed to the sky, where a dark arrowhead of three Raptors was visible just beyond the hills. There was no doubt about it; they were heading their way.

In moments they were in the hut and slamming the door. They threw themselves to the floor, Joss covering the sleeping Lysander with his body. With their hearts pounding in their ears, Allie and Joss lay on the rough boards; it was not long before they heard the rhythmic *swish-oosh, swish-oosh, swish-oosh* of wingbeats growing rapidly louder until they were directly overhead. The hut swayed scarily in the downdraft, and through the gaps in the planks they could see the grass swirling as though caught in a sudden whirlwind.

Joss and Allie lay still as statues as huge dragon-shaped shadows came drifting across the grass, growing ever larger as the Raptors slowly descended.

"They're circling us," Allie whispered.

Joss felt sick. "It must be Lysander," he whispered. "They must have found out about him."

No longer daring to speak, they watched the massive dragon shadows lazily circling. Allie found Joss's hand. She squeezed it tight, and together, hardly daring to breathe, they waited. After what felt like an eternity, Allie noticed that the fearsome shadows were getting smaller, and she realized that the Raptors must be flying higher. "I think they're going," she whispered to Joss. He squeezed her hand in reply. Together they watched the shadows grow ever smaller until they disappeared and the grass became still. Gingerly, Allie opened the door and peered out.

"They're gone," she said, feeling weak with relief.

Together, Joss and Allie looked out at the empty hills. Everything was strangely unchanged apart from the sky, which was rapidly darkening, sending deep shadows across the stone circle.

"It's getting dark," Allie said anxiously. "I've got to go. Like, right *now*."

"But suppose the Raptors come back?" Joss replied nervously.

A harsh shout in the distance made Allie's hands fly to her mouth in horror. "It's Madam!" With that Allie was off, running fast.

Joss hurried after her until he reached the foot of the hill, and then he stopped and stood in the shadows. He glanced up at the sky; there was no sign of Raptors, but Joss knew they were hard to see at twilight. Anxiously he watched his sister's slight figure race across the open grassland, heading toward the forbidding high walls of Compound Zoll. Striding to meet her, he saw a squat figure in flowing robes—Madam Zoll. With a churning feeling in his stomach, Joss watched Allie reach Madam Zoll and sink into a curtsy; he saw their owner drag Allie to her feet and aim a swipe at her head. He saw them set off together with Allie being dragged along by her collar, and then it became too dark for him to see anymore. With tears in his eyes, Joss turned and angrily kicked a stone, sending it flying into the night. He hated seeing his sister treated this way, and even more he hated that there was nothing he could do about it. As soon as Lysander was big enough, he would take Allie away from this awful place. And if the Zolls tried to stop him, they would have a fight on their hands. The worm was about to turn.

Joss hurried back through the darkness to the hut, where he wedged the door closed, curled himself around Lysander, and held the dragon tight. "We're going away soon," he whispered. "We'll start a new life and everything will be all right."

Lysander gave a small snuffle, and then he stretched and wriggled, trying to get comfortable as a new row of scales began to form.

8

Edward and Decimus

In the small hours of the morning, Edward, Decimus, and their two outriders flew home along the steep-sided pass that led through the mountains to Fortress Lennix. Edward had delayed the return as long as possible in the hope that D'Mara might have given up waiting and gone to bed; but as they touched down quietly in the landing yard, Edward's heart sank—the light was still burning in D'Mara's lookout.

Three night attendants ran to greet them. They took the outriders' orders for their post-raid meal and escorted them back to their chambers. Neither Edward nor Decimus was remotely hungry—Edward because he dreaded reporting his failure to D'Mara and Decimus because his Lock's discomfort sat deep inside his own stomach like a rock.

Decimus lowered his head so that he could look Edward in the eye. *We did our best*, he sent.

"Best isn't good enough," Edward muttered, his eyes on the spiky silhouette of D'Mara staring out the window.

Decimus hated agreeing with D'Mara, but he felt that Edward had made the wrong call going at dusk. *Lennix*, he sent, *we must search in daylight next time*. The dragon paused, wondering whether to continue. There was something he had wanted to tell his Lock, but until now Decimus had been caught between allegiance to his fellow Raptors and loyalty to his Lock, and had been reluctant to speak.

"What's up?" Edward asked, sensing his Lock's dilemma.

I hear things, Lennix, Decimus sent. *Raptors getting restless. Trouble brewing.*

"Trouble?" Edward sounded rattled.

A rather powerful group of young ones are dissatisfied. They say the flight's lost its edge.

"Do they indeed?" Edward muttered, frowning. "And who exactly is in this group?"

Decimus would not be drawn. *Oh . . . assorted hotheads. They want more excitement. More . . . blood. And they blame the family.* Decimus glanced around to check that no one was listening. *The thing with that Silver, Lennix, is—and this is not easy to say, believe me—I think D'Mara could be right.*

"Oh?" Edward raised his left eyebrow in surprise. Decimus rarely had a good word to say about D'Mara.

This world is ruined now. It's no good for us anymore. A Silver, if that truly is what we found, would give us access to that other place.

Edward snorted. "Decimus! You don't believe that 'other place' rubbish too, surely?"

Decimus did the dragon equivalent of a shrug—a quick head tilt. *All the old stories tell of a place. Only yesterday we had an old Green holding forth in the Great Hall, droning on with a dreary long poem about it. Must admit I fell asleep halfway through. Started snoring apparently. But you can't deny it, Lennix; there might well be something in the legends. And always it's the Silver that is the link between the worlds. You know the old saying: Every cloud has a silver lining?*

"It's just a turn of phrase," Edward said, unwilling to be convinced.

There is often more truth in these old phrases than we think, his Lock sent. *And dragons have longer memories than humans. Just think, a whole new world for us. Fresh and full of humans. You would have the flight eating out of your hand.*

"As long as they're not actually eating my hand," Edward quipped—and then wished he hadn't. A taste for human blood was a heady thing, and even though he trusted his Lock utterly, there was no point in giving Decimus ideas. Decimus eyed his Lock quizzically, and Edward wondered if the dragon had guessed what he had been thinking. "We'll get that egg. Trust me," he blustered.

Decimus nodded. *We need a plan, Lennix. I suggest we track the flight's path all the way back from the Green Valley. I doubt if Ramon has any idea where he let the darned egg drop.*

Edward nodded. "You're right, as ever," he said. "I'll go over the charts first thing in the morning." He felt a wave of fondness for his Lock. Decimus was the most loyal and dependable creature Edward had ever known. He pressed his beaky nose against Decimus's soft snout in affection. "Thank you, my friend."

Decimus watched his Lock stride purposefully across the landing yard toward the fortified double doors that led to the Lennix quarters and the lighted window at the top of the stairs. The dragon shook his head ruefully—why humans bothered to be married was beyond him. Decimus wandered across the landing yard to the long loggia that led to the Raptor quarters, where he was greeted by a night attendant, eager to do his bidding. Out of the way of D'Mara's baleful gaze, Decimus's appetite had returned. "Dir-ra me faruna ne freemin," he said, the soft sounds of dragonsong seeming incongruous coming from such a scarred warhorse of a beast.

"Four sheep heads," the attendant repeated. "Of course, sir. It will be a pleasure."

Edward Lennix snatched a few hours' sleep and was up before dawn, well before D'Mara woke. Silently, he slipped out of the Lennix quarters and headed off into the chill tunnels of granite that burrowed deep into the vast bulk of Fortress Lennix. The dark gray walls glowed dully in the light from candles tucked into countless alcoves. As he hurried through the gloom, Edward pondered Decimus's words from the night before. His Lock was right: He had known the Raptors were edgy but he had chosen to ignore it. And now, Edward realized, it was as important to him as it was to D'Mara to retrieve the Silver egg. Apart from the fact that his own pride was at stake—it was quite possibly a matter of the very survival of the Lennix family.

As he strode through the cold and the flickering shadows of the tunnels—and very nearly mowed down the night candle trimmer—Edward began to rage at his own stupidity. He had lost the wretched egg through carelessness due to his annoyance at being dictated to by D'Mara. He had been unprofessional. Determined to be utterly focused from now on, Edward arrived at his office and, after spending five minutes clicking his way through the locks on the door, he hurried to the shelves that lined his room and began pulling out endless long rolls of maps from their pigeonholes.

Edward worked steadily through the morning, poring over the maps. His office was an old strong room. It possessed only one small barred window that looked out onto the sheer wall of rock that reared up at the back of Fortress Lennix, which suited Edward, who did not like distractions. But the aspect of his office that suited him most was the thickness of its walls and its reinforced steel door, with multiple locks to which D'Mara did not have the keys. So when, late that morning, D'Mara hammered on the door to no avail and then screamed through the peephole—"Edward, come out! I know you're there!"—Edward never even heard her.

Decimus too woke before dawn. As the sun rose, he slipped out of his vaulted chamber of red and gold and headed up the wide ramp to the landing yard loggia. He emerged into a damp, cold mist that hung gloomily over the fortress and coated the cobbles with a fine sheen of water. It was the kind of weather that dragons disliked—the damp got into their wing folds and made them sneeze—but even so, at the far end of the yard, Decimus was not surprised to see the hazy shapes of five Raptors, one of whom he recognized as Valkea, a young and highly ambitious Red. Decimus kept a mental list of possible troublemakers and at number one— by a large margin—was Valkea. And with her, Decimus suspected that he was likely to find numbers two to five on his list.

As one of the most senior Raptors, second only to Bellacrux, Decimus's presence anywhere was never questioned. However, he did not wish to give Valkea any reason to think he was keeping tabs on her, and so he embarked upon an inspection of the low wall that surrounded the landing yard, wandering slowly along the boundary, knowing that at the far end of it was Valkea. After some minutes seemingly immersed in the state of the stonework, Decimus saw the red barb of a tail just in front of him. He looked up as if surprised. "Stehfa!" he said, apologizing for his intrusion.

Valkea was pleased to see Decimus. She made a point of culti-vating the most senior and influential dragons in the Roost. Valkea was an elegant, fine-boned Raptor and normally stood a head taller than the stockily powerful Decimus. Very subtly, she arched her neck to appear shorter and looked up into Decimus's dark yel-low eyes. "Forsarrwi in hiinke te, somma lae," she murmured, telling Decimus that it was a pleasure to see him, as always.

Decimus returned the compliment and then took care to greet Valkea's companions—two Blues, a Green, and a Yellow, who were indeed numbers two to five on his list. Unlike his Lock, Decimus was a skilled diplomat. Giving the appearance of doing nothing more than enjoying a brief talk with five of his most respected colleagues, he embarked upon finding answers to some pressing questions, which were:

Were Valkea and her companions angry about the loss of the Silver egg?

Did they understand the importance of finding a Silver?

Were they planning trouble?

"A misty morning," Decimus said. "Most vexing for you young active ones."

Valkea dipped her head politely. "We'll manage," she said. "Besides, vexation is something to learn from, do you not agree?"

"Indeed so," Decimus said opaquely. "Ah well, a day of rest beside the fire listening to the storyteller is no bad thing," he added. "Every cloud has a silver lining."

"Silver! Huh!" the Green behind Valkea muttered. "No chance of that, by the look of it."

"No chance of anything much here . . ." This came from the shadowy Blue.

Decimus affected not to hear. It was a useful ploy for an older dragon to appear a little deaf at times. "And the summer will be with us before we know it," Decimus said jovially. "All seems better when the sun shines."

"Indeed it does. And all *will* be better by the summer," Valkea murmured.

"*Much* better," agreed the shadowy Blue, as Decimus's keen eye for movement noted a covert touching of tail tips between the five—a sure sign of conspiracy.

"Ah well," Decimus said, looking down at the wall as if fascinated, "at least it's a good morning for inspecting the stones. The damp shows every fault line." He had no idea if this was true, but it sounded good.

"Is that so?" Valkea said, eyeing Decimus speculatively. "*Every* fault line?"

Sensing danger, Decimus laughed. "So I'm told. But it all looks just fine to me." He looked Valkea in the eye with what he hoped was a clear, uncomplicated I-trust-you-completely gaze. "Wishing you young ones a very good morning, and may the mist clear soon."

"Wishing you a good morning also," Valkea returned, and stepped back, taking her tail-touching companions with her, to allow Decimus to continue with his inspection.

Decimus moved slowly along the remaining stretch of the wall, pondering the answers to his three questions. They were, as he had feared: yes, yes, and yes.

Sometime later, inside his strong room, Edward picked up a send from his Lock. *Time to talk, Lennix. Meet on your roof in ten minutes.*

A worm of worry twisted in Edward's stomach—it was rare indeed for Decimus to do a distant send. He carefully put aside five charts and replaced the rest in their pigeonholes. Then he clambered up the ladder he used to reach the top shelves and pushed open a small hatch in the ceiling. Moments later he was standing in the deep, cold shadows on the flat lead roof, staring up into the mist, watching his Lock negotiate the narrow space between the rock face and the main block of the fortress. Edward smiled; he knew there was nothing Decimus liked so much as a challenging landing.

Together the Locks rose up through the clingingly cold mist and emerged into the brilliant sun above. Decimus found a thermal, and with his great wings outstretched, he soared high into the deep blue sky while Edward looked down at the soft white blanket still cloaking Fortress Lennix far below. Now, away from prying eyes and eavesdropping ears—for it was at times possible for one dragon to pick up another's send—they could talk freely. They were, as ever, of like mind, and it did not take them long to agree on a strategy.

So that's agreed, Lennix. We drive a wedge between Valkea and the tail-touchers. Divide her loyalties. Make them jealous.

We keep her close, Edward clarified. *Upgrade her to First Flight to replace the Blue.*

We split up her followers. Send them off to the four compass points on reconnaissance raids. Alone, Decimus sent.

And while the troublemakers are out of the way, Edward said, *we get that Silver egg.*

You bet we will, Lennix, Decimus sent. *You bet.*

Pleased with their strategy, Decimus began a slow descent toward the mist and the problems that lurked beneath.

That evening, at dusk, in a ceremony in front of the entire Raptor Roost, accompanied by dramatically flaming torches and the solemn beat of a drum, Valkea was inducted into the First Flight while her four conspirators looked on with thinly disguised envy. As they prepared reluctantly to leave on their own solitary missions, they kept glancing at Valkea, hoping that with her new status she would intervene. But Valkea turned away and headed off to join her flight. Valkea's ex-comrades were sent off to the four points of the compass with deliberately vague orders to "search out rebellion" and not to return without proof. It was a nightmare mission in its vagueness and it was dangerous too, for a lone Raptor was a tempting target for isolated tribes seeking revenge. No one expected to see them again.

Decimus watched the four Raptors flying away into the lonely night. *Well done, Decimus; a masterstroke, if I may say so*, Edward's send came into Decimus's thoughts. Decimus gave a bow of his head in acknowledgment and headed off to find his supper.

The next five days at Fortress Lennix saw the First Flight leave at dawn and return at dusk. The first day, armed with his precious charts, Edward was confident of tracking the Silver, but they returned with nothing. The second day was the same. And the third, fourth, and fifth. By the sixth day, Edward was in despair; there was no sign of the Silver egg whatsoever. Where could it possibly be?

9

Visiting Time

Sirin was waiting for the social worker.

She was sitting in the neat and tidy front room of Ellie's house, stroking Sammi's soft fur while she listened to the patter of rain falling on the dustbin in the tiny front garden. Ellie had gone to her skating lesson and her mum was upstairs working. Sirin had her homework to finish but there was no way she could concentrate on it. How was she meant to care about the history of the vacuum cleaner when she was already late for her visit to Mum?

A short buzz on the doorbell sent Sirin running to answer. Ellie's mum appeared at the top of the stairs. "You all right to get it?" she called down to Sirin.

Sirin pulled open the door. Standing on the doorstep was her social worker, Anna, who she had met only yesterday. Anna's pale yellow hair was pulled back into a long ponytail, she wore jeans and sneakers and a big orange, puffy jacket. She smiled very brightly at Sirin. "Really sorry I'm late, Sirin," she said. "I expect you want to leave right now."

Sirin kissed Sammi good-bye, grabbed her coat, and, aware that Ellie's mum was watching her go with relief, she hurried out, carefully closing the door behind her.

"So," said Anna cheerily as Sirin settled into the front seat of her tiny car, "how are things today?"

"Okay," Sirin mumbled, looking at her watch and thinking she'd only have half an hour with Mum tonight, if she was lucky.

"Are you and Ellie friends again?" Anna asked as she turned onto the main road and joined a long line of cars.

Sirin shook her head and stared at the traffic, wishing the cars would start moving. For the first few days, she and Ellie had had a great time together: talking late into the night, giggling and telling each other their secrets. But it had all gone wrong when Sirin had shown Ellie her dragonstone and Ellie had gotten jealous of it and then laughed at Sirin for believing in dragons. After that things had changed. At school Ellie had told their group of friends about the "stupid stuff" that Sirin believed in, and now they were all laughing at her too.

"That's a shame," Anna said. "Is there anything I can help with there?"

Sirin shook her head again and stared at the rain trickling down the window. There was nothing anyone could do about *anything*, she thought miserably. The car inched slowly forward while Sirin watched the minutes left for visiting time tick slowly away on her watch. "One drop of rain and everyone gets in their cars," Anna said cheerfully. "Don't worry, we'll be there in time."

But they weren't there in time. The hospital parking lot was full and Anna had to drive around it three times before she found a space. They arrived on the ward just as visiting time was ending. At the nurses' station, Anna asked if Sirin could see her mother "for just a couple of minutes." The nurse glanced anxiously down at Sirin and then back to Anna. "I'm so sorry," she said. "We left a message. Mrs. Sharma has been moved to Intensive Care. She had an emergency procedure this afternoon. There were some . . . complications."

"Well," Anna said to Sirin as they left the ward and headed for the elevators once again, "you didn't miss visiting time after all." Sirin wondered if Anna would be quite so cheerful if it were *her* mother in Intensive Care. She stared at the lighted numbers of the floors flashing by until they reached floor ten. Then the doors swished open and they set off down a hushed corridor with two double doors at the end, above which an illuminated sign reading INTENSIVE CARE UNIT shone with a dull yellow light.

They stopped outside the doors and Sirin felt a big knot of worry tighten in her stomach. Anna pressed the entry button and while they waited to be let in, Anna took Sirin's hand and gently squeezed it.

10

Flights and Fantasies

While the First Flight searched in vain for the Silver egg, its ex-occupant stayed safe in the stone circle and the young dragon's days settled down into a routine.

Every morning Allie came with the breakfast basket and reassurances that the Zolls had no suspicions whatsoever, and every morning Joss questioned her closely, just to make sure. Joss could not relax; he was living for the moment when Lysander was big enough to fly them away and he was terrified that something would happen to stop it. Luckily Lysander seemed to have no worries at all. He ate his way steadily through the egg case and grew fast and strong. He slept all day and woke as soon as Joss put his foot on the first step up to the hut. Then they would race around playing chase-my-tail until Lysander fell asleep.

Lysander grew fast. "Quicksilver by name, quicksilver by nature," Allie reminded Joss one morning when Joss showed her how Lysander now almost filled the entire hut. "And it won't be much longer before he'll be big enough for us to fly away," she said happily.

Joss smiled. That day could not come too soon.

On the evening of the seventh day, with no sign of the Silver egg, Decimus and Edward took another solo flight above the mountains. "It's not good, Decimus," Edward said as they cruised below the highest peak of Mount Lennix, watching the first stars of the evening appear.

Indeed, Decimus agreed. *Valkea is using our failure as an excuse to make trouble again. We need to move her forward in the flight formation so we can keep an eye on her.*

"I wasn't thinking of Valkea," Edward said gloomily. "I was thinking of D'Mara. She is livid."

Decimus had no wish to waste his thoughts on D'Mara. *Look, Lennix*, he sent, *I know we didn't spot it last time, but maybe Ramon really did drop the egg near that stone circle.*

"I am beginning to think the same," Edward admitted. "You remember that shepherd's hut in the stone circle? Suppose the shepherd has hidden it there?"

Or in the sheepfold? Decimus said.

The two Locks pondered in silence for some minutes as Decimus flew out of the shadows and into the clear light of the evening. A magnificent panorama spread before them, wide grassy plains billowing like long, lazy ocean waves, and in the dim distance it was just possible to see the twinkling lights of the Zolls' compound.

Edward broke the silence. "We need to go back there. Check it out properly."

Just you and me.

"At first light tomorrow."

We'll stand the flight down. Give them a day's rest. Apart from Valkea. I'll keep her occupied with some raid-planning.

"Good thinking," Edward said.

Pleased with their decision, Edward and Decimus glided slowly back to Fortress Lennix. They landed in the light of the newly lit torches of the landing yard, and as a night attendant ran to greet them, Decimus saw the familiar figure of D'Mara in her lookout window. He sent a message to his Lock: *You're welcome to spend tonight in my chamber, Lennix.*

"Good plan, Decimus," said Edward, who had also spotted the spiky silhouette. "Very good plan indeed."

11

The First Portal

Decimus and Edward were not the only Locks up early the following morning—in a growth spurt just before dawn, Lysander finally outgrew the shepherd's hut. The sudden push of a thick and muscular dragon tail was the last straw for the decrepit old planks, and they fell apart with an audible sigh of relief, taking the roof with them and sending it tumbling onto the dewy grass outside.

Joss awoke with a shock and found himself staring up at a starry sky. He scrambled out from beneath Lysander's wing, picking up a triumphant send from his Lock: *Hey, I've killed the hut!* Lysander hated sleeping in the hut and did not understand Joss's refusal to allow him to sleep outside. But now, Lysander thought, Joss would have to.

Joss jumped down from the wreckage and surveyed the remains of the hut in dismay. Lysander sat majestically on what was now a trolley surrounded by wooden debris; how the dragon had fit inside the hut Joss could not now imagine. He watched Lysander slowly stretch out his wings to their full span, the skin between the wing fingers shimmering like fine silvery leather. With his scales glimmering in the predawn light, Lysander lifted his head to the sky, flared his nostrils, and took a long, deep breath of fresh air—he looked magnificent. Joss thought he also looked rather smug. *It's not funny, Lysander*, Joss sent. *Anyone can see us now.*

Lysander was unconcerned. He was a dragon—a *silver* dragon—he was almost fully grown, and the world was at his feet. What did he care who could see him? *Hey, Joss, don't fuss*, he sent, and then very slowly Lysander brought his wings down, then up, then down, and to both his and Joss's wonder, he rose up into the air, squeaking with delight.

Joss watched as Lysander, sparkling in the rapidly lightening sky, flew in a perfect circle, just above the tops of the ancient stones. A shiver ran through Joss as he followed every wingbeat, and he knew that he was not the first person to watch a silver dragon fly the circle. And neither, something told him, would he be the last. Lysander swooped gracefully in to touch down with such ease that it was hard to believe this was his first-ever landing. Lysander neatly folded his wings and, with his head to one side, regarded Joss as if to say: Look what I've just done!

Lysander, Joss sent. *That was amazing.*

You fly too! Lysander sent.

Joss laughed. "I can't fly. I haven't got any wings."

Lysander made a snorting noise that Joss thought might be a laugh. *I can see that. Those two little sticks with the bits on the end won't get you very far. So you'll have to borrow mine, won't you?* With that, Lysander knelt down.

Joss did not need telling twice. He scrambled onto Lysander's shoulders and slid down the smooth scales into the small dip just in front of the dragon's shoulder, which felt like the natural place to sit. As soon as he was there, Joss felt at home. He placed his hands on either side of Lysander's neck and, as Lysander stood up on all four feet, Joss felt the power of the muscles beneath him. Joss felt Lysander stretch out his wings, he felt a great sweep downward, and then it happened: Joss and Lysander rose up into the air on their first flight together.

"Whoo-hoo!" Joss yelled, exhilarated at the speed the ground was disappearing beneath him and the sensation of the chill morning air rushing past. His knees gripped the muscles of Lysander's neck and his hands rested easily upon the lower neck crest, which fitted his hand perfectly. Up, up they went until Joss saw far below the circle of stones like a small wheel of dots on the bright green of the grass, with the exploded hut as its hub. The sun was rising now, a huge pink ball creeping up over the misty green of the hills, and as he flew upon his silver dragon up into the pale blue sky dotted with little pink clouds, Joss knew he had never been so happy.

And it was at the precise moment when all seemed perfect that a shadow moved over them. Joss looked up to see, far above, the great white belly of a massive red dragon marked with the three-pronged symbol of a Raptor. He froze, watching in terror as the Raptor tipped over into a steep dive, its huge black talons outstretched as it headed straight for them.

"Lysander! Get out of the way!" Joss screamed. Lysander did not need telling—he was already wheeling away—but to Joss's horror the dragon was shooting upward toward the oncoming Raptor. "No, no!" Joss yelled out as Lysander went rocketing past the Raptor's snout, which belched a spume of brilliant orange fire, missing them by a whisker. As they zoomed past, Joss saw the dragon's rider: a stocky, powerful man in a leather suit and winged black gloves, wearing a red sash emblazoned with the Lennix badge, and Joss knew this was Edward Lennix on Decimus. They were in deep trouble.

Lysander flew even higher, rising like a skylark high into the sky, following a powerful instinct to find safety far above, with Decimus climbing rapidly after them. Joss wrapped his arms around Lysander's neck, glancing back to see if they were outpacing Decimus. It did not look good. Lysander was a novice flier without his full muscle strength, and Joss saw at once that they had no hope of outflying their immensely powerful and determined pursuer. They rose upward, the chill of the air creeping into Joss's bones. Joss looked down at the ground far below and felt quite dizzy—the stones in the circle looked like tiny dots. But even more frightening than the height was the sight of Decimus and Edward drawing ever nearer.

Edward's ferocious bellow reached Joss. "Give up, boy!" he shouted. "Take your dragon down or we'll send you down in flames!"

But Joss was not about to give up yet. He had seen a few Raptor battles and he knew that a small maneuverable dragon had advantages of his own, even against such a beast as Decimus. *Lysander*, Joss sent. *You have to swerve, duck, or dive. Do something he doesn't expect.*

And so Lysander did just that. In a sudden change of direction, he shot to his left and headed off, faster now that he was no longer climbing. Joss saw Decimus wheel around in confusion, and then, urged on by Edward's shouts, set off in pursuit, flying fast and steady, giving the impression of limitless power at his disposal.

Lysander, make zigzags, Joss sent.

But Lysander was tiring fast and could manage no more than a token wobble. Joss looked back to see Decimus coming up close behind them. In horrified fascination, he stared at the Raptor's wide-open mouth, the lines of glistening yellow fangs, until he could bear it no more and squeezed his eyes tight shut. And then Joss felt a burst of heat as a spume of dragonfire hit Lysander's tail.

The flames fell away from Lysander's silver scales like water from oiled feathers, but the shock of it caused him to shoot rapidly forward, hurtling toward a small cloud still pink with the dawn. Lysander felt strangely drawn to the cloud; it felt safe and welcoming as he plunged into it. At once Joss and Lysander felt a jolt run through them, as though they had been struck by lightning, and Joss screamed, thinking that Decimus had finally caught them.

But it was not Decimus who had caught them: It was something much more powerful—a hidden portal to the place D'Mara called the Lost Lands. A portal that only a Silver could find. And so, like iron filings dragged to a magnet, they fell into a vortex of blinding white light, spinning as they went—and then, seconds later, as if they had been spat out, they went shooting into a misty sky, and Edward Lennix and Decimus were nowhere to be seen.

Lysander's send came through loud and excited: *Hey, Joss, we did it!*

"*You* did it," Joss said breathlessly. "That was amazing flying. How did you do that whirling stuff?"

I don't know, Lysander admitted. He stretched out his wings to relax his tired muscles and settled into a long, low glide. But as they slowly lost height, Joss began to get the feeling that something was not right. Although the familiar stone circle was coming into view below, it was somehow different. Not only was the hut gone, planks, trolley, and all, but the whole landscape had changed. The hills had flattened out into rolling downs of rich green rather than the Raptor-scorched earth that Joss was used to. There were strange bands of black laid across the green like ribbons, and fast-moving boxes of different colors were traveling along them. Joss could hear a constant low rumble like a grumbling volcano, and he thought the air smelled very odd. But the strangest thing of all was that his stone circle no longer stood alone but had buildings close by, rather like Compound Zoll, and the stones were surrounded by a tall fence as though they were in prison. And through the misty haze, Joss was astounded to see what looked like long lines of people walking around the outside of the fence. He had no idea that so many people existed.

"Where are we?" Joss whispered.

I don't know! Lysander sent excitedly. And then: *It smells funny.*

Lysander was right. The air was damp with a strangely metallic yet earthy smell. And there was an odd, low rumble coming up from the ground that made Joss feel uncomfortable. It was like nowhere he had ever been before. A legend that his mother had once told him now came back to Joss: how Silvers, unlike other dragons, could travel to another world—"the Lost Lands," she had called it. And something about the strangeness of the place told Joss that his mother's story might actually be true—that he and Lysander were indeed in the Lost Lands. A chill ran through him. "Lysander, can we go home?" he whispered. "Please?"

Lysander felt the fear in his Lock, although he didn't understand why. He wanted to explore this interesting new place, but if Joss didn't like it, it was no fun. He stopped the glide and began to ascend. Anxiously, Joss wondered if Lysander would know how to return to their own world, but it seemed that his Lock was learning fast. Before Joss knew it they were diving into a cloud, hurtling through the tumbling, twisting tunnel of light and then shooting out into a brilliant blue sky. At once Joss knew they were home. It smelled right, it felt right, and far below in the middle of the stone circle lay his shattered hut. Joss felt weak with relief. He wrapped his arms around Lysander's neck and whispered, "Thank you, Lysander, thank you."

Lysander wasn't sure what Joss was thanking him for, but he was beginning to learn that humans were not entirely like dragons. They seemed, Lysander thought, to be jumpy creatures, screaming in fear one minute and then coolly making plans the next. He found it interesting. And oddly endearing.

Right then Joss was still feeling jumpy. Anxiously, he scanned the sky for Decimus and Edward, and to his relief he saw they were already far away, heading toward the distant jagged line of the Black Mountains. But the early morning sunshine was glinting off Lysander's scales, and Joss knew that all Edward Lennix had to do was turn around and he would see them, shining like a beacon. "Lysander," he said, "we need to get down fast."

How fast? Lysander asked, thinking it was high time for some play.

Lysander had, Joss thought, a smile in his voice. "Really, *really* fast," he replied.

Lysander liked a challenge. *Hold tight*, he sent.

Joss wrapped his arms around Lysander's neck. Lysander put his snout down, his tail up, his wings back, and then suddenly Joss was staring down at the stone circle far below. It looked like a target with the exploded hut as the bull's-eye. For a moment they seemed to hang motionless, and then they were off, plummeting to the ground as though they'd been shot. The air rushed by so fast that Joss was sure any moment now his head was going to fly off. Breathing was out of the question. He closed his eyes tight shut, and in his ears he heard a wild noise: *Aaaaaeiiiiiiieeeeeeeeeeee!*

Some seconds later, with his head still miraculously attached, Joss dared to open his eyes. Lysander had taken them down to below the highest hills—no Lennix could see them now. The dragon settled into a glide, and an exhilarated Joss unwrapped his arms from Lysander's neck.

My ears hurt. A reproachful send from Lysander came into Joss's head.

So do mine, Joss sent back.

But my ears hurt because you were screaming in them, Lysander replied as he flew in long, lazy circles, wheeling above the ancient stones, dipping down elegantly with each turn. Joss was wishing the flight could last forever when a shout from below broke into his thoughts.

"Joss!" Allie's voice came winging up through the morning air. "What are you *doing*?"

Joss waved to his sister. "I'm flying!" he yelled.

Allie shaded her eyes, looking up at the sky. Lysander looked magnificent, his wings spread wide, the sunlight glimmering through the silvery skin as he drifted in long, languorous circles. She watched as dragon and boy came gently down to land on the soft grass, as confident and comfortable as if they had already spent a lifetime together. She saw the silver dragon lift his head up to the sky and stretch out his wings as if in triumph, and she could hardly believe that sitting on this beautiful creature was her brother Joss, looking as though he had been born to it. Allie sighed. Lysander was going to change their lives, for sure. She just hoped it was going to be in a good way.

12

Silver Schemes

Edward Lennix and Decimus flew into the freezing shadows of the lower reaches of the pass that led up to Fortress Lennix. Edward paid no attention to the towering, sheer walls that reared up on either side of them; his mind was buzzing with the brilliant dancing image of a small silver dragon.

They were at the point in the pass where it became dangerously narrow and Decimus had no more than a few feet on either side of his wingspan. With some effort, Edward forced the silver dragon from his mind: He must be calm in order to allow his Lock a clear head for navigating through this particularly treacherous part of the approach to Fortress Lennix, which Decimus always found a little tricky. Edward unfocused his mind and observed Decimus half folding his wings and, at a heart-stopping last moment, just managing to slip through the bottleneck that marked the end of the pass. Now they were out, but the dangers were not over yet. The Needles—three sharp pinnacles of rock that had torn many a novice dragon's wings—reared up before them. Decimus was not fazed by these—he gave a powerful thrust that sent them soaring up and safely above.

Over the worst now, Edward relaxed and enjoyed the rest of the dramatic approach across a series of granite precipices and plateaus that formed the sprawling outposts of Fortress Lennix. It was a steep climb that took them through pockets of cold, clammy mists that hung around the higher reaches of the mountains. Isolated turrets of rock poked through, some topped with deserted settlements now falling into ruin. Still they ascended; the air became thinner, but powerhouse that he was, Decimus rose steadily upward, heading toward Fortress Lennix, set on the highest plateau in the upper foothills of Mount Lennix, the tallest of the Black Mountains.

Through the drifting mist Edward Lennix now glimpsed the uncompromisingly square shape of Fortress Lennix, and smiled to himself at the thought of the meeting with D'Mara. The dark shadow cast by Mount Lennix made the orange landing cross hard to see that morning. Decimus, however, knew it so well he could have landed with his eyes closed, which he sometimes did to alleviate the boredom of routine journeys. He settled perfectly onto the very center of the cross and waited while Edward swung himself down. Once again Decimus saw the spiky silhouette watching from the lookout window. *Enjoy your meeting*, Decimus sent.

This time I will, Edward sent. *And thank you, Decimus. Superb flying.*

Edward walked jauntily into D'Mara's lookout and sat down in the comfortable chair by the window, leaning back with the happy knowledge that for once he knew something D'Mara didn't, and determined to savor every moment of it. He glanced over to his wife, who was ensconced behind her desk in her impressive ebony chair fashioned from three sinuously carved dragons. She was looking at him expectantly, but was saying nothing.

Edward waited just long enough to annoy D'Mara with his silence, and then he sat up and looked at her coolly. "It's hatched," he said.

It had the desired effect. D'Mara stared at Edward. "*What?*" she said.

Edward folded his arms in the way that D'Mara always found annoying, and a smug smile crept across his thin lips. "The Silver," he said slowly, determined to enjoy his moment for as long as possible, "has hatched."

D'Mara leapt to her feet. "*Hatched?* You've seen it?"

Edward nodded. "I saw it flying. With a boy."

"With a *boy*? It's big enough already to fly a boy?"

"That's what I saw, D'Mara. The Silver with a boy."

D'Mara began to pace the room in short but rapid steps "Quicksilvers," she muttered. "They call them quicksilvers. So *that* is why. They grow fast too." She stopped beside Edward's chair and stared down at him. "So where is it?" she demanded. "And, more to the point, why isn't it *here*? Now?"

Unperturbed, Edward met D'Mara's gaze. "I could hardly let Decimus catch a precious young Silver in his talons, could I? Not without damaging the creature."

D'Mara had to admit that was true. She looked at Edward suspiciously. "You are sure it was the Silver?" she asked. "Sometimes sunlight on scales can make a Blue look like a Silver."

"I am one hundred percent sure," Edward said. "We did a fire test. The flames rolled off it like butter off a hot knife. Not a mark on it."

D'Mara looked at her husband with something approaching respect. "You got close enough to do a fire test?" She set off once again, pacing the room, her eyes glittering with excitement. "A Silver," she said. "We have a Silver!"

"To be precise, D'Mara, the Zolls have a Silver," Edward said.

"The *Zolls*? So the egg was dropped where the Blue said?"

"Looks like it," Edward said.

"But who is the boy? The Zolls have no children."

Edward shrugged. "Who cares about the boy?"

D'Mara ground her teeth with impatience. "I do, Edward. The boy might have Locked with it." She went over to the bookshelves and took down a heavy book titled *Tenant Register*. "The boy. How old?" she snapped.

"Oh . . . about eleven, I suppose. Or twelve, maybe. I don't know. Very skinny. Don't suppose they feed him much."

D'Mara ran a surprisingly workmanlike finger down a list. "All the farmhands are late teens. There's a house girl and . . . ah yes, there's the girl's brother, an indentured shepherd boy—Joshua Moran—who's the right age. It must be him."

Edward got to his feet. "I'll take the flight down immediately and demand they hand it over."

D'Mara closed the register with a bang. "Sit down, Edward!" she ordered.

Edward sat down. He wondered how he had managed to lose the advantage so quickly. D'Mara was a clever woman, he thought, there was no doubt about it.

D'Mara eyeballed Edward, pleased to have him under control again. "Edward, just for once think it through," she said. "Clearly the Zolls don't know about the Silver."

"They don't?" Edward was puzzled. How did D'Mara work this stuff out?

"If they did, they would hardly let a shepherd boy ride it, would they? So if you and the flight turn up demanding the Silver, we'll have to pay for it—and then some. And even then, they are within their rights to refuse."

"I'd like to see them try," Edward said angrily. "We'd raze the place to the ground in minutes."

"And take the Silver with it?" D'Mara asked. "Or give that awful Zoll man an excuse to take it hostage? Demand a ransom? Maybe even shoot it from his nasty little watchtower? No, Edward, we cannot risk taking the Silver by force."

Edward was stumped. "So how do we get it, then?" he asked.

D'Mara walked over to the window and gazed out to the misty green of the plains just visible through a distant gap in the jagged peaks. "Krane is much stronger today," she said. "He can take me down to the plains. I'll walk from there."

"*Walk?*" Edward Lennix looked shocked. "Why? Where to? What on earth *for?*"

D'Mara turned and smiled, showing a tight row of tiny, pointy teeth, which she had had filed when she was a young teen. "You catch more flies with honey," she said. "Particularly Silver ones."

13

D'Mara and Krane

D'Mara Lennix, her hair flowing free, dressed in multi-colored long, swirling robes and carrying a small backpack and a long walking stave, strode swiftly out of the Lennix quarters. She took the private passageway that ran beneath the landing yard into the Roost, hurried down the Lennix stairs, and took the door marked 4.

Krane's chamber on Roost Level Four reflected the length of time he had been in the Roost rather than his seniority due to his Lock with D'Mara. D'Mara was looking forward to her flight on Krane. Her happiest memories were of the expeditions they had taken to distant lands where they had terrorized the local inhabitants—both dragon and human—and she had turned a blind eye to the occasional human bones that Krane would cough up.

It was on one of these expeditions that Krane had picked up scale fever—a much-dreaded relapsing disease that she knew would blight Krane's life forever. But D'Mara loved her Lock too much to walk away from him as others might have done. She had found a very nearly deserted island on which to nurse Krane in safety and solitude. Throughout the long weeks, she had sat with him, watching his scales fall off and protecting his delicate blue skin with soft grasses until the fever abated and at last the scales began to grow back again. The island's two terrified inhabitants had proved useful. They had willingly provided D'Mara with food and water, and once Krane began to recover, they themselves had—rather less willingly—provided the much-needed protein that tempted the dragon to eat once again and get his strength back. When D'Mara and Krane finally left the island, it truly was deserted.

After that, D'Mara and Krane were inseparable. This did not concern Edward, but when they were younger, D'Mara's children had resented the fact that their mother had endless patience with Krane and his periodic bouts of scale fever, but little with them. They came to realize that they had no choice but to accept that Krane had the biggest place in their mother's heart and it was up to them to squeeze into the small and awkward spaces that Krane left them.

As D'Mara approached the tall blue door that led to Krane's chamber, the attendant—who was nursing a bandaged hand—let her in with a respectful bow. Then she went back to her duties of preparing Krane's supper, rendered a little awkward by the previous day's loss of her index finger and thumb to Krane's sharp snout.

D'Mara stepped into Krane's chamber and looked around approvingly. Krane might only be a Level Four resident, but he had the best D'Mara could provide. Huge velvet cushions in a variety of rich shades of blue were scattered across the floor, which was covered in deep, soft rugs shot through with indigo and gold threads. An azure-blue tracery of beams rose up into a cathedral-like vault, and a line of colored glass windows that looked out onto the mountains sent multicolored sparkles of light dancing across the opulent fabrics. D'Mara smiled. Krane's chamber always made her happy.

Krane was a long, elegant dragon with a vicious-looking snout that possessed the stub of his egg tooth honed to a knifelike point. He was lying half-asleep, his head resting on a pile of cushions, but at D'Mara's entrance he lazily opened one heavy-lidded yellow eye and perused his Lock with an air of extreme puzzlement. *What on earth*, he sent, *are you wearing?*

Expedition clothing, D'Mara sent in return.

Krane flipped out a razor-sharp talon and picked a small sheep bone from his teeth.

So what kind of expedition requires you to be disguised as a small yet colorful tent, Dee? Do tell.

D'Mara walked over to her Lock and stroked the top of his head, noting with pleasure that his scales once more had a healthy shine and had regained their beautiful and unusually deep blue color. *We found the Silver!* she sent.

Krane jerked his head up in surprise. *You* found *it? Dee, that is wonderful news. I can hardly believe it! May I visit it? I'm out of quarantine now.*

Unfortunately, dearest, the Silver is not here yet. It's at the Zolls'.

Ah. The delightful Seigneur and Madam Zoll. Krane flicked the offending sheep bone across the chamber, where it landed neatly into a small bucket of similar bones: Krane was a little obsessive. *No doubt Edward will be liberating it from them as soon as possible.*

Not Edward, D'Mara sent, so loudly that Krane winced. *He'll only mess it up again. I will fetch the Silver myself. However, I wish*

Madam Zoll to have no idea who I am. That way I can get the Silver out from under her long and very pointy nose without any fuss.

Aha, Krane sent. *I am relieved this tent is merely a temporary aberration. It's not a good look, Dee.*

D'Mara smiled. *I know, my love. But it will be worth it. Because if all goes well, very soon you will be having something a little more interesting to eat than sheep.* She walked over to the large brass handle connected to the winding mechanism set beside a massive blue-and-gold hatch that took up most of the wall beneath the multicolored windows. She turned to Krane and asked, *So, my love, I hope you are feeling strong enough today to fly me out of the mountains?*

My wings itch, Krane answered, already getting to his feet. *I'm longing to fly.*

D'Mara wound down the huge blue hatch in the wall of the chamber and allowed it to drop slowly outward until it hung like a diving board on two thick chains over the precipitous drop. Krane joined her at the opening and together they looked out: The small white sun rode in the bright blue sky far above, burning off the swirls of mist that hung around the lower reaches of the mountains and making the snowcapped mountaintops sparkle. The air was cold, but it smelled clean and bright and sent a thrill of excitement through Krane. He lifted up his head and took such a deep breath that D'Mara heard it whistling down into his lungs. *You're wheezing*, she sent anxiously.

And you're fussing, Dee. Come on, let's fly, Krane replied.

D'Mara swung herself up into the rider's dip, and with his Lock resplendent in her robes and seated like a warrior queen, Krane walked proudly out onto the flight platform. A moment later they were soaring up above Fortress Lennix on the first thermals of the day, rising high and fast. D'Mara felt full of joy—flying with Krane always blew her disappointments away.

Krane took a leisurely, practiced glide down through the pass, wheeling this way and that, soaring, swooping, and always in perfect control until ten minutes later he and D'Mara swept out of the shadows of a deep canyon into the bright warmth of the upland plains.

Thank you, my love, D'Mara sent. *You can put me down now.*

Krane glided down in a wide curve and the ground slowly came to meet them. He landed gently, folded his wings, and waited while D'Mara slipped off onto the grass. Krane looked at her quizzically. *So?* he sent. *Why here?*

I'm walking to the Zolls, D'Mara explained.

Krane nodded. *Ah. I get it. And they'll never guess it's you.*

D'Mara laid her hand softly on Krane's snout. *I knew you'd understand. I knew I wouldn't have to explain to you.*

Krane lifted his upper lip in what D'Mara knew was a smile. *Wish I was coming too*, he sent wistfully.

We'll be together again soon, my love. Will you wait for me here? D'Mara sent.

I'll wait anywhere you wish, Dee. But there's a nice little cave up on the outpost plateau. I'll be able to see you coming back. I'll be there.

Preparing to part from her Lock, D'Mara lapsed into speech to make the disconnection easier. "Thank you, Krane dearest. It might be a few days, I don't know. As soon as you see me, would you fetch the twins, please? And a couple of guards with nets?"

Anything for you. Even the twins.

To delay the moment of parting, D'Mara surveyed the vista spread out before her. The scrubby land undulated gently like a rolling ocean, but what had once been fertile grasslands was now a bleak landscape, raked raw by Raptor fire practice. A white, winding track through the scrub marked her path, meandering from one ruined settlement to the next like a lazy snake, and in the far distance, marked by a hazy blue line of hills, lay her destination: the Compound Zoll. An unexpected wave of excitement at the adventure ahead surprised D'Mara. She wrapped her arms around Krane's neck, kissed him good-bye, and jauntily set off. There was something about her hair unbound and the flowing colorful robes that made her feel strangely carefree, as if she were on holiday.

14

Compound Zoll

It was past midnight and Allie was finishing her final task of the day—filling six massive pans with water from the well—when she heard a faint *tap-tap-tap*. The sound was so light, apologetic even, that Allie paid it no attention, thinking it to be just another rat in the wall. But the next *tap-tap-tap* was much louder, with a frisson of impatience, and Allie realized that there was someone at the door who wanted to be let in. Right now.

Thinking to find a farmhand in need of something, Allie opened the door and was shocked to see a stranger outside—a disheveled woman swathed in long, dusty robes, leaning on her walking stave and swaying with exhaustion. "Oh!" Allie said.

The woman ventured a hoarse croak. "Mistress, I am lost and weary. I beg of you a cup of water and shelter for the night."

It was the custom of isolated farmsteads to give travelers a night's shelter in a barn. However, Compound Zoll was different, as Allie was well aware. She hesitated—the woman was exhausted, but did she dare risk taking her to the barn?

"Water, fair mistress," the traveler rasped. "I beg you. A drop of water."

Water, Allie could do. She hurried over to the water pans, dipped a metal cup into the cool, fresh water, and gave it to the stranger. Allie watched while the woman gulped it down, wondering what to do. There was something about the woman that made Allie feel uneasy—a feeling of being watched from under her heavy-lidded eyes. A feeling, almost, Allie thought, of being sized up as if she was prey. Just as Allie was thinking that this was one stranger she would be almost happy to turn away, the kitchen door was hurled open with such force that it hit the wall with a resounding crash. Allie swung around, heart racing, and saw Madam Zoll: a small, sharp-featured woman in a long black flannel nightdress, her gray hair twisted up on top of her head into her nighttime knot. Shortsighted without her spectacles, Madam Zoll stared accusingly in the general direction of the kitchen door and the chill air cascading in from it. "*What* is going on here?" she demanded, sounding triumphant, as though she had caught Allie red-handed in a long-suspected crime.

"A traveler, madam," Allie said. "She has come to beg shelter. I—I'm sorry, I gave her only a cup of water and I was just about to—"

Madam Zoll looked deflated. She had expected to catch the shepherd boy sneaking in out of the cold, but all she had gotten up for was some filthy old beggar. She was about to tell the traveler to go away before she set the dogs on her when the woman spoke.

"Madam Zoll, I beg your favor."

Madam Zoll strode over to the traveler. "How do you know my name?" she demanded.

The traveler smiled but did not answer the question. "I am very willing to pay for a night's board."

"We are not a cheap boardinghouse," Madam Zoll snapped.

"Who said anything about cheap?" the traveler replied.

Madam Zoll looked shocked; few people answered her back.

The traveler took a small leather pouch from a pocket deep inside the folds of her dress. "I am *very* willing to pay," she repeated.

Madam Zoll looked at the bag. It was a quality coin bag, stamped with the Lennix mint seal, and she knew at once it was genuine. Her hands itched to feel the weight of it and the tips of her fingers longed to stroke the dragon-headed coins; the traveler's cool dark eyes met hers and Madam Zoll felt the last trickle of resistance drain away. She held out her hand, and a moment later the soft leather bag nestled in her palm. It was satisfyingly heavy. Madam Zoll pulled at the drawstring and took out a gold coin, thick as a pat of butter, and held it between thumb and forefinger. It glimmered a soft, rich yellow in the candlelight and Madam Zoll lost her heart to it.

Madam Zoll told Allie to show the traveler to the best guest room and bring her up hot water, a clean towel, and supper. Allie took a candle and led the way through the gloomy corridors of the farmhouse, taking the traveler up the main stairs and along to a room hung with dark curtains that contained a great oak bed. As Allie busied herself lighting the fire, the traveler seated herself in the only chair and, to Allie's discomfort, watched her every movement as she coaxed a flame from the damp wood in the grate until at last the fire took hold. Allie jumped to her feet, glad to be able to go. "Excuse me, ma'am. I'll fetch your supper now." She bobbed a curtsy and hurried away, pleased to get away from the scrutiny of those calculating eyes.

Allie made the supper—a fine collection of cold meats, oil, toasted bread, and mulled wine—and took it up to the traveler's room. It was nearly two in the morning when at last she fell exhausted onto her pallet bed in the outhouse. She slept fitfully, with the gimlet eyes of the traveler stalking her dreams.

Allie forced herself to wake early, and it was still dark when she wearily set off along the winding track toward the hills, carrying Joss's food basket. Several glances back at the gate in the compound wall told her that no one had followed her. Allie knew that no one from the Zoll household would dream of going to the trouble of getting up early to follow the kitchen maid on her daily visit to the shepherd boy—she and Joss occupied a status lower than Seigneur Zoll's hounds—but this morning it was not anyone from the household that Allie feared: It was the traveler. She had a bad feeling about the woman.

Allie hurried on her way until the path took her behind the first low hill of the grazing lands, and she was able to slow down and relax a little now that she was hidden from the compound and no gimlet gaze could see her. The day was overcast and the air felt heavy as the gray light of the dawn began to filter through the clouds. Allie climbed the track as it followed the foot of the hill, and when it turned the corner she stopped for a few moments to catch her breath and look down at the stone circle below. In the center lay the remains of Joss's hut, splintered planks strewn in a circle with the hut's bare metal chassis in the middle. Of Joss and Lysander there was no sign, but Allie expected that. They had agreed that it was best if from now on Joss and Lysander bedded down in the sheep shelter. Allie hurried down the hill, across the springy sheep-nibbled grass of the circle, and headed along the winding path to the sheepfold. The sheep were gone and the gate was wide open, which was unusual because Joss was very particular about gates, but Allie thought nothing of it. She checked inside the shelter and saw Lysander curled up and sleeping, his shimmering silver flanks rising and falling in long, slow breaths. Allie stood for some minutes, watching the dragon: He was so beautiful that it took her breath away. Then she sighed, set down the basket, and went to find her brother.

Allie scanned the low range of hills before her, but there was no sign of Joss or the sheep at all. She listened for the telltale plaintive bleat—Joss's flock were a moany lot—but the hills were oddly silent. A flicker of worry nudged at Allie: Suppose Joss and the sheep had been taken by Raptors? Telling herself not to be so silly, that Lysander would not be sleeping peacefully if something terrible had happened to his Lock, Allie stood very still and listened. After some minutes she heard a faint thudding of footsteps, and then the wild figure of Joss came hurtling down the path toward her, running so fast that it seemed to Allie he must surely trip over his own feet. Allie hurried to meet him, and as they neared each other, Joss's feet did at last forget where they were and he came tumbling forward, knocking Allie to the ground.

They lay winded on the dewy grass for a few seconds until Allie got up and pulled Joss to his feet. It was now she saw that Joss was mud-stained and pale, and dried teary streaks ran down his cheeks. "Hey, what's happened?" Allie asked.

"They've gone," Joss said, sniffing and angrily rubbing his sleeve across his face. "All of them. Every single stupid sheep has *gone*."

Allie stared at Joss, uncomprehending. "What do you mean, *gone*?" she asked.

"Gone. Gone, gone, *gone*" was all Joss would say.

She threw her arm around his shoulders and guided him slowly down the track. "Hey, Joss, tell me. What's happened? Was it Raptors?"

Joss shook his head miserably. "Not Raptors. It's all *my* fault." He gulped.

"No, Jossie, it can't be your fault. You love those silly sheep."

Joss sniffed loudly and Allie handed him her handkerchief. "It *is* my fault," Joss said fiercely. "I was so stupid. Last night me and Lysander went into the fold. Lysander promised not to frighten the sheep and he didn't. Well, he didn't mean to. But I let him go in first. And the sheep panicked. They went crazy. They stampeded. They pushed me over and were out of the fold before I could stop them. They ran up the hill so fast . . . I went after them and then . . . well, you know the old quarry?"

"Oh," said Allie.

"Yes," said Joss. "It was dark and they didn't see the edge and they all went over."

"What, *all* of them?"

"Yeah. One by one, even when I was shouting at them to stop. Stupid, *stupid* sheep. So I climbed down into the quarry and they were piled up. Dead on the quarry floor. Well, they weren't *all* dead. Some were injured and bleating. So . . . so I had to hit them on the head. To put them out of their pain. It was . . . oh, it was *horrible.*"

Allie hugged her brother tightly. She thought of what he had been going through last night, and all the time she had had no idea. All she'd had to worry about was some creepy traveler. "Oh, Jossie," she said. "I am so, so sorry."

"The Zolls will kill me when they find out," Joss said. "And I'm not exaggerating."

Allie felt like she had swallowed a stone. "I know you're not," she said quietly.

They walked slowly back to the sheepfold where Lysander lay, breathing deep and slow. "We have to get out of here," Joss said. "Right now. On Lysander."

"Is he big enough to carry both of us?" Allie asked.

"I think so." Joss sounded a little unsure. "He doesn't have to take us far. Not at first. We can find somewhere to hide out while he gets bigger. Then we can go wherever we like."

Allie allowed herself to feel just a little hopeful. "Oh, Joss. That would be so wonderful. But . . ."

"But what?" asked Joss, nervously glancing back at the door.

"But we'll have to go really soon," Allie said. "If I don't go back they'll come looking for me, and then they'll find Lysander. And no sheep."

"So we go now." Joss looked at Allie, his face glowing with excitement. "Right now!" Gently, he put his hand on Lysander's soft, silvery snout and whispered in the dragon's ear, "Wake up, Lysander. Wake up . . ."

But Lysander did not stir.

A little less gently, Joss rubbed Lysander's ears and said, "Please, Lysander, it's time to wake up now." There was no reaction at all.

"Is he all right?" Allie asked anxiously.

"He's fine," Joss said, knowing that if anything was wrong with Lysander he would feel it at once. "Lysander! Wake *up*!" he said as loud as he dared. But the dragon did not stir. He breathed slowly and deeply and his eyes did not even flutter beneath their firmly closed lids. Joss looked up at Allie, his hands over his mouth in dismay. "Oh," he said. "Oh *no* . . ."

"What is it?" Allie asked, trying to ignore a growing feeling that things were going wrong.

"I think it might be his first long sleep."

Allie looked puzzled. "What do you mean?"

"You remember that book on dragon development that Dad had," Joss said.

Allie laughed. "The one you read so much it fell to bits?"

Joss looked sheepish. "Yeah. Well, the thing is, it said that an immature dragon will have three long sleeps of at least twenty-four hours, during which it is impossible to wake them. And each sleep allows a particular thing to develop. The first is navigation skills, the second is dragonsong, and the third is fire. And then they're all grown up."

"Oh," said Allie. She looked at Lysander, who was so still that she could hardly see him breathing.

"So there's no way he'll wake up until this evening," Joss said miserably. "Oh, Allie."

It took a huge effort, but Allie was determined not to let the setback get the better of them. "Okay," she said a little too brightly. "So I'll come back then."

"But can you get away?" Joss asked, his voice flat with disappointment.

"I'll make sure I can. And anyway," Allie said, trying to make the best of things, "it would be better to go under the cover of darkness when no one can see us. It's only a few hours to wait, and then we'll fly away and leave this horrible place forever." She forced a smile. "And his navigation sleep means he'll know where to go, won't he?"

Joss hugged his sister. Suddenly he dreaded being alone all day. "I'll be counting every second," he said.

"Me too," Allie said, reluctantly letting go of her brother. The sun was well up over the hills now, and she dared not waste another moment. "I have to go now, Jossie. I'll be back this evening." She hurried off, running down the path from the sheepfold, across the stone circle, and then climbing the short, steep incline up the hill that hid the circle from Compound Zoll. Then she ran down the well-trodden path, scooted around a tight bend at the foot of the hill, and ran straight into something tall, bony, and swathed in flowing robes.

It was the traveler.

15

A Purchase

Speechless, Allie stared at the traveler with undisguised horror. Fighting the urge to knock the clumsy servant girl to the ground and kick her in the ribs, D'Mara Lennix forced a steely smile. "My, that was a surprise," she said. "I hope I didn't startle you?" It annoyed D'Mara that the girl just stood in the way, gaping like an unattractive fish served up for supper. D'Mara did not like fish and she didn't like the girl either. "I expect you've been to see your brother," she said.

Allie's eyes opened wide with surprise. How did the traveler know she had a brother? "I always take him his morning food basket," she replied guardedly.

"What a faithful friend he has, to be sure," D'Mara said. "He's a lucky boy."

"It depends what you mean by lucky," Allie retorted, and then wished she hadn't. The most important thing was to get the nosy woman away from Lysander, and being rude was not going to help. She thought fast and started again. "I am sorry to be snappy. It's just that I . . . I'm scared. There are wolves prowling by the sheepfold. My brother has taken the sheep to safety over the hills and the wolves are hungry. It is not safe here, ma'am. Shall I show you the way back?"

D'Mara looked quizzically at Allie, weighing up what to do. The girl did seem very flustered and she was clearly running away from something. D'Mara was not entirely convinced, but neither was she prepared to meet a ravenous wolf pack around the next corner. "That is most kind. I thank you for the warning; early morning wolves are best avoided. Let us return to the compound. Perhaps the seigneur will send out his marksmen."

The last thing Allie wanted was to have Seigneur Zoll and his men stalking around the sheepfold with their trigger-happy fingers on their shotguns. But she kept her cool. "Seigneur Zoll says that wolves must have their freedom. That is why he sends my brother out with the sheep."

D'Mara nodded as if in agreement. "I understand. And I thank you for escorting me to safety. By what name shall I call you?"

Allie disliked telling the traveler her name; it felt as though she were giving away the very essence of herself. "Allinson," she said, giving her formal name to ward off any feeling of familiarity.

"Allinson," D'Mara murmured. "I shall make sure to remember that name." A shiver ran down Allie's spine. It sounded like a threat.

For the rest of the day, Allie went about her chores feeling very edgy. She longed to run and find Joss and warn him to stay hidden, safely away from the traveler, but she was trapped by her own deceit. The traveler had reported the presence of wolves and Seigneur Zoll was up in the watchtower with his shotgun. There was no way Allie could make a move until darkness fell. But as soon as it did, Allie promised herself, she would be off, and then she and Joss would fly away and leave this horrible place behind forever. And no one, not even the cold-eyed traveler, was going to stop them.

All through the day Allie surreptitiously collected her meager stock of possessions and packed them into the small backpack she had arrived with two long years ago. She hid it under her straw pallet and distractedly went about her work: scrubbing the floors, keeping the fires supplied with wood, peeling the vegetables, and washing the mud-encrusted clothes of the farmhands. By the time twilight was falling, Allie was exhausted, but the thought of very soon flying to freedom kept her going.

Allie was clearing up the farmhands' supper when at long last the cook went to her room and Allie found herself alone in the kitchen. Outside, the compound was deserted, and heavy footsteps in the Zoll's private chambers above told her that the seigneur had come in from the watchtower. Allie left the pile of dirty plates and with a feeling of excitement ran to get her backpack. It was time to go.

She slipped out of the side door and stopped to check that all was clear. The wide compound was empty: swept clean, neatly stacked with wood, and all the work done for the day. From the long, low farmworkers' annex set along the far wall came a sudden outbreak of shouting. Taking advantage of the noise, Allie moved quickly through the shadows at the foot of the wall, heading for the door. She was no more than a few yards from her goal when the door opened—and Joss and the traveler walked in.

It was all Allie could do not to gasp out loud. Trembling, she watched the two figures walk across the compound. The traveler had her arm around Joss's skinny shoulders and they were talking to each other as easily as if they were mother and son. Allie leaned back against the wall to steady herself. She felt weak with shock as the prospect of freedom suddenly turned to dust. And then, as Joss and the traveler disappeared into the farmhouse, Allie began to feel very annoyed. *What did Joss think he was doing?*

There was nothing for Allie to do but creep back the way she had come and hope to sneak into the kitchen unnoticed. Minutes later, fighting tears, Allie was back at the sink, washing the dirty dishes with shaking hands, her mind racing with a hundred questions. She was so immersed in her thoughts that she did not notice the kitchen door opening and the housekeeper—a gaunt woman who had never spoken to Allie directly before—walking in. "Allinson," the housekeeper said, "your presence is required in the Great Hall."

Allie spun around and gawped at the woman, her hands dripping cold, greasy water onto the floor.

The housekeeper looked at Allie as though she were a piece of dog dirt. "Dry your hands, girl, and take that filthy apron off. Put a comb through your hair too, if you have one. Be outside the hall in five minutes and I will announce you. Do *not* be late."

As her mind whirled with all kinds of scenarios—all of them horrible—Allie did everything the housekeeper had demanded of her. And five minutes later she walked down the wide passageway, her feet sinking into the deep, soft rugs, toward the stark upright figure of the housekeeper, who stood grimly on guard outside the Great Hall—an executioner waiting for her victim. Allie felt as though she were sleepwalking toward her doom. If she had not known that Joss must be somewhere near, she would have turned and run and taken her chance. But right now, there was no choice. She must present herself to the housekeeper, offer her clean hands up for inspection, and wait while the housekeeper rapped sharply on the heavy double doors.

The doors opened and the comptroller of the household—a large, round man with a glistening bald head and a tendency to hit first and ask questions later—put his fat, heavy hand on Allie's shoulder and marched her in. Allie took in the scene, trying to understand what it meant. A fire blazing in the huge fireplace . . . the soft light of candles . . . the shine and scent of polished wood . . . and at the far end of the hall, the high table where three figures had turned and were watching her walk toward them: Madam Zoll, the traveler, and *Joss*. All of that Allie could just about make sense of—but what she could not understand at all was the expression on Joss's face. He was smiling broadly and his eyes were shining with genuine excitement. Joss looked, Allie thought, as though someone had lifted the cares of the world from his shoulders.

The comptroller pushed Allie forward, and as she walked slowly down the length of the hall, she felt the warmth of the fire seeping into her and realized that she had been shivering ever since she had seen Joss with the traveler. Joss made a move to run to her but the traveler laid a warning hand upon his shoulder. He held back but the excitement in his eyes did not diminish. Joss was on a high and Allie had no idea why.

"Allinson. At last." Madam Zoll's squeaky voice broke the silence.

"Yes, madam?" Allie said meekly.

"You are a fortunate girl. Not that you deserve it." Madam Zoll indulged her trademark sniff of disapproval. "You and your brother will be leaving us tomorrow. Out of the goodness of her heart, our guest has bought both your indentures for an exceedingly generous sum."

Allie now noticed that Madam Zoll was holding a soft leather bag stamped with the sign of the Lennix mint. With the bitter taste of disappointment on her tongue, Allie looked uncomprehendingly at Joss. Why was he so happy to give everything up just as they had been about to shake off their indentures forever? How could he abandon their plans for freedom so easily? Tears pricked Allie's eyes. She felt utterly betrayed.

The traveler now spoke. "Allinson, I can see you are understandably concerned for your future," she said. "Let me assure you, you will be going to a place where you and your brother will no longer be servants. And when you reach your age of majority, I will tear up your indentures and you will be free. Until then, I promise that I will not expect any domestic chores from you. Neither will I expect any shepherding duties from your brother."

Allie was stunned. "But . . . but why?" she asked.

The traveler smiled, and Allie saw that it did not reach the cool dark eyes. "In payment and appreciation for saving me from the ravening pack of wolves this morning." Allie looked puzzled, forgetting for a moment the story she had spun in her panic.

Madam Zoll sniffed once more. "We saw no wolves," she said.

"Ah," said the traveler, "but it is the creatures you do not see that are the most . . . troublesome. Is that not so, Joss?" Allie saw Joss's face light up with shared understanding and her heart sank: *The traveler knew about Lysander.*

"I trust you will behave yourselves for your new mistress." Madam Zoll's drilling squeak cut into Allie's panicky thoughts. "Now, Joshua and Allinson, you may both eat your supper in the kitchen tonight, and Allinson, your brother will sleep in your room."

Allie nodded. At least she'd get a chance to talk to Joss soon.

Madam Zoll sighed at the problems of losing two servants, which were not at all easy to replace with the increasing shortage of young humans. She caressed the soft bag of gold to remind herself that the trouble was well worth it. "Well, girl," she barked at Allie. "Say thank you to your new mistress."

"Thank you, mistress." Allie forced out the words.

"Thank you, mistress," Joss said brightly. "Thank you *very* much!"

"Good-bye," Madam Zoll told them coldly. "I doubt we will meet again."

Not if I have anything to do with it, Allie thought. *Not in a million years.*

Madam Zoll saw the unspoken words in Allie's expression. "Get out," she squawked, and aimed a swipe at Allie's head. Allie ducked. She grabbed Joss's hand and pulled him roughly along behind her as she headed for the double doors at the end of the hall.

Allie closed the kitchen door behind them. "What's going on, Joss?" she demanded. "What happened to all our plans? We were going to be free and you've just gotten us sold again! And what about Lysander—have you sold *him* too?"

Joss retreated to behind the huge, scrubbed table in the middle of the room. He had never seen Allie so upset. "Allie, I know what it looks like—"

"I know what it actually *is*, Joss. You betrayed us. But what I don't understand is *why*?"

Joss sat down at the table and put his head in his hands. "Please, Allie. I did my best for us, I promise you."

"Huh!" Allie snorted in derision as she paced around the table. "I hope I don't ever get to see what your worst is."

Joss looked up. "Sit down, Allie, *please*. Just let me explain."

Noisily, Allie scraped the chair back opposite Joss, sat down, plonked her elbows on the table. "Okay, Joss. Explain away."

Joss took a deep breath and began. "After you went, I fell asleep. I was so tired . . . so anyway, I got woken up by Lysander licking my nose." Joss smiled at the memory. "I saw it was late afternoon already, so when I heard a kind of rustling noise outside I thought it was you and you'd gotten away early. I just didn't think. I called out your name and ran outside and—"

"It was *her*. Snooping around," Allie finished for him.

"She wasn't snooping, Allie," Joss protested. "She was just walking past the sheepfold. She said hello and I said hello and then . . . well, we got talking. She seemed really nice."

"Okay, I get that you had to talk to her once she'd seen you, but there was no need for you to show her Lysander," Allie said.

Joss shook his head. "I didn't show her. Lysander came out."

Allie sighed. "And then what happened?"

"Well, she was amazed. I mean, of course she was. And she told me all about her dragon—she's got a Blue—and how much she loves him and how she'd nursed him through scale fever and that flying with him was the only thing in her life that made her happy. So I told her how happy I had felt when I flew with Lysander and she looked horrified. She asked if I knew how dangerous it was for a Silver to fly with a human—even one as small as me—before they are fully grown. She said Silvers have really soft backbones and you can actually bend them permanently, which I didn't realize." Joss dared to glance up at Allie. "So you see, I knew then there was no way we could fly away tonight. I knew we were stuck here. And that very soon the Zolls would see all the crows above the quarry and discover the sheep were dead and then they'd find Lysander and . . ." Joss trailed off and put his head in his hands.

"So when she offered to buy our indentures, it seemed like a way out," Allie said flatly.

"It *is* a way out," Joss protested. "She's offered us a *home*, Allie. A proper home where we can keep Lysander and not be servants anymore. I know it's not what we wanted but it gets us out of here. And Lysander. And you. I insisted she took you too."

"Well, thanks for that," Allie said sourly.

Joss looked at his sister miserably. "Why don't you like her?" he asked.

Allie shook her head. "She's creepy, Joss. Can't you see? Her eyes are dead. I don't think she cares one bit about you. And I know she doesn't care at all for *me*. She just wants to get her hands on Lysander."

Joss shook his head. "That's not true. You didn't hear her talk about her Blue. No one who loves a dragon so much can be a bad person. No one."

"I just hope you're right," said Allie.

At that, the cook came into the kitchen. She slopped two bowls of stew on the table and left, slamming the door behind her. Joss and Allie ate their gristly mush in silence.

16

A Journey

Joss and Allie left early the next morning with the traveler—who, Allie noted, had still not told them her name. They headed out along the path to the sheepfold, footsteps dark in the early morning dew, Allie trailing behind.

Lysander was lying in the empty sheepfold gazing dreamily up at the sky. At the sight of Joss, he got to his feet and went over to nuzzle him. Warily, Lysander allowed the traveler to stroke his soft snout, but with a dragon's inborn suspicion of divulging his identity to a stranger, he would not give Joss permission to tell the traveler his name.

As they stood by the sheepfold fence, the traveler explained that it was a whole day's walk to her home and she hoped that would not be too tiring for them all. She then suggested that it would be wise to lead Lysander—or the Silver, as she called him—on a halter just in case something spooked him and he flew off. Young dragons were very skittish at times, she said with a smile as, from the depths of her voluminous robes, she produced a large, leather halter with heavy brass buckles.

Allie stared at the halter in disbelief. "You're not going to let her do that, are you?" she whispered to Joss.

Joss watched the traveler gently tickling Lysander under his chin—a hypnotizing skill at which D'Mara excelled. Joss noted how Lysander's eyes were slowly closing and felt a feeling of calm emanating from his Lock. In fact, right then Joss was feeling pretty mellow himself too.

Allie, however, was not. "Joss, look at that halter!" she hissed. "It's horrible."

"It's all right," Joss said in a low voice. "Lysander will be fine. Anyway, she's right, he might fly off. We might lose him. Which would be awful."

"But he's your *Lock*, Joss," Allie hissed. "Lysander's not going anywhere without you."

The traveler looked around at the outbreak of whispering behind her. She gave Allie a long, cold stare and then said sweetly to Joss, "Joshua, would you like to help your dragon put this on?"

Allie watched in dismay while Joss helped to fit the halter around the back of Lysander's head and over his snout. Lysander submitted, although Allie thought the dragon seemed uneasy.

They set off along the track that led away from the stone circle, and soon they reached the borders of the Zoll farmlands where the grassy pastures turned to stony ground and scrub. Joss walked beside the traveler, chatting happily about dragons while Lysander followed, head bowed awkwardly with the restricting halter, and Allie trailed after them. And so the day progressed: every step taking Allie away from a place she loathed, but toward somewhere that she could not help but dread. As they trudged over the bleak landscape, past empty, eyeless cottages and through eerily deserted villages, they drew ever closer to the jagged line of the Black Mountains, dark against the clear blue sky. Slowly, Allie began to piece together a jigsaw in her mind—and she didn't like the picture she was making one bit.

At midday they stopped by a small stream to eat the bread and cheese Madam Zoll had reluctantly provided and to allow Lysander a much-needed drink. In response to Allie's questions, the traveler explained that they were heading for the foothills of the mountains. "The foothills below Fortress Lennix?" Allie asked. "Isn't it dangerous living there, so close to all those Raptors?"

"Not to us," the traveler answered smoothly. "They pay us no attention at all."

"They might when they see a Silver dragon," Joss said anxiously.

The traveler was dismissive. "They have far too many of their own dragons to bother with such a little runt as yours, Joshua."

Joss looked offended at Lysander being called a runt, but he said nothing. Allie wondered if he was at last beginning to sense that something was wrong. *It's about time*, she thought.

The journey continued through the height of the day as they trudged along the dusty tracks that wound over the empty, parched plains, the sun hot on their skin, their mouths sticky with thirst. They stopped for water at another stream but the traveler seemed anxious to keep going and would not let them rest. By late afternoon they were wearily climbing across the gravelly uplands that led to the Black Mountains and even Joss was beginning to feel scared. It seemed to him that the closer they got to the mountains, the less friendly the traveler became. Twice she snappily told him to "get a move on," and then, as they neared the shadows of a huge, dark canyon that led into the mountains, Joss tripped over a rock and went sprawling. Allie ran to help him but their new mistress got there first. She grabbed Joss's arm and pulled him roughly to his feet, gripping him so hard he could feel her nails digging into his skin. "Look where you're going, idiot boy," she snapped.

Joss suddenly felt afraid. He glanced at Allie and saw his fear echoed in her eyes, and at last Joss understood that he had made a terrible mistake. *Run, Allie! Run!* he mouthed.

Allie nodded, eyes wide. *Now, Joss,* she mouthed in return. *Now!*

Joss wrenched his arm from the traveler's grasp and in a moment he was free. At once Lysander understood that things had changed—his Lock no longer wished him to submit to the halter. Lysander reared up and the weight of him pulled the halter snaking out from the traveler's grasp, burning the palm of her right hand as it went. She gasped with the pain and sank to her knees, nursing her hand.

Joss, Allie, and Lysander took their chance. They went hurtling down the gritty slope, stumbling, sliding in their desperation to get away. For a few heady seconds, Joss and Allie thought they had done it. The traveler was still on her knees, screaming at the mountains, "Krane! Krane! Krane!"

Lysander drew to a halt. *We fly away,* he sent to Joss.

"Why've you stopped?" Allie demanded anxiously.

"Lysander wants us to fly with him. But remember what the traveler said?"

"She's a liar," Allie told him. "Come on, Joss. If Lysander says it's okay to fly, then it is. Hurry up. *Get on.*"

Joss looked back at the traveler, who was now staggering to her feet, still yelling, "Krane, Krane, Krane!" which he assumed was some kind of mountain swear word. "Allie, let's not risk it. Please. Let's just run. What can she do anyway? It's three against one."

And then, at those very words, it was three against one no more. Framed in the patch of sky between the towering walls of the canyon was a massive blue dragon swooping down—and on its white underbelly, Joss and Allie saw the trident Raptor tattoo. And that was not all; behind the Blue came a huge Green, and then an arrow formation of five more Raptors.

"Krane!" the traveler yelled. "Get them!" And then she was racing toward Allie and Joss, the massive blue Raptor keeping pace with her. Allie and Joss turned to run but the traveler threw herself at Joss and caught his neck in an armlock. Allie hurled herself at the traveler but a well-aimed kick sent her sprawling to the ground. Lysander raised his wings and sent out a hiss of hot air, which, had he had his third long sleep, would have been a burst of fire. The traveler jerked her arm hard against Joss's throat, making him gasp for breath. "Anything you try with me, dragon," she snarled at Lysander, "will damage your precious friend here. So I suggest you behave yourself."

But Lysander would not be told. He sent another searing breath of heat straight into the traveler's face. The grip on Joss's neck tightened even further and Allie saw that her brother's face was beginning to turn purple. She scrambled to her feet, ran to Lysander, and placed her hand on his soft snout. "Please, for Joss's sake, do as she says," she whispered.

"Wise advice, girl," the traveler said, and to Allie's relief she relaxed her hold on Joss. Joss fell to his knees, drawing in huge shuddering breaths, and behind him flying out from the shadows of the canyon Allie saw the huge Green carrying two riders, closely followed by the flight of five. With dread in her heart, she watched the Raptors wheeling down to land in the shadows at the foot of the cliffs. Two girls—twins by the look of them—dismounted from the Green and ran toward them, carrying long-handled tridents, nets, and a sack. This, Allie knew, was their journey's end. The exhaustion of the last twenty-four hours caught up with her and she felt all her strength leave. She leaned against Lysander and waited for whatever it was the traveler had planned to happen. Allie didn't know what that would be, but one thing she did know—it wasn't going to be good.

It wasn't. From each of the flight dragons a guard armed with a long stave dismounted and set off after the twins as backup. But the twins needed no help. Working as a highly efficient team, they shoved the sack over Lysander's head. At once he lay down upon the ground in defeat—the old way of subduing a young dragon who had not reached fire maturity worked every time. Then they turned their attention to Allie. They pulled her arms behind her back and roughly tied her hands, then threw a net over her and wrapped her up so tightly that she could hardly breathe. Allie began to gasp in panic.

"Loosen it, Mirra," the traveler barked. "We don't want to lose the girl just yet."

"Aw, Ma, don't be such a spoilsport," one twin said, pulling the net even tighter.

"She'll be quieter if she can't breathe," said the other.

Allie was panicking now, flailing like a fish pulled out of water. One of her hands shot out from the net and by luck landed a punch square on the midriff of a twin. The girl bent double.

The traveler laughed. "Serves you right, Tamra. Do as you are told and loosen the net."

The net loosened a little and Tamra Lennix hissed at Allie. "You'll pay for that. No one punches me and gets away with it."

As Allie took a shuddering gulp of air, Tamra kicked the back of her knees and Allie fell to the ground. "Don't even think of moving," she snarled. Allie lay still and watched Joss being trussed in his own net and then unceremoniously rolled along the ground so he lay just a few feet from her. She saw Lysander led off like a tame pony and the traveler shooing everyone else away, leaving her and Joss on the ground. *Like bait*, Allie thought.

The traveler looked down at them with a quietly triumphant smile. "Joshua, Allinson, allow me to introduce myself. I am D'Mara Lennix, chief of the Lennix clan. All that you see here, I own—including you and your dragon. I bid you welcome."

Joss and Allie watched D'Mara swing herself up onto the large blue Raptor. They felt the rush of air from the downdraft of wing-beats as the Raptor hovered above them and then neatly plucked them off the ground, so that it held one in each foot. And then, as they dangled helplessly in the air, swinging from the Raptor's talons, it took them on the most terrifying journey of their lives: deep into the heart of Fortress Lennix.

17

Prisoners

In a tiny cell in the depths of Fortress Lennix, Joss and Allie lay trussed in their nets, shivering with cold. It was pitch dark, it smelled of rat pee, and the only sound was the distant *drip, drip, drip* of water.

"Allie," Joss whispered. "I'm sorry."

Allie looked at her brother; he seemed so small and defenseless: like a soft little moth spun with silk awaiting the attention of a spider. She supposed she looked equally vulnerable, but right then Allie didn't feel it—she felt angry. Not with Joss, but with D'Mara Lennix, who had used her brother's trusting nature to get what she wanted and then thrown him away like a piece of trash.

"You've nothing to be sorry for," Allie told him fiercely.

"Yes I have," Joss said. "I got us into this. I believed what she said."

"You shouldn't have to apologize for believing what people say," Allie said.

Joss shook his head. "But you told me we shouldn't trust her. You told me and I didn't listen. I was so *stupid*."

Allie heard Joss sniff. "Hey, don't cry," she said.

"I'm not," he said, and sniffed again. After a while he whispered, "What do you think they're going to do with us?"

"I don't know," Allie whispered in reply. She had been thinking of all kinds of horrible things D'Mara Lennix might do with them, but there was no way she was going to mention them to Joss.

"I suppose they might just leave us here . . ." Joss said. "You know, forget all about us. If they did, no one would know, would they?"

"*Lysander* would know," Allie said.

"Poor Lysander," Joss said.

They both fell silent. In the distance they heard the clang of a door opening and then the thud of heavy footsteps. They lay still, their ears to the floor, hearing the footsteps coming ever closer and then stopping outside the cell door. They heard the clang of bolts being drawn back; then the door was thrown open and a beam of light shone in, so bright that they screwed up their eyes. And then, dark against the light, a burly figure dressed in the padded black uniform of a Roost guard marched in. In one hand he carried a lamp—and in the other a long, thin knife of glinting, polished steel.

Allie felt sick. She heard Joss scream out, "No, no, *no*!" and saw him kicking and struggling, trying desperately to get to his feet. But she found herself frozen with fear, transfixed by the blade of the knife that shone so bright it hurt her eyes.

The guard perused his two prisoners. Noting that Allie was quieter, he headed for her. As he leaned over her and the knife drew near, Allie saw how thin the blade was, how delicate the point, and she closed her eyes. She hoped it would not hurt too much.

Allie waited. She heard Joss whimpering now, "*No . . . oh no . . . no . . .*" and then, close to her ear, she heard the growl of the guard, "Look, I've only come to cut the nets off. Gimme a break. I don't go around stabbing kids. Sheesh. What a bleedin' cheek."

Allie felt relief run through her like water.

"Sorry," Joss said weakly. "I thought . . ."

"Yeah. Well, I don't blame you, son. Now, hold still while I get this net . . . Jeez, it's tough, innit?" Allie lay stone still as the knife did its job and the net fell away. She scrambled up, shaking her hands to get the circulation back and watching as the guard carefully sliced his way through Joss's net. Then she helped Joss to his feet and together they jumped up and down, getting a rush of pins and needles into their feet.

"Thanks," Allie told the guard.

The guard laughed grimly. "Don't often get thanked around here. Now, follow me. You're just in time for the prisoners' supper."

"So we're prisoners?" asked Joss.

"Yes, sonny. And that's what you'll stay too. For the rest of your life."

"The rest of our *lives*?" Joss said despairingly. He had exchanged nineteen years with the Zolls with *forever*. He reached out to grasp Allie's hand and held it tight. Allie's hand was icy cold, just like the fear Joss felt creeping into his bones.

"Well, I'd not worry about it," the guard said as he shoved Joss and Allie through the door. "You won't be here long anyways. Eighteen months is the record, I believe."

"Record for what?" Allie asked as she and Joss were propelled along a narrow passageway of stone, black with mold and dripping with water.

"For the longest time a prisoner has survived. You see, it's just a *teeny* bit dangerous. Take the left turn here, will you? Jolly good.

Now up we go, up them stairs. You go first and don't try to run away. I'm right behind you and there's a guard at the top."

They were marched down another dank corridor into a large, vaulted cellar swarming with young teens. Allie and Joss were shocked to see how ill they looked—pale, thin, and dirty, many with deep, jagged cuts on their arms and faces in various stages of healing. They were crowding around a long table, grabbing hand-fuls of bread and moldy cheese and shiny green slices of meat.

"You got two more minutes of food time before night shift," the guard told them. "Grab what yer can, for there won't be no more until tomorrow evening." He propelled his bemused charges into the throng, shouting, "Make way! Newbies here. Make way!" No one moved. "Come on, be nice to 'em now, they been netted!" A tall, gaunt boy with a thick bandage around his head and a very pale girl with her entire right arm wrapped in a bloodstained cloth reluctantly made way for them. As they pushed past, Allie noticed the blood on the cloth was wet.

Joss and Allie were making half-hearted attempts to chew some stale bread when a bell clanged and a group of new, much fiercer guards marched in, yelling, "Prisoners—atten-*shun*!"

At once, the teens shoved their food into their pockets and sprang to attention. "You two." One of the guards pointed at Joss and Allie. "Stand up straight. Hands by your side. I'll have no sloppiness here or you'll be doing the Bellacrux run before you even get started. Prisoners—*out*!"

The double doors at the end of the hall were thrown open with a bang. The teens turned in unison and marched out. Many, Allie noticed, were limping. Joss and Allie went last and followed the ramshackle bunch into a wide corridor with a long red line painted down the middle of the floor. The teens lined up and guards walked up and down the line, allocating jobs for the long evening shift ahead. "You, you, and you: landing yard cleanup. You lot: sheep-killing. You foulmouthed troublemakers: feeding duty." The last was greeted with a stifled gasp of dismay. "Shut it" was the response.

The guards reached Allie and Joss last. "You"—this was directed to Joss—"Raptor nursery. Go with that lot." The guard pointed to a group of three next to him in the line. Joss glanced helplessly at Allie. "Get a move on before I send yer to the feeding party." A guard gave Joss a shove.

"See you later," whispered Allie.

"I doubt that very much," the guard said as Joss hurried away after his group.

Allie was paired with a pale, redheaded girl whose hair looked as though it had been chopped with shears. She had come in late and stood quietly beside Allie. She had, Allie noticed, a long, deep cut on her leg, and there was a pool of blood on the floor beside her foot. With a feeling of dread, Allie followed the limping girl out of the hall, heading for something called "Bone Grind."

The redheaded girl led the way through a maze of subterranean corridors. Although they were no longer accompanied by a guard, Allie could see at once that there was no prospect of escape: Every door they passed was barred and at each branch of the corridor a guard stood brandishing a long dagger. The girl spoke not a word to Allie until a fearsome roar echoed along the passageways, so loud that Allie instinctively covered her ears.

Without breaking stride, the girl swung around and said, "Bellacrux. Death dragon."

A smell of rancid meat and blood began to fill the passageway and, as she followed the girl around the corner, Allie discovered why. They had reached their destination—a huge circular pit sunk into the floor with a narrow walkway around it. And piled into the pit were bones. The bones were not, however, nice clean white bones; they were covered with scraps of rotting flesh and sinew and swimming in a pale pink slime. Allie retched.

The girl put her arm around Allie's shoulders. "You'll get used to it, kid," she said. "By the way, my name's Carli."

"Allie," Allie just about managed to say, and then retched again.

"Hey," Carli said, pulling her over to the pit. "Not on the floor; we've got to walk on that. Throw up in there."

And so Allie did. Things, she thought as she leaned over the putrid, stinking mess, could not get any worse.

18

Taken Away

It was Friday afternoon and school was over for the week. Sirin was in the cloakroom, taking her time. She looked through her bag, checking that she had all her homework, and then very slowly put on her coat. Sirin wanted to make sure that by the time she came out, Ellie would be well on her way home. That way she wouldn't have to see Ellie ignoring her yet again and stalking off along the street defiantly on her own. It had not been good staying with Ellie, Sirin reflected. Their friendship had not survived living in the same house, and everything Sirin did now seemed to annoy Ellie. Anna had said that it was probably because Ellie found it difficult sharing her mum with Sirin. That wasn't, Sirin thought, a lot of help—if she had had to share her mum with Ellie for a few weeks, she wouldn't have found it difficult at all. She would have just been happy to have Mum around to share.

Sirin hoisted her backpack onto her shoulders and headed out of the battered swinging doors into the playground, damp and dull with drizzle. A quick glance told her Ellie was not there. Relieved, Sirin pulled up her hood and, head down, she walked through the school gates and out into the street beyond the tall black railings.

Sirin hurried along the narrow sidewalk, bumpy with roots from the plane trees, crowded with garbage bags, trash cans, and parked cars. At the end of the street she rounded the corner and caught sight of a group of older girls gathered in a boarded-up shop doorway on the other side of the road. Sirin picked up speed—these were the kind of girls you really didn't want to be near, especially when you were alone. But as she hurried by, a frightened voice yelled out, "Sirin!"

It was Ellie.

Sirin stopped, uncertain where Ellie's voice had come from. And then, as the girls in the doorway all turned and looked at her, she saw behind them the pink of Ellie's rucksack and then Ellie herself in the doorway, hemmed in by the girls. Sirin's heart sank. This was big trouble.

"Sirin!" Ellie called again. "Sirin, please. Please help!"

Sirin knew she could not ignore her friend. Feeling very nervous, she crossed the road and stopped at the doorway, just out of reach of four girls who wore their own interpretation of the uniform of the high school up the road—school ties cut short, skirts even shorter, ripped black tights and new white sneakers. The girls regarded Sirin with hostile stares. "They want their toll," Ellie said in a small, scared voice. "I . . . I promised it yesterday and I haven't got it and . . . oh, Sirin, have you got any money?"

Sirin fumbled in her pocket and took out all she had—a two-pound coin, with which she had been planning to buy Mum some strawberries. She gave it to Ellie, who handed it to a girl with the darkest eye makeup Sirin had ever seen. The girl pocketed the coin.

"Okay, kid. You can go," she told Ellie. "And next time have the money, right?"

Ellie nodded and mumbled. "Right."

Sirin didn't want to hang around, but as she turned to go, someone seized her arm. She swung around, and found the tallest girl eyeballing her. "You," the girl said. "Where's your toll?"

"What toll?" Sirin managed to say.

"For walking this side of the street. On our patch. You owe us. So hand it over."

"But I just gave you the money," Sirin protested.

"No you didn't," the girl said. "You gave your *friend* the money. Not us. So now you pay *us*. Right?"

Sirin stared at the four in dismay. "But that's not fair," she said.

"Ooh, that's not fair," one of the girls mimicked.

Another grabbed Sirin by the collar. "Life's not fair, kid. Get used to it. We want our money."

"But I haven't got any more," Sirin said, glancing desperately at Ellie.

"She'll bring it tomorrow," Ellie said. "She *will*. I promise."

"Five pounds tomorrow," the girl said. "Each."

"*Each?*" Ellie squeaked.

"Yeah. And get out of here before we make it a tenner each."

Suddenly Sirin felt angry. They had taken Mum's strawberries and now they were asking for crazy money that neither she nor Ellie had a hope of getting hold of. "Why should we . . ." she began, but Ellie stopped her, grabbing her hand and pulling her away at a run.

"Don't argue with them," Ellie said as she hurtled along the street, hanging on to Sirin. "They've got knives."

Back at Ellie's house all the previous week's irritations fell away, and Sirin found that she and Ellie were friends once more. They played with Sammi and laughed together all through their best TV show, and then Ellie's dad cooked Sirin's favorite supper. They were sitting by the fire drawing dragons when the doorbell buzzed. It was Anna, but she went straight into the kitchen to talk, so they began coloring the dragons—Sirin used a bright green highlighter and her dragon shone. She had just finished the tail when the door to the sitting room opened and Anna came in.

When Anna left, both Sirin and Ellie were in tears. Anna had come with the news that a foster home had been found for Sirin and she'd be leaving in the morning. *Why*, Sirin thought miserably, *does everything good always get taken away?*

19

Kaan Lennix

Despite his quicksilver development, Lysander was only an infant dragon and he did not fully understand the new, harsh world in which he now found himself. The sense of security and belonging that he had found with Joss had been violently snatched away, and Lysander now found himself utterly alone in a strange place and—despite that place being a warm chamber, well lit, strewn with soft rugs, and provided with good food and water—he felt desolate.

Lysander knew he was in a Bad Place, but that did not bother him nearly as much as the knowledge that his Lock was in an Even Worse Place. He tried sending comforting thoughts to Joss, but he and Joss had never communicated without being next to each other and Lysander could feel nothing coming back from Joss at all. But Lysander would not give up. He lay disconsolately on the soft rugs, placed his head on the herb pillow filled with dragon-balm, and kept on trying to make contact with Joss. Which was why, when Edward and D'Mara Lennix walked quietly and respectfully into Lysander's chamber, pushing before them a stocky boy with floppy blond hair and a bad-tempered mouth that looked like a sharp little knife, Lysander paid them no attention. His thoughts were with Joss and Joss alone.

D'Mara gave her youngest son an irritable shove. "Go on, Kaan. Say hello to your new Lock."

At the word *Lock*, Lysander raised his head. He watched the boy approach him sideways, like a crab unsure of his reception by a particularly large lobster.

"It's a Silver, Kaan," Edward called out. "So remember your manners."

But Kaan had never possessed any manners to remember. He stretched out his hand, grabbed the delicate crest on top of Lysander's head, and pulled. Lysander was outraged—and in pain too. He reared up and his automatic fire response kicked in. There was no fire, but to Lysander's great satisfaction, a blast of scorching air enveloped the boy, who turned and scooted back to his mother.

"Mamma," Kaan whined. "It's a nasty one. I don't want to Lock with it. You know I wanted to Lock with a red one. You *know* I do. So why *can't* I have a—"

"Quiet!" barked Edward. "You will have what you're given and be grateful. You and the Silver will be doing a trial flight this afternoon and you had better make it work, Kaan. You're lucky to have any Lock at all after you treated your last one so abominably. And to have a Silver—well, you should be thrilled."

"But I wanted a *Red*," Kaan muttered sulkily, taking care that his father did not hear.

Lysander watched his visitors leave, the boy looking over his shoulder, glowering. Lysander returned the stare and then settled back down to think of Joss and ponder how very different human boys could be.

That afternoon a girl with short, spiky red hair came into his chamber carrying a halter. She stepped through the wicket gate, closed it behind her, and then stopped dead and stared at him. Lysander watched her—and particularly the halter—warily.

Lysander's visitor was Carli. The guards had noticed that she and Allie got along well and had taken Carli away from Bone Grind and put her back on dragon duties. Carli loathed dragons—as the guards knew well. Kidnapped on a Raptor raid and carried to Fortress Lennix in the talons of Valkea, Carli had experienced the very worst of Raptor cruelty and now hated every moment she spent near them. Carli eyed Lysander just as warily as he was eyeing her. He was, she had to admit, stunningly beautiful, but Carli knew that beauty often hid cruelty. However, she was determined not to let Lysander see her fear. Steadily, she met the dragon's gaze, and as she looked into his sorrowful green eyes, Carli began to feel confused. It seemed to her that here was a dragon who was just as vulnerable, sad, and lost as she was.

Wondering what Carli was going to do next, Lysander quizzically tilted his head to one side. Carli did the same. "Hello," she murmured.

Lysander dipped his head in greeting and then returned to eyeing the halter with suspicion. Carli understood his fear. "I'm really sorry," she said. "But they told me to come and get you. With this."

Lysander began to back away, fear in his eyes. Carli was shocked. She had never seen a fearful dragon before. "Hey," she murmured. "Don't be afraid." She put the halter down on a nearby cushion and walked slowly across the chamber, and then stopped at a respectful distance from Lysander. Lysander regarded her mournfully with his big green eyes, and for the very first time Carli understood that the relationship between human and dragon did not have to be one of fear. This silver dragon was a beautiful, gentle creature. He was someone, Carli thought, who could be a true friend.

"I'm really sorry about the halter," Carli said. "It's a nasty thing. But they ordered me to come and fetch you with it. And if I don't follow orders, I'll be in big trouble."

Lysander did not want to cause Carli any extra trouble. It seemed like she had enough of that already. So he got to his feet and walked over to the halter, flipped it up onto his snout, and waited for Carli to fix it. "Thank you so much," she whispered as she slipped the halter over Lysander's head. "And I am truly sorry."

Lysander rested his soft snout on Carli's arm for a moment, and then she pushed open the main door to the chamber and they walked out into the wide corridor, at the far end of which was the Raptor nursery. As they headed past the nursery's double doors, from which raucous squeaks and squeals echoed, Lysander suddenly had the feeling that Joss was near. *Joss, Joss are you there?* Lysander sent. But unfortunately, at that very moment, a hatchling was screaming at Joss for food and the tiny Raptor's high-pitched, ear-drilling shriek drowned out Lysander's call. Downcast, Lysander followed Carli up a long, winding ramp, wondering what lay in store at the top.

Waiting for them in the landing yard was a daunting group of people: Edward and D'Mara Lennix, their elder son, Declan, and an apprehensive Kaan wearing a new silver sash around his waist. D'Mara had threatened Kaan with a night in the dungeons if he did not Lock with the Silver, and Kaan knew his mother was serious. Declan, who had a happy and close Lock with a sensitive Yellow named Timoleon, was there to help Kaan understand how to Lock with Lysander. He was not happy about it. "Kaan hasn't a hope," Declan had told D'Mara. "I reckon that Silver's already Locked with the kid you brought with you."

D'Mara had disagreed. "The Silver's too young to know the difference. After a few days it won't remember the other kid at all."

"Of course it will remember," Declan had objected. "A Lock is for life. And even if the Silver's still free, you can be sure that Kaan will hurt it like he did his last Lock. It's wasted on him."

"Nonsense, Declan," his mother had told him. "You've always been jealous of your little brother and it's high time you grew out of it."

And now Declan stood with his family, watching a girl with spiky red hair lead the most beautiful dragon he had ever seen toward them. He felt a pang of envy. It was so unfair that Kaan should have a chance to Lock with such a beautiful creature. The redheaded girl stopped respectfully in front of them and his mother grabbed the halter and handed it to Kaan. Lysander snorted and jerked his head upward, giving Kaan's arm a painful tug. Declan and the girl exchanged amused glances and then hurriedly the girl dropped her gaze. It was forbidden for a prisoner to make eye contact with a Lennix.

Edward now addressed Lysander. "Fair Silver, we pray you look well upon your young Lock. We wish you a long and fruitful partnership together."

Lysander gave a disdainful snort and spat a gob of dragon spit onto the ground. The spit hardened upon contact with the ground and the underside of it stuck to the cobbles. Edward Lennix wrinkled his thin, beaky nose. He loathed dragon spit on his precious landing yard; it was a sign of bad dragon management, and notoriously difficult to remove. "You, girl," he snapped at Carli, "get rid of that stuff."

While Carli knelt and began scraping at the rubbery spit with her fingernails, Declan stroked Lysander's nose and murmured the soft, calming words of a dragon whisperer: "Oosh-ma-roo, sali-lamu, tara-mee, tara-tru." Even though Lysander did not yet know the meaning of the words, they made him feel warm and happy deep inside. He relaxed and leaned his head against Declan's shoulder.

"You can get on now, Kaan," D'Mara said impatiently.

Kaan went to clamber on and Declan noticed his brother's boots: metal-tipped heels with tiny daggers sticking out at the back. "Wait," snapped Declan. "You take those disgusting boots off."

Kaan scowled. "But they're my dragon spurs, dumbo."

"Kaan, do as Declan says and take them off," Edward said. "You will never Lock wearing things like that." Scowling, Kaan obeyed, and then, helped by his mother, he climbed barefoot onto Lysander and settled into the place where Joss had sat only two days earlier.

Lysander did not like the feel of Kaan at all. The boy was lumpy and heavy like a lead weight, his sharp nails found the soft skin under his scales and jabbed into him, and he squeezed Lysander's lower neck crests, which were already shaped for Joss's smaller hands.

"Now," Edward said, "send the Silver a thought message. Ask him what his name is."

Kaan screwed up his face with concentration. "He won't tell me," he said. "I expect because it's something stupid, like Binkie."

Declan sighed. "I just don't understand you, Kaan. You've been given the chance to Lock with the kind of dragon people dream of and you're behaving like a total dingbat."

"Oh, go boil your stupid fat head," Kaan said. "We're off, aren't we, Binkie?" And with that, he kicked Lysander's sides sharply with his heels.

Lysander had had enough. He raised his wings and, with a neat vertical takeoff, he rose straight up into the air to the sound of applause from Kaan's admiring parents.

"You see, Declan," D'Mara said. "The Silver is flying with him. Kaan will be fine."

Frowning, Declan watched the dragon shoot rapidly upward; then he turned on his heel and walked away. He stopped briefly beside Carli, who had already broken two nails trying to scrape away the ball of dragon spit. "Here, have this," he murmured, surreptitiously handing her his small pocketknife. "It works on this stuff, I've tried it."

Carli took the knife, a look of astonishment on her face. She nodded her thanks and went back to her job.

D'Mara hurried after Declan. "Take Timoleon and go after them," she said. "Just to make sure they're . . . you know, all right."

Declan went to find Timoleon. Sometimes, he thought, he wished he weren't a Lennix. One day he would fly away from this nasty, cruel dump and never come back. One day.

Lysander soared up and away from his prison, vowing just the same as Declan—he was never going back. But as he circled high above the compound, looking down at the grim, gray granite of the fortress that squatted dark upon the mountain plateau, he at last heard from Joss: *Lysander. Where are you? I miss you so much.*

Lysander felt a stab in his heart. Joss was here after all. *Joss, Joss! It's you! I miss you too.* He sent the words winging down through the air, hoping that somehow they would penetrate those thick, grim walls and find their target. He looked down at the heavy mass of stone and knew that now he would have to return. He could never leave Joss alone in this terrible place.

As if jealous of Lysander's thoughts being elsewhere, Kaan gave Lysander two hard kicks to his flanks. Shocked, Lysander reared backward, and Kaan shrieked so loud that the balance organs in Lysander's delicate ears seized up and he no longer knew which way was up. His head spinning with confusion, Lysander shot upward. The higher he went, the louder Kaan screamed and the dizzier Lysander became. *Joss*, he sent as loud as he could, *Joss!*

Down in the Raptor nursery among all the biting, snapping hatchlings, mopping a pool of hatchling poop, Joss heard Lysander's send. He threw down his mop and yelled, "Lysander! Lysander! Where are you?" The other nursery prisoners looked at Joss and then turned to one another and exchanged glances—it wasn't unusual for kids to go crazy, but it usually took longer than *this*.

Joss saw the covert glances and hurriedly went back to cleaning up the pale yellow, sticky sludge. He didn't care how foul the poop smelled; he was just so happy to have heard Lysander. As he squeezed the poop into a bucket, he concentrated on silently sending a message: *Lysander! Lysander! Where are you?*

But there was no reply—Lysander was gone. He was spinning through a whirling maelstrom of blinding white light, heading fast for another world. And on his back was Kaan Lennix, shrieking like a banshee.

20

Sirin Alone

"Sirin," a voice said gently. "Sirin, it's time to go now."

Sirin did not move. She stayed staring out of the grubby window, thirty floors up, into the emptiness beyond. The thick clouds hung low in the sky, and their gloomy grayness mirrored Sirin's feelings exactly—right then all she wanted to do was lose herself in the soft clouds and never have to feel anything again. But the voice behind her was becoming more insistent. "Sirin. Come on now. Your mum wouldn't want you to—"

Sirin wheeled around angrily. "Don't bring Mum into this," she said. "You have no idea what Mum would want. No idea *at all*." Sirin glared at the woman, who was a new social worker standing in for Anna, who had the weekend off. Sirin was learning fast that when she really needed someone, they went away.

The social worker gave her a sad smile. "You're right, Sirin; I don't know your mum, but I do know that all mums want their children to be safe. And you'll be much nearer to your mum too. We've found you a placement just a few blocks from the hospital. They're a lovely family and they're looking forward to meeting you." The social worker picked up a large bag. "I've put all you need in here for now," she said.

"Except for Sammi," Sirin said.

"I'm sorry, Sirin," the woman said patiently, "but as I explained before, your foster family's little boy is allergic to cats."

"So me and Sammi will stay here, then," Sirin said, stubbornly.

The social worker suppressed a sigh. She didn't understand how Sirin and her mother had managed to even have a cat—pets were banned in the tower block. "Sammi will be fine," she said. "He'll be rehomed."

"Yeah. Rehomed just like me. Except Sammi *won't* be fine and neither will I," Sirin said in a rush. "And Sammi's a *she*, not a he."

"*She'll* be fine," the social worker corrected herself. "And so will you, Sirin. And when your mum's better you can come home again," she added, far too brightly.

She doesn't think Mum will get better, Sirin thought. "There's something in my bedroom I want to get," she said. "A keepsake. It was Mum's. I mean it *is* Mum's."

The social worker nodded, pleased that Sirin seemed to be accepting the situation. "Of course," she said. "You take a few moments on your own."

Sirin ran into her room, stuffed her arm underneath her mattress, and pulled out the small leather pouch with the dragonstone that she had put there for safety. Then she took a shoelace out of an old sneaker, threaded the dragonstone onto it, and tied it around her neck, making a promise to herself that she would not be parted from the dragonstone until Mum was back home again. Sirin kept her hand on the stone, and feeling its warmth spread through her, she walked over to the window and gazed out at the drizzle that drifted lazily down through the misty skies. She looked out over the lines of shiny black roofs to the boxlike shape of the hospital just visible by the river in the distance. Somewhere in that box was the place called Intensive Care where Mum lay trapped in a web of tubes like a fly in the lair of a spider. Sirin held the stone up to the window, hoping that somehow Mum would know she and the dragonstone were here together, thinking of her and wishing her better.

Suddenly a brilliant flash of silver came from a low cloud nearby. Sirin leapt backward with a gasp—she hated lightning—and squeezed her eyes tight shut. She waited for the thunder but none came, and so she slowly opened her eyes. A random shaft of the setting sun glanced off something silver and then it was gone, leaving Sirin staring at the darkening sky, wondering what it was she had seen—and why it made her feel oddly happy.

A gentle cough at her bedroom door brought Sirin back to reality. The social worker had mistaken Sirin's gasp for a muffled sob. "Sirin, are you all right?" she asked.

Sirin nodded. "Yes. Yes, I am, thanks," she said. And it was true, Sirin thought, she *was* all right—the flash of silver light was surely a sign that Mum would get better. Sirin tucked the dragonstone on its dirty white shoelace beneath her sweatshirt and cast a last glance out of the window toward the big box by the river. "Okay," she said. "I'm ready now."

21

Kaan's Journey

Lysander flipped in and out of strange, thick gray clouds, trying desperately to orient himself. Flying with a human who was not a Lock was not easy for any dragon, but flying with a screaming boy who was half throttling him—Kaan's brawny arms were wrapped around Lysander's delicate neck like a vise—was almost impossible. It was a vicious circle: The more terrified Kaan became, the tighter his grasp; the tighter Kaan's grasp, the less air Lysander could take into his lungs and so the more dizzy he became—until at last, Lysander blacked out, his wings folded in like an umbrella, and he plummeted toward the ground.

As Lysander dropped like a stone through a cold, clutching mist, Kaan fell silent and became weak with terror—and that was what saved them both. Kaan's grip loosened, allowing Lysander to take a shuddering breath. As the dragon's senses kicked in once again, he spread his wings and his headlong dive morphed into an upward glide. Kaan, exhausted by fear, slumped over Lysander's neck like a damp dishcloth.

With Kaan shocked into silence, Lysander flew slowly through a patchy, cold mist, taking in long, deep breaths and getting his strength back. Meanwhile, Kaan stared down through the gaps in the mist to the ground far below.

There were very few things Kaan Lennix had a talent for, but one thing he could do better than anyone else was to accurately see objects at a great distance. Kaan's vision was keener than that of any hawk. And what he saw far beneath him took his breath away. It reminded him of the old maps of mythical cities that his mother used to show him that she said belonged to a place called the Lost Lands. Kaan had loved those stories, for it was the only time his mother paid him any attention, but what he now saw was even more exciting, because he could see things actually *moving*. Kaan enjoyed snooping on people so much that he had his own spyglass. Excited, he took the small brass tube from his pocket, pulled it open, and focused it on the scenes below as they drifted in and out of the mist.

Kaan gasped in amazement. Long boxes of various colors, which he thought must be dragons wearing a weird kind of armor, were moving slowly through the streets of a huge city. Dragons in colored boxes Kaan could understand, but what shocked him was that scurrying along beside them were humans—*hundreds* of them—like little black ants. Kaan was stunned. "Hey, dragon!" he said to Lysander. "Where *are* we?"

Lysander did not react.

"Don't suppose you know anyway," Kaan muttered. "Don't suppose you, dumb dragon, can even see all those people down there. Well, I'll tell you where we are. We're in the Lost Lands. My ma told me all about this stuff. Stories and all that. I thought she was talking garbage. We all did." Kaan laughed. "But hey, maybe she was right, eh, Binkie? Just wait till I tell her. Ha ha!"

Lysander ignored Kaan and concentrated on the itchy feeling between his eyes, which he was pretty sure was leading him toward the portal back to his own world. Lysander headed steadily upward into the thick, cold cloud, and soon even Kaan's spyglass showed only misty whiteness. It was now that Lysander became aware of a clattering noise in the sky, growing ever louder. He became aware of a disturbance in the air and a strange metallic smell, which did not feel good at all. And then, suddenly Lysander saw another huge silver dragon coming out of the cloud, heading straight for them. It was terrifying: Its wings whirled around the top of its body like a windmill, and it had a fat, blunt snout with a powerful beam of light streaming from it. Kaan began to scream, but in the din of the great dragon's ear-shattering noise, Lysander didn't even notice. Blinded by the beam of light shining straight into his eyes, Lysander shot upward, and guided by the tingle between his eyes, which was now so strong it made him want to sneeze, he went rocketing toward the portal.

And then he was there, spinning into a tunnel of light. Kaan's screams were silenced, the silver dragon with the clattering wings was gone, and all was beautifully calm. In perfect control now, Lysander allowed the portal to pull him through its vortex and send him shooting out like a cork from a bottle into the blue skies and sunshine above the Black Mountains. Kaan gave a great whoop of relief to be back in familiar surroundings, and as the boy fidgeted in the pilot dip, Lysander coasted slowly down toward the forbidding stronghold of Fortress Lennix. As he drew closer, Lysander saw a yellow Raptor flying rapidly up toward him and he recognized Declan as the rider.

Not wanting to spook the young Silver, Declan and Timoleon kept their distance. But they were close enough to see Kaan sitting astride the dragon as though he were a returning hero, riding one-handed and kicking Lysander to show who was boss. Declan noted that the Silver was not reacting to his brother at all, but was staring down at Fortress Lennix as if searching for something.

There's no way they've Locked, Declan sent to Timoleon.

Totally disconnected, Timoleon agreed as they drew level with Lysander and Kaan.

"Hey!" Declan yelled across to his brother. "Where have you been?"

"Wouldn't you like to know?" Kaan shouted back smugly.

Declan sighed. *What an idiot*, he sent to Timoleon.

An idiot who's had a good flight though, Timoleon returned. *I wonder where they disappeared to?*

I suspect we'll soon find out, Declan sent. *Kaan looks full of it.*

Declan and Timoleon followed Kaan and the Silver as they glided down toward the landing yard, where, to Declan's surprise, the Silver ignored the landing cross and, flying only a few feet above the ground, headed for the back of the yard. Kaan began to panic. "Stop!" he yelled. "Stop and land, you stupid dragon!"

Declan watched with interest as the Silver blithely ignored its rider's commands. It was now hovering right above the poop slide, which led straight down to the poop pit some twenty feet below. In a slick maneuver that impressed Declan—it had clearly thought this through—the Silver tucked its tail in and performed a perfect backflip. With a piercing shriek, Kaan plunged neatly headfirst into the very center of the pile of steaming poop, leaving only his bare feet sticking out.

Declan knew he shouldn't laugh—but he did.

22

Silver Dreams

D'Mara Lennix sat in her ebony dragon chair presiding over a family meeting. A scrubbed and very pink Kaan sat sulking next to his mother, and opposite him Tamra and Mirra pointedly held their noses. Declan sat at the far end of the desk next to his father, both of them silent.

D'Mara surveyed her family, her eyes glowing with suppressed excitement. "This afternoon," she said, "Kaan saw something very interesting indeed."

Tamra and Mirra spluttered with laughter. "Yeah. The inside of the poop pit!"

"Be quiet, both of you," Edward snapped. Mirra looked shocked; her father was normally such a pussycat with them. She glanced at Tamra, who shrugged and pulled a face.

"Today," D'Mara announced, "Kaan went to the legendary Lost Lands."

Mirra looked at Tamra in dismay—had Kaan done something right at last? But Tamra was riveted by the news. "*The Lost Lands? You mean Kaan went there for *real*?" she asked, her eyes glowing with excitement. For the first time, Mirra noticed uncomfortably how much Tamra and her mother looked alike.

"I mean exactly that," D'Mara told her daughter. "You all know that I have always believed these lands exist. And now, thanks to Kaan and my Silver, I know they do." She flashed Edward a look of triumph.

Edward made a harrumphing noise. He was not convinced. Kaan was a notorious liar—but this time he intended to get to the truth. D'Mara knew what her husband was thinking. "Declan," she said. "You tell us what you saw up in the sky."

"I saw Kaan kicking that beautiful Silver," Declan said, glowering at Kaan. "And he'd wanted to wear those disgusting dragon boots too. That is no way to treat any dragon, let alone a precious young Silver. Kaan got everything he deserved, if you ask me."

D'Mara sighed; she wished her sons didn't dislike each other so violently. "Calm down, Declan," she said. "Please tell us what you saw up there—"

Kaan interrupted angrily. "Why are you asking *him*? What does *he* know? Only I can tell you what I saw. And I can tell you something else too: That stupid Silver is no good. And I'm not going on *any* dragon ever again unless it's a Red. *So there*."

D'Mara and Edward exchanged glances. "We will discuss that later, Kaan," his father said. "Meanwhile, you will be quiet. Please continue, Declan."

"Kaan and the Silver were flying just above Mount Lennix," Declan said. "There was a brilliant flash of silver light and that was it. They were gone. Totally vanished."

D'Mara turned to Kaan. "Now, Kaan, you may tell us what happened."

Kaan, annoyed at having been told to keep quiet, shrugged and said sulkily, "Nothing much. There was a tunnel thing with light and then there was a big cloud and a long way down I saw stuff like one of those old maps with a load of people running around and moving colored dragon-boxes and then we came home. Just stupid, boring stuff on a stupid, boring dragon."

D'Mara smiled at her family, revealing her sharp white teeth. "What Kaan is saying is that the Silver took him through a portal. And that he saw a city full of humans."

Edward leaned forward. "How many humans, Kaan?" he asked.

"Dunno. Tons of them. They were like ants."

D'Mara looked at Edward, her eyes shining with triumph. "I told you so," she said.

"So you did," Edward said tersely, and turned his attention back to his youngest son. "Now, Kaan. You will write a report on what happened. You will draw a map of the place you saw. You will estimate how many people you saw and then—"

"No *way*," Kaan interrupted.

"And then," D'Mara added, "you may go to the Roost and ask Valkea if she would consent to be your Lock."

Kaan's eyes lit up. "*Valkea?*"

"Valkea?" Tamra echoed. "But, Ma, you can't do that! You *can't*. Me and Valkea, we've got an agreement. We—"

"Don't be ridiculous, Tamra," D'Mara said. "You are already Locked with Trixtan."

"It's not a full Lock. You *know* it's not. I have to share him with Mirra. And it's so *boring*."

"Be quiet, Tamra," D'Mara snapped. She turned the full might of her cold-eyed stare upon her daughter and Tamra shrank back, like a snail before salt. *One day*, Tamra thought, *I'll show my mother who's boss. And then she'll be sorry.*

D'Mara turned back to her son. "Valkea is a fine Red and Krane tells me she would like to Lock with a Lennix. So you stand a good chance. I advise you to be on your very best behavior. Valkea is not a dragon to be messed around with. Do you understand?"

Kaan was already on his feet. "Oh yes! Yes, I understand. I'll be really nice to her. I will, I promise."

"But first you do the report for your father. It will be good practice. If Valkea allows you to Lock, you will have to write up a log for each flight. You understand that?"

Kaan nodded impatiently. "Yep, yep, I get it. Can I go now?"

D'Mara nodded. Through half-closed eyes, Tamra watched Kaan scrape back his chair. He unwound his silver sash, threw it to the floor, and ran out, leaving the door open behind him. Silently, glowering like thunder, Tamra stood up. Declan, Mirra, Edward, and D'Mara watched her as she picked up her notepad, neatly tucked her chair into the table, and walked toward the door, head held high. She closed the door quietly behind her and they heard her light footsteps going slowly down the stone stairs, then there was silence.

D'Mara frowned. Tamra's considered silence worried her. She would have much preferred a door-slamming tantrum.

———

Later that night, D'Mara and Edward stood on the roof of D'Mara's lookout and watched the skies. It was a clear night with a bright moon that illuminated a few small clouds in their usual place above Mount Lennix.

"Can we be sure Kaan went through a portal?" Edward asked. "You don't think he was just boasting, telling stories? He's not the most truthful of our children, to put it mildly."

"I believe him," D'Mara said. "You can always tell when Kaan is lying. He looks up to the left and fiddles with his right earlobe."

"Does he?" Edward was surprised.

"I wouldn't expect you to spot subtle signs like that, Edward, but yes, he does. Every time. And this time he didn't. Not once. And he wasn't boasting, was he? He didn't really want to talk about it."

Edward was surprised. He thought D'Mara hardly noticed their children. "Well," he admitted, "Decimus thinks the Lost Lands might really exist too."

Now it was D'Mara's turn to be surprised. "Well, well. And I always thought that Lock of yours was a bit of a bonehead. Good for him."

Edward was thinking. "So if the Silver took Kaan through a portal," he said, "why are you giving him Valkea to Lock with— surely he should stay with the Silver?"

"Kaan is no good for the Silver," D'Mara said. "I see that now. He's too big, too clumsy. The Silver is a delicate beast. He'll damage him and we can't risk that."

"Kaan didn't look right with him," Edward agreed.

D'Mara nodded. "And they didn't Lock, that's for sure. There was absolutely no communication between them. But we have the Silver now and that is what matters. Because with it the Lost Lands are lost to us no more!"

To Edward's shock, D'Mara grabbed his hands and looked down into his eyes, holding his gaze uncomfortably. "Edward, don't you see? *This* is why I wanted that Silver egg. *This* is why I walked all that way to the ghastly Zolls' place to get that dragon. Our world is no good anymore. We've used it up. There is nothing left for us or the Raptors. This wonderful Silver is the key to our very survival. With it we can go to a place full of humans just waiting to be used. We can go through to those Lost Lands and make them our own. Edward, those lands and all in them belong to *us*."

"I understand. Believe me, I do," Edward said, desperate to escape the piercing gaze.

D'Mara laughed and, to Edward's relief, let go of his hands and spun around to look out of the window up at the sky, where there lay a myriad of invisible links to a whole new world that they now had access to. "We Lennixes are not finished yet, Edward. Just think how grateful our Raptors will be to eat human flesh again," she said, touching a subject she knew Edward held dear.

Edward became animated. "It will be just like the old days, before we had to go over to sheep. It's never been the same since."

"It is so simple," D'Mara said. "The Silver is our key."

"But a key needs a Lock, D'Mara," Edward said. "And clearly, that's not going to be Kaan. So what do we do?"

"I've been thinking about that," D'Mara said. "I rather suspect that Declan was right, the Silver already has a Lock—that shepherd boy."

Edward was aghast. "Well, that's a disaster," he said. "There's no point if the Silver's not Locked with a Lennix."

D'Mara's eyes glittered in the moonlight. "So we'll make that shepherd boy a Lennix," she said. "We'll adopt him into the clan. He'll be so grateful he'll do whatever we want."

Edward felt giddy with admiration. "D'Mara Lennix, you're amazing. Absolutely *amazing*."

For once, D'Mara's smile reached her eyes. "I know," she said.

23

Joshua Lennix

Early next morning Allie was on her way to Bone Grind. Carli was with her, sent back after D'Mara reported her for "smirking." They were late, and hurrying through a crossing point where six passageways met, when Carli stopped and frantically flapped her hands. "Back! Get back against the wall," she hissed. Marching toward them was a phalanx of guards in the impressive Lennix household livery of gold and black with the colored sashes of their own Raptor Locks. "Something's up," Carli whispered. "The household guard never *ever* come down here."

Wide-eyed, Allie stared. Not at the guards who looked so impossibly clean and bright in their finery—but at the slight, ashen-faced figure being marched between them. "Joss . . ." Allie breathed. "It's *Joss*."

"*Shh!*" Carli hissed.

For a fleeting moment, Allie met Joss's panicked gaze, and then he was gone, swept past her in a *clacker-clack, clacker-clack* of steel-tipped boots. Allie watched the backs of the guards disappear around the corner, taking Joss away from her, to what fate she had no idea. All she knew was it looked bad.

"Come on," Carli said, pulling Allie along with her. "We're even later now." Blindly, Allie followed Carli as she ran along the passages to Bone Grind. As Carli pushed open the door, she saw tears streaming down Allie's face. "Hey, kid," she said gently. "It's not so bad. At least we're going to be warm today. We're burning bones for ash for the new eggs' nests."

Allie nodded. She stared at the pile of bones waiting to be scrubbed clean and placed into the furnace, and she realized that she didn't feel the slightest bit sick. In fact, she didn't feel anything at all. And she didn't think she ever would again.

Joss, on the other hand, felt sick with nerves. Something terrible was about to happen to him, of that he was sure. Why else would he be sent under guard to the Lennix quarters? He'd heard all about Madam D'Mara's cruelty to prisoners, the way she singled some out for particularly dangerous duties, and as he was marched up a flight of wide stone stairs, he guessed that now it was his turn. He'd heard enough stories in the Raptor nursery to know what to expect: D'Mara reveled in the occasional push from the launching platform and had even been known, so they said, to dump prisoners into the bone crusher.

Joss was trying to decide which fate would be the least terrible when the posse of guards threw open a heavy set of doors, marched him through, and—with much stamping of feet—halted. Joss stared in amazement at the opulently furnished hall that lay before him. Polished weapons and trophies lined the walls, which were festooned with red and black silk banners on which was emblazoned the Lennix symbol: a red inverted triangle enclosing an upward-pointing black arrow. Down the middle of the hall was a long, narrow table; at the nearest end was a large candle and three ebony chairs with red velvet seats. Two of the chairs were already occupied: one by D'Mara Lennix and the other by Edward Lennix. The chair between them was empty.

The guards bowed and backed out of the room, softly closing the doors behind them, and Joss was left alone to face the Lennix clan chiefs. They looked up, appraising him with a cool gaze as though, he thought, they were looking at something and deciding whether to buy it.

D'Mara spoke first. "Welcome, Joshua, to Fortress Lennix." Joss said nothing; his mouth was too dry to speak. D'Mara continued smoothly. "Joshua, clan Lennix is an inclusive family. We like to welcome the very best of people into it. At Compound Zoll I saw at once that you were one of these people. I believed you were destined for great things."

Confused, Joss stared at D'Mara. He heard what she was saying but the words made no sense at all.

D'Mara and Edward exchanged anxious glances. Was there something wrong with the boy? He looked utterly gormless. D'Mara steamed ahead. "But before I could offer you anything, I had first to prove your worth to my husband. He did not believe me."

Edward flashed an annoyed frown at D'Mara, who paid no attention. "And so, Joshua, you were put into the Roost as a prisoner as a test of your character, which I am delighted to say you have passed with flying colors. Of course, I knew you would, despite Edward's—"

Angry at being used as a scapegoat by D'Mara, Edward thumped the table with his fist. "Enough," he snapped.

D'Mara glared at him. "Edward, this is for the good of the Clan," she hissed.

"I realize that." Edward spoke through clenched teeth. "It's your methods I'm objecting to."

Joss watched the two Lennix chiefs with bemusement. They seemed to be fighting over him. It made no sense at all.

Edward decided to take over before D'Mara bad-mouthed him anymore. He looked Joss in the eye and said, "Joshua, welcome to clan Lennix."

Joss stared uncomprehendingly. What did they mean, *welcome to clan Lennix*? Were they playing games with him? Was this some kind of test too?

D'Mara saw they were getting nowhere, and decided to try a less formal approach. "Joshua dear, come and sit with us," she said, patting the soft red velvet seat of the empty chair. Feeling as if he were in a dream, Joss sat down uneasily between the two Lennixes. He felt like a vole caught between two competing eagles. Unsure which beak to look at, he gazed at the table in front of him, where a scroll tied in red ribbon lay beside the candle, pen and ink, and a stick of black sealing wax.

"Well, Joshua," D'Mara said, reaching for the scroll. "This is a special day for us all. Family is so important, don't you agree?"

Joss tried to ignore the empty space inside him that always seemed to open up when anyone mentioned family. He glanced up at D'Mara and she gave him a smile that almost reached her eyes. Joss remembered how he and D'Mara had sat in the sheepfold and talked about dragons and how she had listened and sympathized with all his fears about the Zolls. Maybe, he thought, this was what she had been planning all the time. Maybe Allie was wrong after all. Maybe the netting and being a prisoner really was, as D'Mara had said, a test—which he had passed. Joss tried his very best to convince himself that the Lennixes were more misunder-stood than murderous and felt himself very nearly succeeding.

D'Mara untied the red ribbon and flattened out the scroll in front of him. Joss stared at it, uncomprehending.

"You *can* read?" Edward asked.

Joss nodded. He could read well enough, but the Lennix script was crisscrossed with curlicues and squiggles and was so cramped and narrow that the only words he could make out were his own name.

D'Mara handed him the pen and Edward placed a well-manicured index finger on an empty line at the foot of the document. "Sign there, Joshua. And then it will be done."

At last Joshua found his voice. "*What* will be done?"

"The adoption, of course," D'Mara said.

"*Adoption?*" Joss asked.

"Indeed. You will become our son."

Joss stared at the Lennixes in astonishment.

"That's right," D'Mara said. "From now on your name will be Joshua Lennix. You will be part of our family and treated no dif-ferently from our own children. Indeed, we already regard you as fondly as we do our own sons, do we not, Edward?"

Edward Lennix nodded. That was easy enough—he was not particularly fond of either of his boys.

A strange feeling began to creep through Joss. He had forgot-ten how it felt to be thought of as special—and to feel safe too. And there in the Lennixes' hall, for the first time in two long, frightening years, Joss felt both these things. He was with two powerful people who would protect him and even seemed to value him. They weren't his parents—no one could replace his parents—but they were *something*. Very deliberately, Joss pushed aside all the terrible things he had seen and heard in Fortress Lennix, and when the image of the blood on the pale girl's bandage stubbornly refused to go, Joss gritted his teeth and told himself that it was probably not nearly as bad as it seemed. And besides, once he was part of the Lennix family, he could help to make it all better. For everyone. Couldn't he?

But there was one thing that Joss could not talk himself out of caring about. "My sister," he said. "Will you adopt my sister too?"

A microsecond's glance passed between Edward and D'Mara. At times like this they understood each other perfectly. D'Mara chose her words carefully. "Don't worry about your sister, Joshua," she said. "We will look after her too."

Edward nodded his agreement.

"And Lysander?"

"Lysander?" Edward asked suspiciously. "Who's he?"

But D'Mara had guessed. "Is Lysander the Silver's name, Joss?"

"Yes," Joss admitted, feeling cross with himself for letting Lysander's name slip out. *But*, he told himself, *I'm one of them now. So it's fine. It's all fine.*

"So I take it you are already Locked with Lysander?" D'Mara asked.

Joss nodded.

"Well done, Joshua. We are proud of you," D'Mara told him. Joss smiled. It felt good to make someone feel proud of him. "To be Locked with a Silver is a great honor," D'Mara added. "A great honor indeed."

"Almost as much of an honor as being a Lennix," Edward muttered.

"Thank you, Edward," D'Mara said, throwing him a warning look. She turned her attention to Joss. "Now, Joshua, I expect you will wish to live with Lysander in his chamber while he becomes accustomed to the Roost? We Lennixes like to live with our Locks in the early stages."

Any niggling doubts now vanished. "Live in Lysander's chamber?" Joss asked, incredulous. "Just me and him? Oh, yes, *please*. I would *love* to." He reached for the pen, not noticing the looks of triumph the two Lennix chiefs exchanged. He was too busy trying to get the right amount of ink to stay on the delicate pen nib. Joss had not used a pen for two long years, and his hands, more accustomed to grabbing sheep, felt clumsy.

Slowly, carefully, Joss began to sign his name at the foot of the scroll. When he reached the *a* at the end of *Joshua*, D'Mara leaned forward and said, "Don't forget to sign with your *new* name." Joss nodded, and with a sense of unreality, he wrote: *Lennix*. He looked at his new signature, a little shaky and shining with wet ink, and he knew he had done something that would change his life forever.

24

Bellacrux

It had been a long, hard day in Bone Grind. The nursery had had a flurry of hatchings, and Allie and Carli were now part of a team of six, all working to produce enough bone ash to line the nests and make bonemeal to mix in the hatchlings' feed. But now at last, as the light in the window slits faded and the shadows fell over the bone pit, Allie, Carli, and their four coworkers had very nearly finished. Hands shaking with exhaustion, Allie tamped down the last of the bonemeal into the final sack and Carli tied the top with twine. They shoveled out the ashes of the final batch of burned bones and heaved them into the ash cart. Then they rang the bell for the nursery attendant to fetch the sacks and cart.

The boy who came was Joss's replacement, and Allie found the courage to ask him if he knew what had happened to Joss. The boy smirked. "Some kids have all the luck," he said. "He got adopted."

"Adopted?" Allie stared at the boy, bewildered. What could the boy possibly mean?

"Yeah. He's a Lennix now."

"What do you mean, *he's a Lennix*?" Allie demanded angrily. "Of course he's not a Lennix. How could he be?"

The boy shrugged. "Like I said. He got adopted by them. And now we're going to have to bow and call him sir and all that stuff.

But I'm telling you, he'd better not come down here without a guard. We don't like turncoats."

"Joss isn't a turncoat," Allie said indignantly.

The boy spat on the floor in disgust. "Well, *I* wouldn't take the filthy Lennix name, not for a thousand crowns."

Allie walked silently along the maze of passages. Carli stayed with her but the other four hurried ahead—Allie guessed none of them wanted to be seen with the sister of a "turncoat." As they went, Allie tried to make sense of what the boy had said. Why would the Lennixes want to adopt Joss? And why would Joss agree to such a thing? Surely it could not be true?

In the dining chamber, Allie was greeted by sullen silence; it seemed everyone knew about Joss. The prisoners were crowded around the table, cramming as much bread and lumps of meat into their mouths as they could in the five minutes they had to eat. Allie felt faint with hunger. She pushed her way into the crowd only to be met with sharp elbows and turned backs. She had just managed to grab a piece of bread and had retreated to a quiet corner when there was a collective gasp and everyone sprang to attention.

Mirra and Tamra Lennix stood in the doorway. "Allinson Moran," they said in unison. "Come with us."

The attitude in the dining chamber changed. Glances of sympathy were thrown Allie's way—Tamra and Mirra were notorious bullies. Prisoners they picked on did not last long. Shocked, Allie looked at them blankly.

"Move!" Tamra screamed.

"Now!" Mirra yelled.

Allie's exhaustion made her reckless. "Why?" she asked.

Tamra came up to her. She stood a head taller than Allie, and her gimlet dark eyes looked down with a cold loathing. "Because, Allinson Moran, you are going on a little visit to Bellacrux."

Mirra laughed. "For a nighttime snack. Ha ha."

Allie was aware of a soft hissing all around her. She realized it was the horrified intakes of breath from her fellow prisoners.

Tamra lost patience. "Guards!" she yelled. Two Roost guards marched into the dining room. They gave the Lennix salute to the twins and then strode over to Allie, took her by the elbows, and marched her out. The door slammed behind them and shocked silence fell in the dining chamber. It was finally broken by Carli: "She doesn't deserve that."

"No one deserves to be sent to Bellacrux," another said flatly. "No one."

The prisoners finished their supper in silence.

Allie was marched along a maze of passageways to the service stairs that went up inside the center of the Roost. With the guards hurrying her along to keep up with the prancing figures of the Lennix twins, Allie stumbled up the seemingly endless steps, her mind racing. Bellacrux, Bellacrux, *Bellacrux* . . . surely this must be the very same Bellacrux who had killed her great-aunt Ettie? Dragons lived for a long time—she had even heard some lived for centuries, and it was perfectly possible. Fear settled deep into Allie's stomach as she climbed ever higher, out of the damp and airless depths of Fortress Lennix, into the fresher air of the upper levels. But Allie knew that the better the air became, the nearer she drew to the dragon.

At last they reached the top, where a finely carved block of stone announced they were on Level One. Instructed by the twins, the guards marched Allie along the landing, and for the first time since she had been taken prisoner, she saw the sky, glimpsed through a stone window slit. It was dark, which surprised her, and a sprinkling of stars gave her a twinge of nostalgia. She remembered nights in Compound Zoll sitting on the kitchen doorstep, watching for shooting stars. Never had Allie expected to remember her time at the Zolls' with anything like affection, but now it seemed to be almost idyllic in comparison.

At the end of the landing was a heavy door set in a deep archway, above which Allie read the sign: SENIOR RAPTOR ROOST. NO UNAUTHORIZED ENTRY. While the guards unlocked the door, Mirra and Tamra took the opportunity to slam Allie against the wall. "Payback time," Tamra hissed. "You don't punch a Lennix and get away with it." The door was thrown open and Tamra gave Allie a vicious shove forward.

"We'll take the prisoner from here," said the taller guard abruptly. Allie got the impression the guard liked the twins as little as she did.

"Health and safety, miss," the other hurried to explain.

Tamra snickered. "She can forget about safety," she said.

"Not so good for her health either," Mirra added.

Their snorts of laughter followed Allie as the guards led her along a long, wide corridor, the walls whitewashed and bright, lit by torches with flames guttering in a cold breeze. At the end of the corridor, Allie saw a huge, vaulted circular atrium, and on its far side a pair of arched doors at least thirty feet high, hewn from dark wood and peppered with reinforcing bars and studs, above which was a faded gold sign reading: LENNIX GRAND: BELLACRUX. A feeling of dread went through Allie—she was near her journey's end. Another snicker came from one of the twins, and Allie decided that whatever was about to happen, she would not give them the pleasure of showing them how terrified she was.

They progressed into the atrium, and Allie now saw the reason for the breeze: To their right was an opening in the wall that gave out onto the night. As they walked past, Allie saw a wide runway stretching out into the darkness and caught a stomach-churning sensation of the massive drop below. She had a sudden fear of the twins throwing her off the runway, and felt glad of the guards' almost protective grip upon her shoulders. They walked slowly on toward the arched doors and came to a line painted on the floor, just out of arm's reach from a small wicket set into the doors. There they stopped.

"Where's Harry?" Tamra asked, her eyes on a small door to the left where Bellacrux's attendant slept.

"Mr. Harry is not here, miss. It's his night off," the taller guard explained.

"Good. Just checking," Tamra said. "You can shove her in now."

The guard went pale. He hadn't expected this. He had thought the twins were merely frightening their prisoner. "In . . . in there, miss?" he asked.

"Don't ask stupid questions," Tamra snapped. "Yes, in there."

"But, miss—" the other guard began.

"Do what you're told," Mirra snapped. "Or you'll be going in too."

Bravely, the guard dared to reply. "I beg pardon, Miss Mirra, but I just want to make certain. As you know, Bellacrux is now incubating the Green's egg. It's a highly dangerous time to invade her territory. And the girl's going in with no food offering neither."

The guard's matter-of-fact words sent a rush of panic through Allie, and she had to fight the urge to fall to her knees and beg for mercy. There was no point, she told herself. The twins would love to see her beg. They'd just laugh and throw her in anyway. And so, to the twins' annoyance, Allie stared studiedly into the distance while Mirra laughed at the guard. "Ha ha. *She's* the food offering."

The guards exchanged horrified glances. "Actually, miss, it's not strictly our job to *feed* prisoners to—"

Tamra cut the guard short. "Just do it!" she screamed.

"Or you'll be next," Mirra yelled.

The tall guard turned to Allie. Under cover of rattling his keys, he said rapidly in a low murmur, "Ladder on the right. Walkway at the top. Get into the refuge."

Allie nodded. Her mouth was too dry to speak.

"Stop your whispering and get on with it," Tamra snapped at the guards, who still hesitated. "Oh, you brickheads, *I'll* do it. Give me the key."

Reluctantly the guard handed over the key. Tamra opened the wicket and Mirra grabbed Allie. "Get in," they snarled, and shoved Allie through.

Allie tripped over the threshold and fell hard onto the marble floor. Dimly aware of the shimmer of an ocean of green scales not so very far away, she scrambled to her feet and raced up the long metal ladder. Allie reached the top in the fastest time anyone had ever run up a thirty-foot-high ladder. She stopped to catch her breath and take stock. The walkway was a wide stone ledge with red railings. It ran all around the top of a huge, domed chamber, which was lined with green tiles punctuated by the occasional gold stripe. On the far side of the chamber, directly opposite, was a small, enclosed area with a turreted roof and a narrow window, which Allie guessed was the refuge. However, it could have been on the other side of the world for all the hope it gave her, because the only way to get there was along the exposed walkway. And far below, Allie could hear long, deep intakes of breath, like the wind being drawn through a tunnel, and an ominous scratching, which sounded like a dragon sharpening her claws.

Allie knew she had no choice but to try to get to the refuge. Keeping close to the smooth green tiles of the wall, she began to crawl in slow motion along the walkway. She counted each painfully slow hand-step forward: *one ... two ... three ... four ... five ... six ... seven ...*

And then came a roar like thunder. It sent Allie reeling backward, her hands clamped over her ears, convinced her eardrums were exploding. Like a wave crashing upon the beach, the chamber's renowned echo took up the roar and sent it ricocheting off the walls, engulfing Allie in a wall of sound, washing her away into nothingness. Allie threw herself flat upon the cold stone walkway, covered her head with her hands, and waited for the end to come.

Outside the doors, Tamra and Mirra heard what they'd been waiting for. They did a dance of victory and ran off shrieking with laughter.

The guards waited until the last vibrations of the sound had died away, and then the tall one spoke. "Shall we go in and, er, you know, see if there's anything we can do?"

The other guard shook his head. "We go in there and we won't come out again. The kid's just the starters. We'll be the main course."

Allie opened her eyes and immediately wished she hadn't—looking straight at her was a brilliant green lozenge-shaped pupil the size of a plate. Unblinking, the eye regarded her steadily. Allie stared at the eye's swirling reflections, which felt like mysterious gateways to another world. She saw the delicate folds of the greenish-brown skin that formed the eyelid and the precise, shimmering green scales that ringed it. Allie knew she should make a run for the refuge while she still could, but she was mesmerized. Slowly, she got up so that she was kneeling, and not once did she take her eyes from the dragon's limpid green gaze.

Bellacrux turned her head so that she was facing Allie full on, and it seemed to Allie that all time was suspended. She looked deep into Bellacrux's eyes and waited for whatever the dragon would do. Allie knew and accepted that there was no escape now, but somehow it no longer mattered. Her whole world lay within those mysterious eyes. Bellacrux took a long, deep breath, and Allie felt the breath from her lungs being drawn into those dark, wind-tunnel nostrils, and then put her hands over her eyes and prepared herself for what must surely come next: dragonfire.

But what came next was a distant voice somewhere deep inside her mind: *Allie. I, Bellacrux, know you.*

Allie thought she must be imagining things. Cautiously, she peeked through her fingers and saw Bellacrux tilting her head to one side in what seemed to be a quizzical glance: *Allie. You are from Ettie. The sweetest Lock I ever had. My darling Ettie.*

"Ettie?" Allie whispered, and the echo took up the name: *Ettie Ettie Ettie Ettie Ettie Ettie . . .* "My great-aunt Ettie?"

Allie. Ettie. Twin souls.

Allie was transfixed. She crawled over to the guardrails and, thinking that this was the stupidest thing she had ever done in her life, she reached out and placed her hand very gently on Bellacrux's snout. It felt like warm velvet with a touch of dampness. Bellacrux did not react, so Allie let her hand lie there, thinking how strange it was that it made her feel so happy. But as Allie sat gazing at Bellacrux and the stillness between them seemed to fill the chamber, her grandmother's words came back to haunt her: *My darling sister, Ettie, Locked with the Lennix Grand—a vicious Green named Bellacrux. The next day, it killed her.*

Bellacrux blinked slowly, and Allie saw a tear escape from the dragon's right eye. As she watched the tear find its way down the scales, these words came into her head: *Allie. Please, never believe this terrible lie. It was not I who killed my dearest Ettie; it was the Lennixes. They killed her in front of my eyes, for daring to be my Lock.*

"Was that you talking to me?" Allie whispered to Bellacrux.

The big green head nodded.

It was very unsettling having someone else's voice appear in your mind, Allie thought. But she decided to try to send her thoughts to Bellacrux: *Bellacrux. Can you hear me?*

I can hear you, Allie, came the reply. Allie looked deep into Bellacrux's eyes. *I'm so sorry,* she sent. *So sorry for you and for Ettie.*

Bellacrux lowered her head. *It is the Lennixes who will soon be sorry,* she sent to Allie. *I, Bellacrux, have a long memory. I have waited through the slow turning of the years for vengeance, for everything the Lennixes have done. I have bided my time. And now that time has come.*

Allie felt a thrill of excitement. "Good," she whispered, too excited to think of sending her thoughts. "And the Lennixes will deserve everything they get. They are monsters."

Fighting talk, Allie heard Bellacrux say. *I like that, Allie. Ettie was the same. She was so brave. She knew it was dangerous to Lock with me but still she did it. You remind me of her. Very much.*

"I'm glad I do," Allie whispered. "Because I want to be brave too. It's not always easy, but sometimes being brave is the only thing you have left."

Wise words, Bellacrux said. *Wise and brave.*

Allie thought it was much easier to be brave with a huge green dragon by her side, but she said nothing. And then these words came into her mind: *Allie. It is true, two are always braver than one. And so, I, Bellacrux, ask you this. Will you be my Lock? My last and best?*

In the echoing dragon chamber, there was silence as Allie sent her message deep into Bellacrux's mind: *Oh, Bellacrux. Yes, I will be your Lock. I will be your last and best.*

As the shadows from the moon moved across Bellacrux's chamber and two guards sat dejectedly outside, Allie climbed down the ladder and curled up beneath Bellacrux's wing beside a large green rock.

Sleep now, Allie, my Lock. Bellacrux's words came to Allie. And so, exhausted, Allie slept.

25

Locks

While Allie was falling into a deep sleep beneath her Lock's wing, Declan was showing Joss the Lock's room: a simple space containing a bed, a chest, a desk with a few books on dragon care, and, most important, a small blue door leading directly to Lysander's chamber.

Rather self-consciously, Joss wore the Lennix Roost uniform. It was a smart black tunic and trousers edged with the dark Lennix red, and around his waist was the impressively shiny silver sash that Kaan had recently thrown off in a temper. By far the best thing about the uniform, Joss thought, was the Lennix watch. A big, square timepiece, it sat on his wrist while the seconds, minutes, and hours ticked relentlessly over. Joss had never seen anything like it and he could hardly stop looking at it.

Joss was tired; he had spent a long day learning all about Lennix family history. He knew he should be interested, because however strange it seemed, he was a part of them now, but he had found it hard to stop thinking about Lysander. After the history lesson there had been a tour of the Lennix quarters and then a strained supper with his new brothers and sisters, three of whom had refused to acknowledge his presence. But at long last, here he was, only a few steps away from Lysander.

Lysander was the newest member of the Raptor Roost, and so under its strict hierarchy he had been allocated a chamber on the lowest floor, Level Twelve. It was an airy and comfortable space; its walls were painted a calming blue with a silver frieze of interlocking swirls below a dome of dark blue scattered with silver stars. A circle of silver lamps sat high on the walls, lighting the chamber with a soft glow. The floor was, like all the Roost chambers, strewn with rugs and huge soft cushions, although on Level Twelve these were a mixture of plain colors—Lysander's being all in various shades of blue—rather than the more exotic rich patterns found in the upper levels. Comfortable though Lysander was—and also full of a supper of three roast chickens—he felt lonely and unhappy. He missed Joss terribly. He lay mournfully on the rugs, his head resting on a cushion, thinking of the last terrifying time he had seen his Lock: trussed in a net and being flown away in the talons of a huge blue Raptor. And then, suddenly, Lysander's eyes flickered open—Joss was near. *Joss!* Lysander sent excitedly. *Joss, Joss, Joss!*

Joss laughed out loud. Declan looked at him quizzically. "All right?" he asked.

Joss grinned. "You bet. I just heard from Lysander. Can I see him now?"

Declan grinned and pointed to the blue door. "He's through there. See you tomorrow," he called after Joss as he headed for the door. "Don't forget, it's family breakfast at eight a.m. prompt. You'll find a Roost timetable on the noticeboard. Don't be late, okay?"

Joss turned and nodded. "I won't be late, not with this watch. But thanks for telling me. There is so much to remember."

"You'll get used to it." Declan came over to Joss and shook his hand. "We're brothers now," he said. "We're in this together."

Joss smiled. "Thanks, Declan," he said, then, heart beating fast, he pushed open the little blue door and raced into the dragon chamber. "Lysander!" he yelled. "Oh, Lysander, Lysander. I've missed you *so* much!" He threw his arms around Lysander's neck, and as he buried his face in the soft folds of skin beneath Lysander's ears, he felt a long, rasping dragon tongue, warm and damp, on his cheek.

Joss, Joss, I missed you too. Lysander's happy squeak filled his head. *I was so sad. They put you in a net. They hurt you.*

Joss tried not to think about the terrifying ride in the net. It was certainly some test that D'Mara had set for him and just the thought of it made him feel sick. Lysander caught some of Joss's terror at the memory and his excited squeaking faded away. They sat quietly together in the chamber, Joss leaning back against the dragon's soft stomach, which burbled in a companionable way.

After a while, Lysander sent: *Hey, Joss, I know how to open the outside door. We could fly away. We could go right now!*

Joss patted Lysander's stomach affectionately. *I can't go. Not yet. Allie is here too and I can't leave without her.*

Lysander did not understand. *Why? You're not Locked with Allie.*

Joss searched for a way to explain it. *Allie is my sister. She is like . . . my human Lock.*

Lysander snorted scornfully. *But you can't fly with her. What use is that?*

But the truth of it was that it wasn't just Allie making Joss reluctant to leave; it was the new and exciting possibilities that had opened up for him. Now that he—and very soon Allie—were to be part of the Lennix family, Joss felt that at last he belonged somewhere. The idea of leaving did not fill him with the kind of hope he had felt when he and Lysander had planned to escape from the Zolls. And besides, he really liked Declan.

Joss was wondering how to begin to explain all this to Lysander when the wicket in the large door to Lysander's chamber burst open and Tamra and Mirra came hurtling in. Lysander leapt up and raised his wings to an attack stance. Joss placed his hands on Lysander's neck and whispered, "Shh . . . it's all right. It's all right."

Tamra and Mirra stopped dead and stared at the silver dragon—he was a startlingly beautiful sight with his raised wings shimmering in the light of the lamps, his head held high, and his brilliant green eyes glittering with anger. Mirra's and Tamra's mouths dropped open in amazement. Mirra stood silent, over-awed by such beauty, but Tamra quickly recovered herself. "Hey, little bro," she sneered. "Tell your shiny friend to keep his temper, will you?"

Joss looked at the two girls, who were now officially his sisters. They stood a head taller than him, their identical dark curls scraped back into ponytails, their Lennix Roost uniform sporting green sashes for their Lock, Trixtan. He thought how lucky he was to have Allie as his sister; he couldn't wait for her to become a Lennix too. As soon as she was part of the family they'd hang out together all the time, and there was no way they would have anything to do with the twins. But right now, Joss knew he had to remember he was a Lennix. "Sorry," he said. "I think you frightened him."

"Yeah," Tamra said, laughing. "We're good at that. Frightening things."

Joss made an effort not to respond. The sooner the twins left him alone, the better. But it seemed they were not finished yet.

"So you're our brother now, right?" Mirra said, leaning nonchalantly against the wall and kicking at the rug.

"Yeah, I am." Joss forced a smile.

"So what does that make us, Sheep-boy?" Tamra sneered.

"Well, you're my sisters," Joss said, trying his very best to sound pleased about it.

"Yeah. We're your *sisters*," Tamra said.

"Yes," Joss said, feeling the smile growing tight upon his face and his cheek muscles aching. The twins were working up to something, and he really did not want to know what it was.

Tamra walked slowly over to him, taking care to keep an eye on Lysander, who was standing at the ready, guarding his Lock. But even Lysander could not guard Joss from what Tamra had come to tell him.

"Well, we're the *only* sisters you've got now, Sheep-boy."

From beside the door, Mirra spluttered with laughter.

Joss's stomach felt as though it were suddenly full of ice. "What do you mean?" he asked.

"I'll give you a clue." Tamra stuck her face so close to Joss he could see the rash of pimples on her forehead. "It's two words. And it's . . ." She trailed off and looked back at Mirra. Joss could tell they had practiced this and were enjoying every minute.

"Dragon food!" Mirra yelled.

"What?" Joss felt like the world was spinning out of control. Behind him he heard Lysander take in a deep firebreath. Unaware that Lysander had yet to have his fire sleep, Tamra hurriedly backed away. "Hey, calm down. Don't set fire to your bed, ha ha."

She joined Mirra at the door and Joss suddenly lost his resolve to stay cool. He hurtled across the chamber and dived at them, but the twins were too quick for him. They leapt through the wicket and slammed it in his face.

"What have you done to her?" Joss yelled after them. "What have you done to Allie?"

The tiny inspection flap in the wicket flipped open and Tamra's face appeared.

"Fed her to Bellacrux," she said. And the flap snapped shut.

Joss stared at the flap, waiting for it to flip open again and for Tamra to tell him it was a joke. It stayed shut. A feeling of numbness spread through Joss as he stood stone still, unable to move, unable to think or even feel. Slowly he became aware of Lysander nuzzling his hair with his long, rough tongue, and he turned to his dragon and wrapped his arms around his warm, silvery neck. And there they stayed, while Joss's tears ran down Lysander's scales and dropped onto his polished Lennix shoes.

He thought how scared Allie must have been and how, while he'd been all dressed up in the stupid Lennix uniform acting like he was someone important, Allie was being thrown away like a piece of garbage. He wondered what he'd been doing at the very moment Bellacrux had taken Allie's life. How come he hadn't known what was happening to his own sister? Joss threw himself down onto one of Lysander's cushions and buried his head in its dragony-smelling softness. And then he sobbed and sobbed for the unbelievable awfulness of everything.

Lysander placed a protective wing over Joss and waited patiently until he found a space in all the grief to send: *Joss, Joss. Please don't cry. Maybe the nasty girl was lying.*

Joss raised his head and looked up into Lysander's eyes. Too upset to send any thought, he spluttered out loud, "She wasn't lying . . . I could tell. She did it. She really did it."

Why don't you try to send Allie a message, Lysander suggested.

Joss shook his head. "It's not like that with humans. We can't send thoughts. Or hear them. Not from humans."

Lysander put his head to one side. *Why ever not?*

"I don't know," Joss wailed. "I don't know anything anymore. All I know is that Allie is dead. And I'm never, ever going to see her again."

26

In the Chamber of the Grand

Late the next morning, Allie opened her eyes and found she was hugging a warm green rock with a strangely soft texture. For a few moments she had no idea where she was; all she knew was that for the first time in years, she felt safe. She stretched, rolled over, and looked up at what seemed to be the roof of a leathery green tent. And then she remembered. The events of the previous day came rushing back, and Allie understood that she was under her Lock's wing and her Lock just happened to be the Lennix Grand. "Bellacrux!" she said.

A gentle voice came into her head: *Shh, Allie, my dear.*

The leathery tent above Allie's head moved and revealed a rippling wall of green scales—somewhat faded and battered-looking, but impressive even so. A long, muscular neck with a jagged crest arched down, and Bellacrux's wise old eyes regarded her new Lock fondly. *Do not speak out loud*, Allie heard. *They must not know you are alive. Remember what they can do.*

Allie looked up at Bellacrux and concentrated hard on sending her a message. *I won't ever forget. I won't forget my parents, I won't forget your Ettie. And we will make sure they never forget either.*

The big green head nodded. *We will indeed, my little Lock. Now, tell me, did you sleep well with our egg?*

Allie put her hand on the green "rock." Of course, it was a dragon egg. *Very well indeed*, she sent.

The best sleeps are those beside an egg. There is a quietness within that soothes, Bellacrux told her. *And how do you feel this morning, my little Lock?*

Allie wasn't quite sure how she felt. Despite the fact that she trusted Bellacrux completely, she was still a little shocked to find herself in the Chamber of the Grand and actually be alive. Carli's words, *death dragon*, still haunted her. *Bellacrux, may I ask you something?* she sent tentatively.

You may ask me anything you wish, Allie dearest.

I was . . . er, I was wondering why everyone is so scared of you.

Ah, well, sometimes I . . . Allie thought she detected a wisp of embarrassment from her Lock. *Sometimes I behave a little . . . badly. But I choose no one who does not deserve it. Do not forget, my little Lock, that I am a Lennix Raptor and must at times be seen to behave like one if I am to avoid suspicion.*

Allie decided to ask no more. It was, she told herself, none of her business. But there was one other thing she did not understand. *Why do you stay in this horrible place?* she asked. *You could fly away whenever you want to.*

Bellacrux gave a long sigh that ruffled Allie's wispy hair. *Well, Allie, my dearest. Over the centuries, I've learned how to play the long game. I am here for now, biding my time, understanding all I can about the Lennixes.*

Allie smiled. *Keep your friends close, but your enemies closer.*

Bellacrux lowered her head so that she was looking Allie in the eye. She winked. *Indeed. And we will not be here much longer, my little Lock. Because the thing I hoped for has finally happened.*

What's that? Allie asked.

A Silver has been born, and now he is here, in this place. He is our key. With him I believe we can at last save what is left of this poor Raptor-ridden world.

Allie was puzzled. *But Lysander's only little,* she said. *How can he possibly save a whole world?*

Lysander? Bellacrux sounded puzzled.

That's the Silver's name, Allie sent. *My brother, Joss, Locked with him. I'm sure that's why D'Mara Lennix kidnapped us.*

Well, well. Who would have thought it? Bellacrux sent. *Indeed, I am sure it is why they took you. They want the Silver as much as I do.*

Allie sighed. *I know. Lysander is a beautiful dragon.*

It is not his beauty we want, Allie. It is his power. A Silver is a key to another world. The place my ancestors called the Lost Lands. Some say this world is no more than a legend but I know it is real. My grandmothers' grandmothers lived there once and they passed their stories down to me. It is a beautiful, peaceful place to which I long to return and take my kind with me. We will leave the Raptors and the Lennixes and all the wreckage they have made far behind, take our good friends with us, and go to live in peace with humans once again.

But how will we all get there? Allie asked.

Lysander will take us, Bellacrux said.

But how? Allie persisted.

My little Lock, don't you see? Lysander is a Silver. And all Silvers can travel through the invisible portals that link our two worlds. And if a Silver touches its tail to another dragon, they can both go through. Indeed, you can have a whole chain of dragons going through. This is how our great-great-great-grandmothers came here all those long, long years ago.

Allie was silent for some time, taking in what Bellacrux had told her. It was staggering. She knew the stories of the other world, but she had never believed they were real. Now Allie understood why D'Mara had made the long trek to find Lysander and why she had bought them from the Zolls. She even began to understand why the Lennixes had adopted Joss—what better way to keep control of Lysander than to adopt his Lock into the family? Although, when she thought about Joss actually agreeing to the adoption, Allie felt a little less understanding.

As she thought about how wonderful it would be to be safe and happy in a whole new world, a terrible thought came to Allie. *We must never let the Raptors go to the other world*, she sent.

Indeed, Allie. We must never let that happen, Bellacrux agreed. *Which is why we must get Lysander away from here as soon as we can.*

Allie and Bellacrux spent the rest of the morning discussing how to get Lysander away from Fortress Lennix. All the while, Allie stayed firmly beneath Bellacrux's wing. She sat close to the egg, her arms draped over it, and every now and then she felt a movement inside like the fluttering of a trapped bird. *Will the egg hatch soon?* she asked Bellacrux.

All too soon, I fear, Bellacrux replied. *And when it hatches, they will take it, tattoo it, and torment it until they turn it into a Raptor.*

Allie thought of the soft green innocent creature sleeping inside its egg. *That mustn't happen*, she sent.

Indeed, my little Lock. It must not. I've had to watch it too many times.

Exhausted by the events of the last few days, Allie eventually fell into a doze. She awoke to find a small box of food and a flask of water placed beside her, and Bellacrux watching her with a tender expression. *Harry came in with a roast sheep and when he wasn't looking I took his own lunch too. Dear Harry, he can't understand what has happened to it. He likes cheese sandwiches; I hope you do too. Would you like some sheep first? I saved the ears—my favorite—for you.*

Oh! Allie sent. *Sheep ears. Wow.*

Bellacrux's amused voice came into Allie's mind. *You don't like sheep ears, do you?*

Er . . . I've never had them. But I'd rather not try.

You don't know what you're missing, Bellacrux sent. *They are so chewy. And deliciously salty.*

Cheese sandwiches will be just perfect, Allie replied.

That night, Allie was awoken by Bellacrux gently nuzzling her face. *Allie dear. There is trouble in the courtyard. I must go. Pile the cushions over the egg and hide underneath. But if you close your eyes and stay calm and still, you will find you are flying with me.*

Allie peered out from her nest of cushions and watched Bellacrux push open the huge barn door in the side of the chamber so that it fell outward and lay flat upon its hinges like a drawbridge. As the chill of the night filled the chamber, Allie watched Bellacrux walk out onto the door and the huge chains settle with the weight of the dragon. And then, with a great downward thrust of her wings, Bellacrux rose into the air and was gone.

Allie burrowed down deep into the nest and wrapped her arms around the egg. Then she closed her eyes and concentrated on becoming calm and still, as Bellacrux had told her. In the warmth of the nest, Allie found it easy to let all her cares slip away, and a feeling of tranquility soon came over her. And then, suddenly, Allie was almost overcome with a dizzying sense of height. It was just as Bellacrux had said; she too was flying. The air was cold on her skin, the mountainside was bright in the moonlight, and above it she saw the stars dusting the sky and below a myriad of flickering lights in the great square mass of Fortress Lennix. And then, too soon, she was swooping down, heading fast toward the wide-open space of the landing yard.

Gathered below, Allie could see the dark shapes of Raptors already in the yard, and in the distance she saw the unmistakable figure of D'Mara Lennix striding toward them. As she came in to land, Allie saw that in the center of the group of Raptors was a small, young Green. She stood at bay: fangs bared, head raised defiantly, her wings half outstretched, and Allie knew that this dragon was no Raptor. And now Allie was on the landing yard, the Raptors were parting, and she was walking through them, heading for the young Green interloper.

Allie felt the sympathy of her Lock go out to the young Green, and then Bellacrux's behavior became suddenly shocking. She was now in front of the Green, looking down at the dragon, and Allie felt the heat of fire in her mouth as Bellacrux sent short bursts of flame flickering across the ground, so that they curled around the delicate feet of the Green and sent her hopping from one foot to another—much to the amusement of the other Raptors. Allie saw the whites of the young Green's eyes as they widened in fear and she felt her Lock feel . . . what was it . . . yes, it was *shame*.

Now the young Green began to hesitantly speak in dragon-song, and Allie understood what her Lock heard. *Fellow dragons, I am Herlenna. I come as ambassador from the Greens. You have taken our entire clutch of eggs. You have stolen our future. I beg of you; let me take one egg back home: just one to give us hope.*

Allie felt the warm, leathery surface of the egg she shared the nest with and realized that it must be from the stolen clutch. She waited for Bellacrux to offer to return it, but Bellacrux did no such thing. *You will get no egg tonight*, Allie heard her say. *Go home while you can still fly.*

Allie was so shocked at the harshness of her Lock's response that for some moments she lost her connection with Bellacrux. It returned with a terrifying image—a massive red dragon, its wings raised in fight stance, its mouth wide open, showing its long, glistening incisors. This was, although Allie did not know it, Valkea. In a sudden movement, the red dragon brought her wings down in such a way that their sharpened barbs gouged deep grooves through the scales of the Green and tore into one of her wings.

From somewhere in the night, through the open door, Allie heard a scream of pain, and she knew it was Herlenna. She threw her arms over her head, trying to get rid of the image of the cruel Red. She wanted to lose the connection with Bellacrux now—she didn't want to see anything else bad happen to the Green—but the connection would not go. Dismayed, Allie saw Bellacrux ordering Herlenna to be taken prisoner; she heard her Lock saying that she did not even believe all the Greens' eggs were gone, that the Green was no more than a low-down spy and she must be made to tell them where they were hiding the rest of the clutch. Allie heard the baying of delight from the Raptors, and the last image that came into her mind was the young Green, streaming dark blood, being hustled away.

The connection with her Lock vanished and left Allie in turmoil. Suddenly needing fresh air, careless of whether she would be seen or not, Allie pushed her way up from the cushion and sat, breathing in the cold air that tasted of stone and, Allie thought, of fear. She looked out onto the night and saw the mountains beyond, their jagged peaks dark against the starry sky. She heard the howling of the wind as it found its way through the canyons below and she felt like a stranger marooned upon a distant planet.

A brisk flurry of footsteps in the atrium outside sent Allie burrowing back under the cushions, her heart racing. Whoever it was had stopped outside the door. She heard the little viewing hatch in the wicket being flipped open, and she lay stone still. She could almost feel the gaze of the watcher traveling around the chamber. At last she heard the hatch flipping down again and she breathed easily once more.

Suddenly Allie felt overwhelmed by loneliness. The two beings closest to her—her brother and Bellacrux—were not who she had thought them to be. Joss had become a Lennix and Bellacrux was no more than another cruel and heartless Raptor. Her brother had betrayed her and her Lock had deceived her. Allie curled up around the egg for comfort, thinking that at least she had something in common with the tiny creature inside: Both of them had lost their true family and were utterly alone in Fortress Lennix.

27

A Farewell

Joss's day had been one long mire of misery. *Allie, Allie, Allie* was all Joss could think about. He had just about managed to get through breakfast by avoiding the twins' smug glances and keeping quiet. D'Mara had put the redness of Joss's eyes down to some kind of allergy. Edward did not notice. Kaan did not care. But it did not escape Declan's shrewd gaze.

Joss had spent the day with Declan on a tour of the lower levels of the Roost, starting with the dungeons, and Declan, assuming Joss was feeling the strain of his new position—being a Lennix was never going to be easy—had been very gentle with his adopted brother. But after a strained family supper when Declan had seen Joss's eyes brimming with tears, he had decided to accompany Joss down to his room at the end of the evening. And there, after some persuading, Joss had told him what had happened to Allie.

Declan was aghast. "I don't believe it," he said. "They can't do that. That's murder."

Joss gulped. He had never thought he would hear that word associated with Allie.

"Stay right there," Declan said, "I'm going to find out." It was Declan's footsteps that Allie had heard, and Declan's gaze she had felt, traveling across the chamber.

Declan was not inclined to search Bellacrux's chamber. The Lennix Grand was notoriously bad-tempered and Declan had no wish to be found rooting around in her precious cushions when she returned from wherever she had gone. He knocked on Harry's door and was greeted with some hostility. Harry was one of the few people in the Roost who was brave enough to show his contempt of the Lennixes to their faces. "What do you want?" he demanded.

Declan explained about Allie. Harry looked troubled. "I wasn't here," he said. "Your sisters deliberately chose my evening off. They knew I'd have stopped their nastiness. But yes, the Roost Guards told me. They pushed a girl in and Bellacrux took her." Seeing Declan's horrified expression, Harry defended the dragon he loved. "You mustn't blame Bellacrux; it's only her nature. But I am surprised even so; she's never taken an innocent child before. But Bellacrux is a bit unpredictable right now. She took my lunch box today and wouldn't give it back. I suppose it's the egg they gave her. She's gone broody."

Feeling shaken, Declan thanked Harry and walked slowly away. Harry watched him go. *That boy's too soft to be a Lennix*, he thought. *Needs to toughen up or he won't last long.*

Declan sat with Joss in the Lock's room, trying to give him some hope. "All I can say is I looked through the viewing hatch really carefully and there was no sign of . . . well, of anything at all. You know, no, er . . ."

"Blood," Joss finished for him.

"Exactly. So it all must have happened very quickly."

Joss gave a sob and Declan put his arm around his shoulder. "I'm so, so sorry. Even Harry is shocked that Bellacrux would do such a thing. He seemed puzzled . . ."

They sat silently while Joss choked back tears. After a while Declan said, "You know, Joss, something does not quite add up."

Joss looked up at Declan. "How do you mean?" he asked.

"Well," Declan said, "sometimes I wonder about Bellacrux. It's true she has a bad track record of kills, but I made a list of the victims once and discovered that every single one of them had killed someone themselves. If she'd taken Tamra and Mirra, I'd believe it right away. But your sister . . . well, it's odd. It makes no sense to me."

"Or to me," Joss said miserably.

"No. Well, of course it doesn't," Declan murmured.

Declan left Joss curled up asleep with Lysander and tiptoed away. Furious, he told the story to his mother, but D'Mara merely laughed. She said that was one less problem to bother about and told him not to be so sentimental. Declan went to sleep almost as troubled as Joss.

The next morning Joss woke up beside Lysander with the feeling that he had decided something while he slept. As he wriggled out from beneath his Lock's warm, soft tummy, Joss knew what his decision was: He must go and see Bellacrux's chamber for himself.

Lysander did not stir as Joss tiptoed toward the Lock's room. At the door Joss paused and sent: *See you later*, but there was no reply. Joss went back to Lysander and gave him a gentle prod, but there was no reaction. *Hey, Lysander*, he sent, *are you in your dragon-song sleep?* There was, of course, no response. Joss smiled. He was so looking forward to hearing Lysander speak the dragons' lyrical language, and he knew that Lysander would teach him too. Declan had told him how speaking dragonsong made you feel even closer to your Lock.

In his Lock chamber, Joss dressed quickly. He picked up his silver sash, and then he stopped. *What was he doing?* He had allowed himself to become part of a family that had killed his own sister. And here he was putting on their sash with no thought about what it really meant. Joss took a deep breath. He wanted to throw the sash to the floor but, he told himself sternly, if he ditched being a Lennix now, he would never make them pay for what they'd done to Allie. The Lennixes had used him to get Lysander, but now they were going to discover they would get a lot more besides a stolen Silver. Angrily, Joss wound the rest of the sash around his waist, checked his timetable—there was a muster at 8:00—checked his Lennix watch: 7:15, stuffed the Roost map into his pocket, and hurried out.

The corridor smelled of disinfectant and was damp from having just been cleaned, but there was no one around. At the far end was an arch leading to a doorway emblazoned with a faded Lennix crest. Upon it was a brass plate reading: NO ACCESS TO LENNIX STAIRS. As he pushed open the door, Joss told himself: *Remember, you're a Lennix now. This place belongs to your family. Don't rush, act confident, and don't smile too much. In fact, don't smile at all. You don't need to please anyone: You are a Lennix.*

The door led into a small chamber hewn from the rock, bright and airy with whitewashed walls and a line of portholes that looked out over the mountains. From here a broad flight of stairs wound upward through the rock, and Joss began the climb. At last he reached Level One where he paused to get his breath back and consult his map: He needed to head for the Grand Atrium. There was only one exit door—over which a faded sign in gold announced SENIOR RAPTOR ROOST. Joss pushed it open and stepped into a wide corridor. Following his map, he turned right and headed toward a huge circular space at the far end of the corridor, passing on his way four large, ornate doors, each one announcing the presence of a Senior Raptor of the First Flight behind it. He walked rapidly past, wishing his footsteps did not echo quite so loudly— and then sternly telling himself that he was a Lennix and could make as much noise as he liked.

Joss walked into the soaring space of the Grand Atrium, goose bumps running down his spine. He looked up in wonder at the domed roof, gilded and decorated with warring dragons breathing fire. They looked almost real. Joss had never seen anything like it. He could have looked at it for hours, but he reminded himself he had not come to gaze at paintings. He had come for Allie. And so, with some trepidation, he headed toward a pair of massive arched doors, above which he saw the words LENNIX GRAND: BELLACRUX. A movement caught his eye and he swung around edgily. In the shadows was the redheaded girl he remembered seeing with Allie.

Carli was on forty-eight-hour duty with no breaks because, upset about Allie, she'd shouted at a guard. She was wearily mopping the floor when she looked up and saw Joss, resplendent in his Lennix uniform, coming toward her. It was forbidden for a prisoner to be alone with a Lennix, and Carli did not dare get into even more trouble. Hurriedly, she pushed open the nearby service door, but in her haste to get away she got the mop wedged across the doorway.

"Hey, let me help," Joss said.

"*You?*" Carli looked shocked.

Joss freed the mop and Carli backed away through the door. Joss put his hand on her arm to stop her from going, and Carli flinched. "Please don't go," Joss said. "There's something I need to know."

Something in Joss's tone made Carli put down her bucket. "Thought you'd know everything now," she said. "Being a Lennix and all."

Joss flushed. "I had no choice," he said.

"We all have a choice," Carli told him. "Some are right, and some are just plain *wrong*."

"My sister, Allie," Joss whispered and then choked up, unable to go on.

Carli's expression softened a little. "She was a nice kid."

Joss heard the past tense, and any hope he'd been hanging on to evaporated. "Do you know what happened?" he asked. "I mean . . . did you see anything?"

Carli nodded grimly. "Yeah. I saw your lovely adopted *sisters* come and take her away at supper the day before yesterday. She's not been seen since. But yesterday morning when I cleaned up here, I heard Harry saying what a terrible fate it was for anyone, let alone a kid."

"Harry?"

"He's Bellacrux's servant. Been with her forever."

"Oh. I see." Fiercely, Joss rubbed the tears from his eyes. "Well, thanks for telling me," he managed to say.

Carli found herself feeling sorry for Joss, despite his hated uniform. She put out a consoling hand. "Look," she said. "You're a Lennix now, so if you want to know more, go ask Harry."

"Thanks," Joss said, the tears beginning again at Carli's sympathetic touch.

"I've gotta go," she told him. "My name's Carli. If there's anything I can do . . ."

Joss nodded, not trusting himself to speak. He watched Carli set off, her mop and bucket clanking as she went, and then he rubbed his face on his sleeve and walked back into the atrium. Gathering his inner Lennix, he paused a moment outside the attendant's room beside Bellacrux's chamber and then he pushed the door open so hard that it slammed against the wall. Harry looked up but did not move. *So this is the new Lennix kid. As rude as the rest of them*, he thought, regarding Joss with a steady glare. Joss was a little wrong-footed at Harry's lack of deference, but he plowed on. "I have come to see the Grand," he said.

"The Grand has already left for muster," Harry replied stonily.

Shocked at how fast the time had flown, Joss glanced at his watch: 7:53. If he ran now he would just about make it on time. But something told Joss that if he didn't go into the chamber right now, he would never find the courage again. "Take me up to the lookout," he said. "I'll wait."

Harry slowly got up and pushed open the small door that led to the stairs to the lookout chamber that doubled as the refuge. "Follow me," he said.

And so Joss walked slowly up the cold spiral stairs, with a feeling of dread settling into his stomach. He was, he told himself, going to say good-bye to his sister. Forever.

28

Dingbat

The Lennix watches flicked over to 8:00. Up on the landing yard, the Lennix family were minus their newest member.

Muster was an old tradition in Fortress Lennix, and no Raptor was considered to have made it until they were part of the muster. It consisted of forty-nine of the fiercest, fastest, and most loyal dragons, all of whom had proved their bravery and resolve. As ever, they were lined up in ranks of Red, Green, Blue, and Yellow in order of size—the tallest standing over fifteen feet high to the top of the head and twenty-five feet long to the tip of their tail. No Raptor could be called small, for there was not one who was less than three times the size of Lysander. The only Raptors not in size order were those in the very first rank, which consisted of the elite twelve members of the coveted First Flight. In the center of the first rank stood Valkea, tall and proud, no longer trying to conceal her height difference from Decimus.

But Decimus was still in charge. He stood facing the Raptors, watching the clouds of steam rising from the dragons' nostrils with approval; not one was out of time. He had drilled them so well that the Flight even breathed in unison. The morning sun, which had just cleared the mountain peak behind the fortress, shone upon the mass of glistening scales below, glinting with a fierceness that made it seem as though the dragons were made of metal. The crests running down their spines were honed Raptor-fashion into dagger points, and the barbs on their tails, held high in the attention stance, were as sharp as a sword. *They are*, Decimus, thought, *the best they have ever been.*

While Edward joined his Lock to congratulate him, D'Mara cast her gaze around for Joss, who, to her extreme annoyance, was nowhere to be seen. D'Mara frowned. This was not a good start. Today was the first chance she would have to try out the boy and the Silver together. She was planning to send them up to find a portal and take Mirra and Tamra on Trixtan along too. She'd instructed the twins to bring back indisputable proof of the other world. Preferably human proof. *A baby would be best*, she had told Tamra. "Where is that wretched boy?" D'Mara fumed. "We *must* have all the family here."

"He's not family," Kaan muttered under his breath.

"We'll get him, Ma," Mirra offered.

"Yeah. We'll teach him to respect the family," Tamra added gleefully.

D'Mara looked at her daughters—sometimes their viciousness worried even her. "Thank you, Tamra. However, you will leave the teaching of your new brother to me. But yes, go and get him at once. I suppose he's sleeping in late, the lazy little tyke."

Eagerly, Tamra and Mirra hurried away.

Annoyed at finding Joss's room empty, Mirra and Tamra rifled through his desk. "You don't think he's run away, do you?" Mirra asked.

"More likely to have *flown* away," Tamra said, throwing open the door to Lysander's chamber with a bang.

To their surprise, Lysander lay on the cushions, deeply asleep. The twins gazed at the silver dragon, once again taken aback by how beautiful he was. "He's so shiny," Mirra whispered. "I'm glad Kaan didn't have him. He would have messed him up."

"Yeah," said Tamra gloomily. "But now Kaan's got Valkea."

"And she'll mess *him* up." Mirra smirked.

Tamra looked at her twin with interest. Most of the time Tamra thought Mirra was a waste of space. But there were times when Mirra actually said something interesting, and this was one of them. "Yeah," Tamra said thoughtfully. "Maybe she will."

They left Lysander sleeping. Back in Joss's room, the twins turned his bedding upside down and did their best to trash the place while they looked for clues to where he might be. Neither of them wanted to go back to their mother empty-handed. A scrap of paper with *Allie* written all over it fluttered out from under the pillow and Tamra picked it up. "You know what?" she said. "I think the kid's gone up to Bellacrux. He probably wants to go and see if there's anything left of her. And then sob all over it."

Mirra giggled. "He'll be crying over a pile of dragon poop, then."

The twins set off up to Level One, laughing.

Meanwhile Joss was following Harry up the spiral stairs to the lookout. At the top, Harry unlocked a narrow door.

"You will leave now," Joss told him.

"All spectators are to be accompanied," Harry said stonily.

"A Lennix is never a spectator," Joss said, a little shocked at how easily pretending to be a Lennix came to him. "Now get out."

Harry did not trouble to disguise his look of contempt. "Very well. Have it your own way."

Joss listened to Harry's footsteps retreating down the stairs until at last they were gone. Then he took a deep breath and walked into the lookout. It was a brick-built circular turret with a small green door on the far side labeled EXIT TO THE CHAMBER OF THE GRAND. Joss pushed open the door and stepped onto the same walkway upon which Allie had so recently crawled in terror. Joss looked up at the magnificent green tiled vault of the roof with its fine gold and red curlicues and then, using all the courage he could muster, he peered over the railings down at the rug-and-cushion-strewn space far below. He was surprised to see a bed of cushions with the tip of a large green egg poking out, but apart from that there was nothing else. He scanned the chamber, trying to take comfort from the fact that there was no blood anywhere; indeed, there was no sign of a struggle at all. The place felt calm and quiet. It felt, Joss thought miserably, as though Allie had never even existed.

Joss sank to the floor and leaned his head against the railings. "Allie," he whispered. "Oh, Allie . . ." The echo took up his question with enthusiasm: *Allie oh Allie oh Allie oh Allie . . .* mocking Joss until he could bear it no more. "Allie!" Joss yelled in despair. *Allieeeeee!*

Gleefully, the echo took up the refrain: *Al . . . leeeeeeeeeeeeeeee eeee . . .*

Joss put his hands over his ears—it felt like the whole world was taunting him. And then, very faintly, he heard something. And it sounded like Allie.

"Joss? Joss, is that you?"

Joss shook his head and groaned. Now he really was going crazy.

Allie's voice cut through the mocking echoes of groans. "Joss! It's me! Joss, I'm down here. Down here, you dingbat!"

It was the "dingbat" that did it: Joss knew he would never imagine that. He leapt up, looked down over the rails, and there he saw Allie's face, wreathed in smiles, miraculously appearing from beside the egg.

Joss hurtled along the viewing platform, clattered down the ladder, and flew into Allie's arms. She pulled him down with her into the nest. "Shh," she whispered before he could say any more. "No one must know I'm here."

Surrounded by cushions, squashed against the leathery dragon egg, Joss's face shone with happiness. "Oh, Allie. Allie. I can't believe it," he whispered. "You're here, you're alive!"

"I am," Allie agreed happily. "I'm alive."

"But how?" he asked. "Isn't Bellacrux dangerous?"

Allie grinned. "Not to her *Lock*."

Joss's mouth fell open in amazement. "*Lock!*"

"*Shh*," hissed Allie. "Yes, we Locked. She's . . . she's just *amazing*."

Joss looked suddenly serious. "Locked! Oh, Allie. Don't you remember what happened to Ettie?"

Allie smile left her. "Of course I do. But it was the *Lennixes* who killed Ettie, not Bellacrux. They killed her because she Locked with their Grand."

Joss was not reassured. "And they'll do the same to you too," he said.

Allie put her finger to her lips. "Which is why no one must know I'm here," she whispered.

Joss sank down deeper into the nest of cushion, shaking his head in disbelief. "I can't believe you've gone and Locked with the Lennix Grand."

"Neither can I really," Allie said. "But it feels so right, Joss. And Bellacrux is on our side. She hates the Lennixes too."

"Are you sure about that?" Joss whispered. "Can you really trust her?"

Uneasily, Allie remembered her desolation of the previous night, when Bellacrux had been so cruel to Herlenna. When Bellacrux had returned she had explained why she had had to do it, but even though the memory still unsettled Allie, in her heart she knew Bellacrux was trustworthy. "Yes, I can trust her. Okay, so sometimes Bellacrux has to do horrible things so that the Lennixes don't get suspicious, but that's what she has to do to survive, Joss. In fact, that's what lots of people in this awful place have to do. Look at Harry. Look at some of the guards too. They all do it."

Joss was not convinced. "But Bellacrux *kills* people, Allie."

Allie leapt to her Lock's defense. "Who are you to talk, Joss?" she countered. "Look at you, wearing that nasty Lennix uniform. You're doing just the same as Bellacrux."

Joss scowled. "I'm not a Lennix anymore," he said.

"Really?" asked Allie.

"Yeah. I'm done with that, Allie, after what they did to you. It's us against them now." Joss squeezed Allie's hand. "Okay?"

"Okay," Allie agreed.

Outside came the sound of footsteps hurrying across the atrium. Joss leapt up. "I've got to go."

Allie caught hold of his arm. "You have to trust Bellacrux. She has a plan to get us all out of here. With Lysander," she whispered. "Can you come back when she's here? Please?"

Joss had no idea how he would manage it, but there was no way he would let Allie down ever again. "Okay." He nodded. "I'll come back as soon as I can." He hurried back up the ladder, and when he looked down from the walkway he saw no sign of Allie—just a green egg lying quiet in its nest.

When he got back to the hide, Joss was shocked to find Harry waiting for him. "Oh!" he gasped. He searched Harry's face for a sign that Harry had seen him with Allie, but Harry was inscrutable. "Misses Mirra and Tamra are waiting for you in the guardroom," Harry said. "I believe your attendance is required at the muster."

Silently, Joss followed Harry down the steps, gathering his courage to face the Lennix nightmare that surely awaited him.

29

The Muster

"Ah," said D'Mara, "here's the boy at last." She watched Joss being frog-marched across the yard by the twins. He looked very disheveled, and as he got closer, D'Mara could see the beginnings of a bruise on his forehead. She decided to ignore it.

"We found him in the Grand's chamber, Ma," Mirra announced triumphantly.

"What on earth were you doing in there, Joshua?" D'Mara demanded angrily.

Joss told himself that it didn't matter how angry D'Mara was. It didn't even matter that the twins had slammed his head against the wall and he was still seeing stars; all that mattered was that *Allie was alive*. "I . . . I just wanted to see the Grand," he said lamely.

D'Mara looked exasperated. "Well, you went to the wrong place. She's here. Watching the muster, as she always does." She pointed over to the loggia, where Bellacrux and Krane were watching the proceedings, although for very different reasons. Krane missed being part of the muster and had come to soak up the atmosphere. Bellacrux was, as Allie had observed, keeping her enemies close. "Our Grand is proud of the flights," D'Mara told Joss. "And so should you be. In the future, Joshua, you will abide by your timetable or there will be trouble. You are a Lennix now, and we Lennixes live according to the rules. Do you understand?"

Joss squared his shoulders and looked D'Mara in the eye. "I understand."

Mirra looked sulky: How come the kid was getting off so easily? He was just some low-down farm kid who had stolen their Silver and their mother was letting him get away with being late for muster. None of *them* got off so lightly. It wasn't fair. Tamra eyed Joss angrily. The kid was up to something, she could tell. Why didn't her mother see it?

Edward Lennix gave Joss an irritated glance. "So, D'Mara, now that he's here, can we get on with it?"

D'Mara nodded curtly.

As Edward stepped forward to address the muster, Tamra moved over to Joss and got in a quick kick to his ankle. Joss stared straight ahead, determined not to react. "I'm watching you, Sheep-boy," Tamra whispered. "I know you're up to something. I'm going to find out what, and when I do I'll . . ." But Edward's booming voice drowned out her threats.

"Raptor flights, I greet you!" Edward Lennix was answered with a fearsome roar that echoed off the mountains and seemed to shake the very foundations of the fortress.

"Two nights ago we broke the Green defenses and demolished their nest. The free Greens are finished. But the free Reds, Yellows, and Blues remain. These are, as you know, a little trickier than the Greens. *They* keep their secrets close and we have yet to find all their eggs. And so now begins the next stage of our campaign—hit and run. Raptors, tonight we shall go in for the kill. We go to the Islands of the Blues where they hold their eggs deep in caves beneath the ocean. From them we shall take a tribute: a living infant that we shall tear to shreds before their eyes, and then we shall leave them in their grief. We shall return again and again and again until the Blues show us the hiding places of their clutches and beg us to take them. And when we have cleaned them out, we shall do the same with the Mountain Reds. And then the Desert Yellows. We shall take every last one of them! Raptors, you are our heroes, you are our hope, you are our future. Raptors, we salute you!"

Another roar, baying for blood, whirled through the air like a tornado, and Joss had to shove his hands deep into the pockets of his Lennix tunic to stop himself from clamping his hands over his ears. He stared down at the open mouths of the dragons below, glistening red caverns bordered their long, curved yellow incisors, and Joss began to understand the titanic power of the Lennixes.

The Lennix family gave the clenched-fist salute—Joss forced himself to do the same—and forty-nine valedictory streams of dragonfire shot into the air, the flight gave its ritual foot stamp, and then all was done. The dragons headed toward the arches of the loggia, where their Grand watched quietly. They filed respectfully past Bellacrux, each giving her a quick bow of their head as they headed down into the Roost, where teams of prisoners were already delivering freshly slaughtered sheep and tubs of pure spring water to every chamber. The Raptors would eat now and then sleep all day to prepare for the first of the night hit-and-runs.

When all the Raptors were gone, Joss watched Bellacrux walk out into the yard, head along the runway, and slowly take off. He still found it hard to believe what Allie had told him—that she had actually *Locked* with Bellacrux. Joss gazed at Bellacrux as she rose seemingly effortlessly up into the air, her huge wings outstretched, dark against the bright morning sky. She flew a wide, elegant circle and then began to descend into the deep valley below, where the open door to her chamber awaited her. Joss smiled at the extraordinary thought that this terrifying dragon, so revered by Lennixes and Raptors alike, was now Locked with his sister.

D'Mara's voice made him start. "Joshua!" Terrified that D'Mara could somehow read his thoughts, Joss pushed Allie from his mind. D'Mara gave him an unusually animated smile. "It's a great day for flying, Joss. I think it's time you took Lysander out. He'll be needing the exercise."

"Oh!" Joss sounded surprised. "I thought you said he was too young for me to fly safely?"

"Did I?" D'Mara was momentarily wrong-footed. "Ah, yes. Well, he's grown a good deal since then. He is strong enough now." To Joss's discomfort, D'Mara looped her arm over his shoulders and walked him away from the rest of the family. "You do know, Joshua, your Silver has a special talent?" she asked.

Unsure what to say, Joss decided to play dumb. A look of puzzlement settled onto his features.

D'Mara resisted a loud sigh. She really hoped the kid wasn't as stupid as he sometimes appeared. Speaking very slowly and clearly, she said, "Joshua. Your Silver, your beautiful Lysander, can go through a kind of invisible gateway in the sky and fly into another world."

Joss stared at D'Mara in dismay. *How did she know that?*

D'Mara resisted a desire to tell the boy to stop looking so pathetically scared. It was very annoying. She patted Joss's shoulder in what she hoped was a motherly way. "Your Silver's talent is nothing to worry about, Joshua. Indeed, it is something to be *very happy* about. And so, Joshua, I thought today you could see if Lysander will take you through one of those amazingly exciting invisible gateways. Your sisters can go with you on Trixtan to keep you company."

Joss forced a look of enthusiasm into his eyes. "Oh yes! That would be such fun. I'd love to." And then, like the sun going behind storm clouds, he changed his expression to desolation. It was a little mechanical but good enough to fool D'Mara. "Oh!" he said miserably. "But my Lock is deep into his dragonsong sleep."

With some difficulty, D'Mara resisted the temptation to scream with frustration. Why did she always have to wait so long for her plans to work out? She let her arm fall from Joss's shoulder, much to his relief. "So soon?" she said, and gave a brittle little laugh. "My, my, these Silvers develop very fast. Well, it can't be helped. We'll timetable it for tomorrow."

"Oh yes. Wow. Great, really great. I am *so* looking forward to it," Joss babbled.

D'Mara gave Joss a puzzled look. *There's no getting around it,* she thought, *the kid is weird.*

Joss hurried away, but before he had gotten far, Edward Lennix grabbed him. "And where do you think you are going, boy?" he demanded.

Joss's heart sank. How was he ever going to get back to Allie? There was no way they were going to leave him alone for one second. He pulled himself back into Lennix mode and said, "Father.

My Lock is in his dragonsong sleep today, but I intend to use my time productively. Declan showed me the lower levels of the Roost yesterday. Today I plan to familiarize myself with the upper levels."

Edward Lennix eyed Joss irritably. There was something about the boy he didn't quite trust, but he couldn't fault his reply. "Very well. Declan is with me all day on flight allocation and route planning. Kaan can go with you."

Kaan! Joss tried not to panic—Kaan would be a disaster. Joss knew that with Edward he must be confident and speak bluntly, and so he did. "Not Kaan, thank you, Father," he said.

Edward looked amused. "Don't blame you," he said, and looked at his watch. "I'm sure you can manage on your own. I'll give you three hours precisely for the upper levels of the Roost, and at eleven fifty-six you will present yourself at the meeting room to observe our planning for tonight's raid. Now, do you have a plan?"

Joss stared at Edward, horrified. *How did he know he and Allie were about to work out a plan?*

"Oh, for goodness' sake, boy. If you haven't, it's not a hanging offense," Edward said. "Here, take mine." From his pocket Edward pulled out his own plan of the Roost. Joss took it, his hands shaking.

"Scared of your own shadow," Edward observed. "You're a Lennix now, boy. No need for that anymore."

"Yes, Father. Thank you," Joss said, and as Mirra and Tamra arrived to claim their father, he walked briskly away, aware of their stares following him. As he heard their voices wheedling a favor, he slipped into the shadows of the loggia and walked down the wide Raptor ramp to Level One.

From the shadows of the loggia, Krane watched Joss go by and waited for D'Mara to join him. Krane was a quiet dragon who heard much and said little—except to his Lock. He was considered something of a spy among the other Raptors and had few friends. As he and D'Mara walked slowly down the ramp, he updated his Lock on the latest gossip. Usually it was some kind of light scandal that amused D'Mara, but this time it was neither light nor amusing.

Dee, Krane sent, *Valkea is stirring up trouble about the Silver.*

Oh? D'Mara asked.

They're all talking about it, Dee. You know, this Lost Land full of humans that they say the Silver can take us into? Well, Valkea is telling the Raptors that you Lennixes are keeping it just for yourselves.

D'Mara sighed. *Of course we're not, Krane. But we'll only let them through accompanied by a Lennix. Valkea can go when I've got proof that Kaan can control her. I'm not having Valkea creating havoc over there too.*

I'll tell her she'll be one of the first to go through, shall I? Krane suggested. *That should keep her quiet. For now.*

Yes, please, Krane, I'd be very grateful if you would. D'Mara reached out and rested her hand on her Lock's smooth blue scales. *Oh Krane*, she sent, *what would I do without you?* Together dragon and Lock walked down the ramp to Krane's chamber, entirely content with each other.

30

A Crushed Owl

It was half term and Sirin was sitting in the chilly dining room at the back of her foster family's house doing her homework. The room smelled of stale Sunday lunch and hamster bedding and, with the foster family's two little boys away at a friend's, the house was quiet and the only sound was Nibbles the hamster going around his wheel. Sirin had a low opinion of hamsters—there was no way that Sammi would spend her time running around a wheel going nowhere. The thought of Sammi made Sirin feel like a little dagger had been jabbed into her stomach, and she tried to push it away. But she couldn't forget the awful moment in the flat when Sammi had refused to get into her cat carrier and scratched the new social worker and then she'd phoned the lady from the animal shelter, who had come and taken Sammi away. Sirin was proud of Sammi for fighting. *Maybe*, she thought as she slowly colored around a complicated coastline, *maybe I should have fought too. Maybe I should have just picked Sammi up and run away with her.* But Sirin had nowhere to run to. She was just as stuck in her foster family as Nibbles was in his cage.

Sirin closed her geography book and put it neatly into her backpack because her foster mother, Mandy, liked everything kept tidy, and so Sirin knew that was what she must do. She didn't belong anywhere enough to be untidy. Or irritable. Or sad. Now she must be how other people wanted her to be. That was the deal.

Mandy put her head around the door and said brightly, "Ready, Sirin?"

Sirin's spirits lifted. As it was half term, they would surely have time to stop in at the shelter and visit Sammi on the way back from the hospital. She hurried out and was soon sitting in Mandy's little black car with its plastic seat covers and Christmas tree air freshener swinging from the mirror. Excited at the hope of seeing Sammi again, Sirin took out the cat toy—a small purple owl— that she had bought from the corner shop. She squeezed it and the owl let out an exuberant squeak.

Mandy jumped. "Goodness!" she said. "What on earth is that?"

"An owl," Sirin said. "It's for Sammi."

"Ah," said Mandy in the tone of voice that Sirin had heard a lot recently. It meant that the person was about to say something upsetting, but they were going to pretend it was okay because they didn't want Sirin to make a fuss.

Mandy explained in her now-don't-get-upset voice that Sammi wasn't in the shelter anymore because she had gone to the vet's.

"Sammi's *ill*?" Sirin asked anxiously.

"Er . . . well, not exactly," Mandy said awkwardly.

"Oh." Sirin was puzzled. Why was Sammi at the vet's if she wasn't ill? "Can I go to the vet and see her?" she asked.

Mandy didn't answer, and Sirin began to get the same feeling in the pit of her stomach that she got when Mum had been moved to Intensive Care. At last Mandy spoke. "Well, er, Sammi isn't actually there anymore, Sirin. You see, Sammi was an old cat and—"

Suddenly Sirin knew. "You killed Sammi!" she gasped. "*You killed Sammi!*"

"Of course I didn't kill Sammi," Mandy said, rather indignantly.

"The vet killed Sammi," Sirin said flatly.

Mandy did not disagree.

Sirin did not say anything more to Mandy. As far as she was concerned, Mandy *had* killed Sammi, because if Mandy had let Sammi stay, if she hadn't made a fuss because one of the little boys was allergic to cats, then Sammi would still be alive. But Sirin knew she shouldn't say that. She knew she must try to be polite and nice because it was Mandy's home and Mandy's car and that was how it was now. So Sirin sat very still and squeezed the owl so slowly that it didn't make a sound while she heard Mandy saying how it was much kinder to Sammi not to leave her to languish in the shelter.

Languish is a strange word, Sirin thought. *Like anguish only longer.*

"And the problem was that Sammi was quite an aggressive cat," Mandy was saying now. "She scratched and hissed, which made it hard to find a home for her. So it was for the best really."

Sirin crushed the owl into a tiny ball until all she could feel was the hard edges of the squeaker cutting into her palm. If only she could have made Sammi understand that if you don't have a home and you want to survive, you have to be good. And nice. And not scratch anyone. But it was too late now. Sammi was dead.

In Intensive Care, Sirin sat beside Mum while the nurses spoke quietly to Mandy. Mum looked small in her big bed, which Sirin thought wasn't much like a bed at all, more like something in an operating theater. Mum had lots of tubes going into her and Sirin had gotten used to them all except for the one in her throat that did the breathing. It made a soft click with every breath and it made Mum seem not quite *Mum* anymore. The nurses had told Sirin that even though Mum seemed to be asleep, she could probably hear what Sirin said, so Sirin told Mum about her homework and going to the park and what she'd seen on TV, which didn't take long. And then she stopped, because there was no way she could tell Mum about Sammi. So she told Mum about the owl instead and made it squeak for her.

Soon Mandy came in and said it was time to go, and the nurses said good-bye and gave her hugs. When she was halfway down the corridor, Sirin turned around to wave to the nurses again, and caught them off guard. And that was when she saw something in their faces that made the little ball of dread inside her grow even heavier.

31

Flight Plans

The ramp took Joss into the echoing corridors of Level One. Quickly getting back into Lennix mode, he strode along, head held high. Prisoners were hurrying to and fro with food and water, but now the whispers of *turncoat . . . turncoat . . . turncoat . . .* did not bother him at all. He walked confidently into the service kitchen, picked up a lunch box, and, watched silently by the bemused servant, he headed off.

When Joss reached the Grand Atrium, he saw he had a problem: Harry. The old man had brought his chair out from the side room and was sitting reading quietly, right in front of the wicket. It seemed to everyone who passed that Harry was merely enjoying the morning sunshine that was streaming in through the high windows. In fact, Harry was acting on behalf of Bellacrux—as he always did—and Bellacrux had asked him to keep all visitors out of her chamber except for one. From his seat, Harry regarded Joss lugubriously. Why Bellacrux wanted to see the snotty new Lennix kid, Harry had no idea, but he would not dream of questioning the ancient dragon. As Joss neared, Harry got to his feet, wordlessly opened the wicket gate, and indicated for Joss to go in.

Relieved that getting into the chamber was so simple, Joss thanked Harry—much to the old man's surprise—and stepped through. Inside the chamber, Joss was almost blinded by a brilliant shaft of sunlight streaming in from the open flight door. Dark against the light, he saw Allie kneeling, gazing into the pile of cushions, and Bellacrux's long and powerful neck arched protectively over Allie, the tips of her serrated spines glinting. Joss felt a great weight of worry lift from him: With Bellacrux at Allie's side, no Lennix could ever hurt her again.

It was only when Joss had silently crossed the floor and was standing right beside her that Allie looked up and saw him. "Oh, Joss," she said. "Look. It's hatched!" And there, hidden in the nest of cushions, lay a small green dragon, chewing on a large, leathery scrap of eggshell.

"Oh, it's beautiful," Joss said. "May I touch it?"

Allie looked up at Bellacrux, who nodded. The tiny dragon tolerated Joss's hand smoothing its soft scales for a few seconds, then it let out a loud squeak and rolled over onto its back.

"Ah," Allie murmured. "Such a cute little tummy."

"And it will have a Raptor tattoo on it by tonight when they find out it hatched," Joss whispered, tickling the hatchling's tummy.

Bellacrux gave an indignant snort, her breath coming hot and damp onto the back of Joss's neck.

"And tomorrow," Joss said, "they want me to fly Lysander through to that other world, you know, the one Mum called the Lost Lands, and take Mirra and Tamra on their Raptor with me." At that, Bellacrux gave an even louder snort, and Joss felt dragon spit drip down the back of his neck. Joss saw a faraway look come into Allie's eyes and he guessed she was listening to her Lock.

"Bellacrux says that the Lost Lands are sad without dragons. They need them back. But no Raptor must *ever* go through," Allie whispered. "She says that we must take only those who are True to the Wing."

Joss looked puzzled.

"It's the old name for dragons who refused to become Raptors," Allie explained.

Joss loved the idea of going back to the Lost Lands and a new life away from Lennixes and Raptors, but he thought Allie was forgetting something. "But first we have to get out of Fortress Lennix," he said. "And they're hardly going to wave us good-bye and wish us luck, are they?"

Allie looked up at Bellacrux for an answer. "Bellacrux says that the First and Second Flights are leaving for a big raid tonight. They will assemble at sunset. She says you must get Lysander under the cover of the preparations and bring him here, to her chamber. She will go to the muster as usual and come back for us when it is safe for us to leave. Bellacrux says . . ." Allie waited and listened to her Lock's thoughts. ". . . that we must be brave and take our chance."

Joss looked up at Bellacrux's deep green eyes. "I'm not sure how I'll do it, but I'll try," he said doubtfully.

Bellacrux gave Joss a look that told him she was not entirely happy with his answer.

"Bellacrux says that trying is not enough," Allie told him. "She says you must *do* it. Oh, and you must also bring Herlenna."

"*Herlenna?*" Joss was aghast. "But she's locked in the dungeon."

Allie was quiet for a few seconds and then said, "Bellacrux says . . . she says you're a Lennix, so you have a passkey." Allie lapsed into sister talk. "Come on, Joss," she said, "you can do this. You know you can."

Joss got to his feet and looked out through the opening of the launch door to the mountains beyond. He so wanted to be free of this gloomy place, free of the tyranny of the Lennixes, their violence and nastiness, and to be able to be with Allie again. But Fortress Lennix weighed him down; it made him feel trapped and powerless. Joss shook his head. "I . . . I *don't* know if I can," he said miserably. "I'm always having to do Lennix stuff. And they're always watching me."

Allie grabbed Joss's hand and looked him steadily in the eye. "Joss," she told him, "you *have* to fix it. You have to be here, in this chamber, at sunset with Lysander and Herlenna. There is no way around it. *That is what you have to do.*"

A prickle of goose bumps ran down Joss's neck. He knew it was not only his sister looking at him; it was also the gaze of an ancient and powerful dragon. He took a deep breath and steadied himself. "Then that is what I will do," he said. "I'll see you at sunset. With Lysander and Herlenna." Joss walked slowly across the chamber and then stopped. "Oh! I nearly forgot this," he said, coming back and handing Allie the lunch box. "My turn, I reckon."

Allie hugged him. "Thanks, Joss. Be careful," she whispered.

"You be careful too," he said. Then he walked over to the wicket door and quickly slipped out. Harry watched him go without a word.

Joss hurried across the atrium, but when he reached the dimness of the corridor, two figures stepped out and barred his way: Tamra and Mirra.

"Hey, Sheep-boy," Mirra said. "Went to find a bone, did you?"

"What?" Joss said.

"A little *sister bone* for a keepsake?" Tamra asked.

"A nice little finger bone to hang around your neck to remember her by. Ha ha!" Mirra echoed.

Joss was speechless—how could anyone be so vile?

"You're lucky Bellacrux had a lamb this morning, or you'd have been meeting your sister again—inside Big B's stomach. Haha!" Mirra added for good measure.

"And you're lucky you laugh at your own jokes," Joss retorted, "because no one else is going to."

Joss walked quickly away, his heart pounding with rage. And as he went, he realized that the malice of the twins had pushed all fear and doubt from his mind. Whatever it took, he would make sure that tonight they would leave this dreadful place. A cool, calm clarity descended on Joss, and a plan began to take shape in his mind. He checked his Lennix watch, which remorselessly flashed up second after second, and decided he just had time to get to Bone Grind, pick up some bone ash, and get to Lysander's chamber before he was due at the raid meeting.

Tamra stared at the double doors guarding Bellacrux's chamber and the immovable Harry sitting in front of them. "The kid's still alive. He's been to see her."

"Nah," Mirra said. "You heard that roar when we put her in. I can tell you where she is right now."

"Where?" Tamra asked with interest. She was unused to Mirra having ideas of her own.

"A little ball of bones in the poop pile! Snarf-snarf." Mirra snorted with glee.

"Sometimes, Mirra," Tamra told her twin loftily, "you are so infantile."

"And you're so *stupid*."

Tamra rounded on Mirra. "No. *You* are stupid. Too stupid to see what is obvious. Our so-called brother is up to something. I am going to find out what exactly it is. And then . . ."

"And then *what*?" Mirra demanded.

"Sheep-boy will wish he had never been born."

Mirra fell silent. Tamra sounded just like their mother—and their mother scared Mirra more than anyone in the whole world.

32

One Hour

At 5:35 precisely, the raid-planning meeting finished. "You have a free hour until Flight Assembly for tonight's Raid Flight Blue," Edward told Joss as he leapt up from his seat. "Don't be late."

"I won't, Father," Joss said, heading out the door as fast as he could. He had just one hour to do everything. One hour before the Lennixes came looking for him.

Declan caught up with him on the stairs. "Hey, Joss. Want to hang out on the jump roof for an hour? Practice emergency landings?"

"No, thanks," Joss said, leaping down the stairs two at a time.

"It's good fun," Declan said, keeping up with him. "Especially after a boring afternoon. I'll show you the zip wire."

"Thanks, but I gotta go," Joss said. He felt mean. He liked Declan—but what could he do?

Declan had one last try. "Kaan hates it. Never goes."

Joss slowed down. "Hey, I'm really sorry. It sounds great. But Lysander's just come out of his dragonsong sleep. I have to check on him."

Declan nodded. "Of course you do. Another time. See you up at assembly."

"Yeah. See you." Joss hurtled off along the cross passage that led from the Lennix quarters to the Roost. He felt guilty and just a little bit sad: If everything went to plan, he would never see Declan again.

Ten minutes later, in Lysander's chamber, Joss found Lysander wide awake after his dragonsong sleep and crooning quietly to himself. He approached with the bone ash bucket, and Lysander spoke to him in a soft, singsong voice: "Harlarla te faa, me soll."

Goose bumps run down Joss's spine at the almost unearthly sound. "Oh, Lysander," he whispered. "When we've left this horrible place, will you teach me dragonsong too please?"

"Yarilla lo!" Lysander replied, nodding his head. Joss rightly took it as a very definite "yes."

Now Joss set about explaining the contents of the bucket to Lysander, which was not, as the dragon had hoped, supper. As he begin to cover Lysander with bone ash, Joss told his Lock the plans for that night while Lysander stayed remarkably still, concentrating hard and giving Joss great confidence. He didn't think anyone had listened to him with such earnestness before. It was a good feeling. Ten minutes later, the bucket was empty and Joss was rubbing the last of the sticky gray stuff onto Lysander's silver scales. He stepped back to check on his handiwork and saw in front of him a dull and dusty dragon. He smiled, pleased with the result: Lysander would blend into the night beautifully.

Joss thought Lysander smelled revolting, but Lysander thought otherwise. The dragon sniffed the air appreciatively, flicked out his long, green tongue, and licked a tiny bit of the delicious camouflage off his snout. *Lysander*, Joss told his Lock sternly, *please don't lick the bone ash. We need you not to shine tonight.*

Lysander sighed. Why was it always the nice stuff you weren't allowed to eat?

From the small lookout window, Joss noticed that the sun was now dropping down behind Mount Lennix and a feeling of apprehension began to creep over him—there was so much that could go wrong. The sounds of the Roost stirring as the Raptors awoke from their rest and then the rattle of the first of the flight doors being wound down made everything feel frighteningly real.

Hey, Joss. Lysander's voice came into his mind. *We can do it!*

Joss nodded, dry mouthed, and began hauling on the ropes that operated the pulley system to open Lysander's flight door. It swung down like a drawbridge and, supported by its chains, it now became a launching platform. Joss leaned out and looked up at the sheer wall of the Roost that rose up into the sky. He saw, one by one, hatches dropping down as the Roost began to stir. The sight gave Joss a strange stab of grief, which confused him until he realized why: The Roost reminded him of a cliff face of seabirds, which was one of the last things he had seen with his parents. They had been attempting to escape a Lennix roundup, and it hadn't worked. He remembered Raptors diving down, taking his parents hundreds of feet up into the sky, and then dropping them into the sea. The memory took away Joss's fear and replaced it with anger. He watched the Raptors walking out, testing the platforms, and stretching their wings as though they were lords of all they surveyed. He saw the glint of sharpened talons, and brief but dazzling flares of dragonfire as they tested their fire stomachs.

And Joss told himself that they would never, ever have a chance to spoil another world.

Lysander, he sent. *I am going now. I'll be back soon. I hope. With Herlenna.*

The answer came winging back: *I will see you both soon.*

Joss went to pat Lysander's neck and stopped himself just in time. He didn't want any more bone ash falling off. He hurried out through the Lock's room and into the corridor. It was deserted but filled with the sound of creaking pulleys, rattling chains, and opening hatches. Joss took the service steps down to Level Thirteen and, using his passkey for the very first time, he unlocked its studded metal door. It swung open with a loud, complaining creak, and Joss froze. He waited, heart beating fast, but no footsteps came running and no voices barked out warnings. Gingerly he stepped inside.

The dungeon was all a dungeon should be: cold and dank with the smell of mildew, and beneath it the sweet cloying scent of rotting flesh. Despite the presence of two dragons—Ramon, the Raptor Blue, and Herlenna the Green, a heavy silence pervaded, broken only by the distant, dismal *plink* of dripping water. It was lit by a few flickering lanterns, which showed the streaks of grime and mold upon the rough walls hewn from the rock. Unlike the rest of the Roost, this was not the work of skilled stonemasons, but of someone with only a pickax and a bad temper.

Just inside the door there was a stand of dragon-baiting rods—long poles with metal points on the end. They were vicious-looking things, but Joss knew he must stay in his role in front of the Raptor prisoner. So he took one.

The dungeon was partitioned into cages with a dragon entrance (but rarely an exit) hatch on the far side. As Joss's eyes became used to the low levels of light, he saw within two of the cages the distinctive shapes of the dragons. Both creatures were lying down, their heads laid wretchedly on the serrated, rocky floor. Joss walked over to the Green and whispered, "Herlenna?"

The dragon raised her head and regarded Joss suspiciously. She had learned enough in her short imprisonment to be very wary of anyone wearing a Lennix tunic—particularly a boy carrying a baiting rod. Kaan Lennix was a cruel and frequent visitor.

Aware that the Raptor in the cage opposite was paying close attention, Joss dropped his voice. "Herlenna, I've come to rescue you. But I shall have to behave like a Lennix—otherwise the Blue will become suspicious. Do you understand?"

Like all Greens, Herlenna placed great value on her intuition. Her eyes regarded Joss coolly and saw something in him that she trusted. She gave an infinitesimal nod of her head to show she understood.

"I ask your pardon in advance," Joss said.

Herlenna nodded once more and Joss yelled fiercely, "Get back, get back!" and aggressively shoved the baiting rod through the bars. Herlenna played her part well; she cowered in the corner and went into a submissive pose, flicking her ears back and turning her head so she was not looking directly at Joss.

"Dragon! You are ordered to the landing yard," Joss barked. "At once."

In the cage behind Joss, Ramon thumped his tail angrily— why wasn't *he* going too? Joss strode over to him and shoved the baiting rod through the bars. "You wait your turn," he snarled. Ramon subsided, thinking that he would be next.

Using all his strength to move the ropes through the rusty pulleys (they were not used much), Joss hauled open the massive hatch door that led to the outside. It fell into position with a loud clang that made Joss terrified someone would come to investigate. But in the hustle of the mass of Raptors exiting the Roost, no one even noticed. Ramon watched enviously as Joss unlocked the door to Herlenna's cage and swung it open. He saw Joss herd the Green out with a few prods and then awkwardly swing himself up onto the dragon's neck and settle into the rider's dip. He watched the Green walk out onto the hatch, stretch her wings luxuriously—*oh, how he longed to do that*—and then rise up into the evening sky. Ramon settled down to wait his turn. It was a long wait.

Outside in the deepening twilight, Joss and Herlenna were buffeted by the streams of turbulence caused by the continuing mass exit from the Roost, and Herlenna, hampered by her torn wing, had to fight to keep the downdraft from dashing them against the rock face of the Roost. Joss looked up and saw the dark shapes of dragons circling above, the flashing white of their underbellies each showing the Raptor trident tattoo as they waited for Decimus to take the lead and begin the landing for the assembly of Raid Flight Blue. The low rumble from the wingbeats reminded Joss of a swarm of bees.

Joss sent an exultant message to Lysander: *Lysander, I've got Herlenna, we did it!* He scanned the line of open hatches on the level above and saw a distinctive gray snout with a tiny touch of silver poking out. Guided by Joss, Herlenna flew up toward Lysander's chamber and as she hovered, gauging the angle of flight into the chamber, a small and highly excitable Yellow shot out from next door to Lysander and very nearly flew straight into them. However, such was the Yellow's eagerness at the prospect of the raid, it paid no attention to the unfamiliar Green being ridden by a Lennix boy and headed rapidly up to join the throng circling above.

With the coast now clear, Herlenna flew neatly into Lysander's chamber and landed just inside the door. The dragons greeted each other in soft dragonsong while Joss fretted about Lysander's camouflage brushing off, and then they peered out of the door, watching the unformed flight wheeling high in the rapidly darkening sky, like crows on a winter's evening over a graveyard.

Joss was surprised at how long the flight was taking to form up. He looked at his Lennix watch and a knot began to tighten in his stomach. In a few seconds he would be late for Flight Assembly, and from that moment on, Edward Lennix would be looking for him. At that frightening thought, his watch flicked over to 6:35.

33

Fights and Flights

Edward Lennix had more pressing things on his mind than the whereabouts of his newly adopted son: He had a crisis to manage. The assembly for Raid Flight Blue was in trouble—Valkea had very deliberately walked away from the flight and picked a fight with D'Mara. Now Valkea's harsh dragonsong, equally matched by D'Mara's raised voice, was carrying across the yard. A tense silence had fallen. There was not a wing creak, talon scrape, or fire snort as every Raptor listened to D'Mara's angry words. Edward was furious: D'Mara was making it obvious to the whole Roost that the Lennixes were losing their grip.

"Valkea," D'Mara was saying, "I will *not* be maligned by an upstart young Raptor such as you. I have not broken my word to you. I promised you nothing. You will get your chance to go through to the Lost Lands, but you will go when I tell you and not before. Now get back to the flight at once."

Valkea did not move.

Edward picked up a send from Decimus. *You have to stop this, Lennix. Look at those young Raptors at the back.*

Edward followed Decimus's gaze to a group of young Yellows at the back of the assembly. Their orange eyes, shining in the torchlight, were all fixed on Valkea. Edward got the impression that at any moment they too would walk away. "Leave it to me, Decimus," Edward growled.

Followed by thirty pairs of watchful Raptor eyes, Edward strode over to D'Mara and Valkea, his boots loud upon the cobbles in the deadly silence of the landing yard. D'Mara gave her husband a furious glance—how dare he interrupt—but she said nothing. In times of trouble, Lennixes always kept a united front.

"Good evening, Valkea," Edward said smoothly. "Raid Flight Blue is ready to leave. Your attendance is required at once."

Valkea raised her head, and in a shocking act of aggression, she opened her mouth to show her well-tended, glistening fangs in a classic Raptor warning display. Edward was horrified. But he decided the best thing to do was to ignore it. "In the first rank," he added.

Valkea considered her position. To be promoted from the rear to the first rank was unprecedented. It was an opportunity not to be missed. Deciding to leave her fight with D'Mara for another day, she turned away without the customary bow of the head to a Lennix and walked slowly back to Raid Flight Blue.

Edward let out a sigh of relief. "Next time you decide to pick a fight, D'Mara," he said in a low voice, "do it in private, would you?" And then he too walked away, leaving D'Mara speechless. It was not her fault, she wanted to say. It was *Valkea* who had picked the fight, not her. D'Mara decided she would speak to Bellacrux about Valkea's behavior. The old Grand didn't have much to do anymore apart from keeping the younger Raptors in order. Clearly Bellacrux was losing her edge.

In pursuit of the ever-united Lennix front, D'Mara joined Edward at the front of the flight and the assembly continued with

Valkea in the first rank next to the twins' Trixtan. It was then that an exasperated Edward realized that neither Kaan nor Joshua were anywhere to be seen. It was Kaan's absence that annoyed him the most, for Kaan was flying Valkea and this was yet another loss of face for the Lennixes. "Where is Kaan?" Edward said in a low growl to D'Mara. Before D'Mara had time to answer, Tamra, who had yet to join Trixtan, came striding over. "Kaan says he has a stomachache and is too sick to fly," she said triumphantly. "What a baby. I told you Kaan can't hack it with Valkea. Bad call, Ma."

D'Mara gave her daughter a look of anger that a few days previously would have reduced Tamra to jelly—but no longer. Tamra stared coldly at her mother for some seconds and then walked pointedly away from the flight.

"Leave her be," Edward growled. "Mirra can fly Trixtan on her own."

D'Mara sent a guard to fetch Kaan. He arrived dragging his feet and looking, D'Mara had to admit, very pale. But if Kaan hoped for any comfort from his mother, he was soon disappointed. D'Mara looked at him as though he were a nasty little worm. "I don't want to hear any excuses, Kaan. You're flying tonight," she hissed. "You must learn to control yourself. And your Lock. I won't tell you again."

Kaan stared at the ground, mortified. "Go and distribute the firestix," D'Mara told him. "One holster to each rider. Try at least to get that right, will you?"

Kaan perked up. He loved firestix. They were vicious weapons: a long metal lance with a tip that, when armed, glowed red-hot and on contact with dragon flesh burst into flames. Fueled by the keratin in dragon scales, a firestik would burn its way steadily through the flesh, ever deeper, like a burrowing worm of fire.

While Kaan distributed the firestik holsters, D'Mara turned her thoughts to her newest problem son: Joss. *Where was he?* Fuming, D'Mara watched Edward take his place on Decimus at the head of the flight. She saw Kaan nervously climbing up onto Valkea, and Mirra settling herself on Trixtan. In the second rank was Declan on Timoleon, who was, in D'Mara's opinion, a timid Raptor who did her eldest son no favors. All were in position now and ready to go. "I wish Raid Flight Blue a great success!" D'Mara called out. "Good hunting and safe return!"

An answering triple stamp in perfect time, which sent goose bumps down her spine, was her reply. D'Mara relaxed: All was well with the flight. Smiling, she watched Edward and Decimus take the first launching run. She felt the rumble come up through the cobblestones as the heavy Red ran along the launching platform, closely followed by Valkea and then one by one the Raptors launched with rapid, well-practiced efficiency. Soon all were airborne.

Tamra watched the dark arrow of Raid Flight Blue wheel away in perfect formation and head swiftly down toward the pass. Then she picked up a firestik and, on a raid mission of her own, she headed down to the Roost. From the shadows of the loggia, Bellacrux watched her go. And then the Lennix Grand walked slowly out onto the empty landing yard and took off. She too was on a mission—and now it was time for it to begin.

34

Knife Edge

From Lysander's open flight door, Joss watched the Raptors' white underbellies flashing like fish in a pool as they wheeled into their turn and dipped down toward the pass. "They've gone," he told Lysander and Herlenna, and as he spoke he saw the magnificent winged silhouette of the Lennix Grand appear, coasting gently down toward her chamber. "All's clear. Let's get out of here!" He swung himself up onto Lysander and turned to Herlenna. "Herlenna, follow as close as you can. We're going up to Level One, into the Grand's chamber."

Herlenna, whose experience of the Lennix Grand had not been good so far, gave Joss a quizzical look. "Trust me," Joss said. "Bellacrux is with us."

The flight up the face of the Roost was nerve-racking, but above them Bellacrux hovered protectively, guiding them into her chamber and then following them inside. Allie met them, beaming, and made sure Lysander avoided the hatchling—he had grown so fast he was no longer sure where his feet were. "I was so scared," Allie told Joss as Bellacrux greeted her two dragon guests. "I kept thinking of all the things that could go wrong."

"Me too," Joss said. "And they still could. They'll be looking for me right now. And Tamra suspects something, I know she does. We've got to get out of here fast."

But leaving quickly was not so easy. It seemed to Joss and Allie that dragons possessed a different sense of time than humans. Bellacrux had apologies to give to Herlenna and she would not fly without making them. The sound of dragonsong began to fill the chamber; it flowed between Herlenna and Bellacrux like the washing of the tide upon the sand, the ethereal ancient dragon language sending swaths of goose bumps down the spines of the listening humans.

Joss and Allie watched Herlenna lift her head and gently touch Bellacrux on the end of her snout, and then Allie heard Bellacrux tell her: *Give Herlenna her young one. I have already given her my sorrow and apologies for her suffering.* Allie carefully placed the hatchling in Herlenna's rider's dip. The little dragon's cling reflex kicked in and it grabbed hold of Herlenna's crest.

To Joss's dismay, the dragonsong continued. He was feeling increasingly anxious—with every second the danger of being discovered increased, and there were more than enough Raptors left in the Roost to give chase and send them crashing to the ground in flames. "Allie, *please*," he said. "Tell Bellacrux we have to go now. We can't wait another second."

"I know," Allie whispered. "But I can't find a space to say it."

I hear you, Allie, came Bellacrux's voice. *We will go now. Herlenna says she will lead us to the Greens' hideout. We shall be their honored guests.*

As Herlenna walked out along the launching door, there was a sudden crash and the wicket door flew open. Three dragons and two Locks swung around to see Tamra, firestik in her hand, staring at them, her mouth gaping in shock.

Confused for a moment, Tamra took in the scene. She'd come to ask Bellacrux for help to find the Sheep-boy so-called brother but he was already here—along with his nasty sister, who was meant to be dragon food. And standing over them, her wings half-raised, was Bellacrux, *protecting* them. Tamra tried to make sense of it. She saw the Green on the landing door next to a small dragon covered in dust with a shining silver snout. And then, at last, Tamra understood: *Bellacrux was a traitor.*

Joss felt almost sorry for Tamra as the growing realization of Bellacrux's betrayal spread over her sharp, watchful features. "Bellacrux," Tamra gasped. "W-what's going on?"

In answer, Bellacrux drew in a long, deep firebreath, and Tamra's eyes opened wide with fear. In a moment she was out of the wicket, slamming it behind her. With her legs suddenly weak as water, Tamra sank slowly to the floor. Bellacrux, their faithful Grand, who had loved them like her own, given them rides when they were little, and taught them dragonsong, had turned.

Trembling with shock, Tamra listened to the sounds of the launching door creaking as one by one the dragons took off. When all was quiet, she nervously opened the wicket and walked across the empty chamber. She stood at the massive opening, staring up into the night sky, and watched as the dark shapes of the three dragons flew steadily away, with Bellacrux leading them past the main exit route toward a pass named the Knife for its narrowness and the razor-sharp rocks that stuck out from its sides. Bellacrux had chosen well, Tamra thought. No Raptor would willingly give chase through the Knife at night.

A wave of pure anger came over Tamra. How dare Bellacrux betray the family? How dare that so-called brother throw all they had done for him in their faces? And how dare that Allinson kid still be alive? The sight of the three dragons disappearing into the Knife galvanized Tamra into action. Bellacrux and those kids would not get away with this. She would hunt them down and avenge their betrayal.

In a moment Tamra was out of the chamber and racing toward the Lennix stairs. She knew where to find a Raptor who was desperate enough to fly the Knife at night—and she was going to get him.

35

Midnight Crossings

The trio of dragons emerged safely from the Knife and set off above the empty plains. Herlenna's torn wing was troubling her, forcing them to fly much more slowly than they would have liked. With the exhilaration of the escape behind them, Joss and Allie began to worry about the slow pace. Neither could believe that they had managed to get away from Fortress Lennix. It was almost too good to be true, Joss thought as both he and Allie stared back into the night, searching the dark mountains behind them for signs of pursuit. Surely Tamra must have alerted the Roost?

It was the first time Allie had ever flown on a dragon. The initial few minutes were pure excitement mixed with a little thrill of terror, and then she began to get the strangest feeling: that Bellacrux's great green wings had become part of her and that she herself was flying. A feeling of awe crept over Allie: In flight, she and Bellacrux were one.

Joss felt almost wild with relief. He had managed to do everything right to make their escape possible, and now, for the first time, he and Lysander were really together. If they could just make it to the Green hideout, there would be no more hiding, no more fear, no more worry. It would be a dream come true. Once again he glanced back to check for pursuers, and to his relief there were still none. The moon was full and the star-dusted sky was clear apart from a few small clouds. There was not a Raptor in sight. Which was strange, Joss thought. Surely Tamra was not going to ignore their escape?

They were flying over the stone circle now, and both Joss and Allie looked down at the ancient stones standing proud in the moonlight, guiding them on their way. Allie watched the Zolls' farmhouse, dark and still in the night, pass beneath her, and she smiled to think how shocked Madam Zoll would be if she looked out the window now and saw her flying Bellacrux, the fabled Lennix Grand.

Leaving the farmhouse behind, they flew steadily onward, following Herlenna and her precious hatchling. Now they were heading out over bare hills toward the forests where deep in a hidden valley, the last of the Greens kept a precarious foothold. A sudden flare of light on his wrist told Joss that he had not entirely escaped Lennix life. He looked down at his Lennix watch and saw 00:00 flash up: midnight. Joss pulled the time tyrant off his wrist and sent it tumbling toward the ground, flashing as if in panic at its fall. It landed in a lone tree, where it spent the rest of its life providing endless fascination for a nest of baby owls.

As the clock outside Intensive Care flipped over to 00:00, Sirin was sitting on a hard chair, watching the swinging doors that led into the unit. A fierce red light was glowing above the door and people wearing what looked like blue pajamas kept hurrying in. Sirin sat and stared at the notices on the opposite wall, but her mind took in not a single word. Next to her sat Mandy. Mandy wore a strained expression and kept glancing anxiously at Sirin, who pointedly ignored her. Sirin didn't want to hold Mandy's hand or have a "nice toffee" or be told not to worry. Sirin just wanted some space in which to remember how it was when she, Mum, and Sammi were happy in their tiny flat up in the clouds, but it felt like a lifetime ago. In fact, it seemed to Sirin that she had always lived with Mandy, Mr. Mandy, their two noisy little boys, and their nasty, nippy hamster.

While the comings and goings from Intensive Care flowed by her, Sirin took refuge in her mother's dragon stories. She thought about how her mother had said you could still find places that remembered the dragons if you knew where to look. There were golden dragon heads hidden in ancient wells, there were dancing dragons of azure blue carved deep into sea caves, and, if you stood on the top of rolling chalk hills at sunset, you could look down and see the shadows cast by the huge ancient dragon shapes that their human friends had dug deep into the turf.

Sirin hugged those images to herself and tried to push from her mind the dreadful moment that evening when the phone had rung and Mandy had begun talking into it in whispers and Sirin's heart had suddenly felt like it was filled with lead. By the time Mandy had come off the phone, Sirin had had her jacket and boots on and was ready to go. Mandy had said nothing at all, just fetched her coat and told her husband they were off to the hospital. And for that, Sirin was grateful.

It was four blocks to the hospital, and the roads had been so packed with traffic that they'd run along the streets, and all the while, Sirin had stared resolutely up at the full moon, riding high above the rooftops, and allowed its peacefulness to take a little bit of the fear away, just for a while.

And now, outside the swinging doors, Mandy was at last silent. She had stopped saying everything would be all right, which Sirin appreciated, because she had a terrible feeling that from now on nothing would ever be all right again. Ever.

36

Pursuit

An open dragon door, freezing wind, and one empty cage greeted Tamra as she strode into the dungeon. Scowling, she stopped and took stock: The captured Green was gone. That figured. She *knew* she hadn't recognized the Green in Bellacrux's chamber. The astounding treachery of their Grand fired Tamra's rage to even greater heights. For a moment she considered going to her mother with the whole story, but Tamra was in no mood to share anything with D'Mara. *Let her find out for herself,* she thought. *And by the time she does, I'll make sure that her precious Bellacrux and her double-crossing toad of a so-called son will be a pile of smoking cinders out on the plains in the middle of nowhere.*

Tamra threw open Ramon's cage and the Blue, all fight quelled by his time in the dungeon, cowered in fear. "Come with me, Ramon," Tamra told him. "Do what I ask, I'll set you free." Encouraged by the absence of a dragon prod, Ramon bowed his head and slunk out.

Tamra led Ramon out onto the dragon door, and as the howl of the wind hit them, she slipped into the unfamiliar rider's dip. Exhilarated by his unexpected freedom, Ramon rose rapidly up past the sheer wall of the Roost, and under Tamra's instructions, he headed for the mountains.

From her lookout window in the Lennix quarters, D'Mara was shocked to see a familiar blue Raptor flying rapidly away. D'Mara snatched up her night-sight spyglass and trained it on Ramon; she was horrified to see her eldest daughter ensconced in the rider's dip. D'Mara banged on the window with her fist. "Tamra! Tamra! Come back here this minute!" she yelled. There was, of course, no response. Aghast, D'Mara watched as the Blue flew into the dreaded Knife pass, and she was left staring into an empty sky. D'Mara fumed with rage. Tamra was up to something, and she, D'Mara Lennix, was not going to let her get away with it. Enough was enough.

Ramon flew fast and confident through the Knife. The wind funneled along its narrow gap, screaming like a banshee and buffeting him dangerously close to the rocks, but Ramon did not care. He was flying for his future. Apart from a small cut to a wing tip, Ramon emerged unscathed. Tamra was impressed. She liked his go-for-it attitude, and if she had not had other plans cooking, she would have been tempted to try to Lock. She was done sharing with Mirra. Ramon, in turn, appreciated Tamra's reckless bravery. Deciding to learn from it, he pushed aside his old, timid self and promised himself to take his chances where he found them. One day, he resolved, he would be known as Ramon the Brave.

Ten minutes later, D'Mara and Krane were heading off into the night in pursuit of Tamra. Avoiding the Knife, they took the long way around and flew up over the mountaintops, and as they coasted down D'Mara put her night-sight spyglass to her eye. In the light of the full moon, she saw a distant shimmer of blue. D'Mara smiled; she was on her daughter's trail. But unfortunately for D'Mara, Krane did not possess the stamina he'd once had; he was no match for Ramon, and soon she was no longer able to see her daughter through her spyglass. The trail was cold.

Tamra was amazed at Ramon's speed. All Blues were fast, but Ramon was breathtaking. The night winds rushed by and they flew rapidly onward through a starlit sky, and it was not long until Tamra glimpsed what she had been looking for—a distant flash of silver in the moonlight. Bone ash could not stick to smooth silver scales for long, especially in the rush of wingbeats, and in the light of the full moon, to Tamra's delight, Lysander shone like a beacon.

Ramon's natural cautiousness made him the ideal tracker. He kept just enough distance from their quarry to blend into the night sky. Whenever Joss and Allie looked back—and they often did— they saw nothing but stars and a few scudding clouds, and they heard nothing but the whistle of the wind in their ears. Once Allie thought she caught a flash of blue in the moonlight, but it quickly disappeared. And so the trio flew slowly, steadily onward, now above a wide expanse of destroyed forest, burned to a few charred trunks standing out like blackened teeth in a damaged mouth. Raptors loved nothing more than to set forest fires, and it was the once-vibrant ancient forest nearest to Fortress Lennix that had suffered the most.

Tamra had now seen all she needed: The traitor Grand and the stolen Silver were following the escaped prisoner Green. The reason for that was obvious—the Green was showing the way. And Tamra knew exactly where that would be: to the Greens' not-so-secret hideout in the middle of the forest. There was no need to follow any farther. Tamra's fury had abated in the cold night air, and she now realized that she and Ramon stood little chance against the might of Bellacrux and that her plan of sending all three dragons crashing to the ground in flames was somewhat unrealistic. What she needed was reinforcements—and fast. She was going to make sure that not one of those traitorous dragons ever got within fire-breathing distance of the Greens' scrappy lump of cave-riddled rock in the middle of the forest. Tamra told Ramon to make a course for the Island of the Blues. At the speed Ramon flew, they would easily overtake Raid Flight Blue, who were flying to conserve energy. Tamra intended to divert the flight to the Greens' hideout and annihilate it—along with the traitor Bellacrux. Then they'd set fire to the rest of the forest and finish what they'd started. She grinned. It promised to be a good night.

Spurred on by Tamra's energy and excitement, Ramon flew faster than ever, and it was not long before D'Mara was shocked to see her daughter hurtling back toward her. "Tamra!" she yelled, her voice traveling through the stillness and silence of the night. "Tamra!"

D'Mara's shout cut into Tamra's dreams of fire and destruction and sent them vanishing into the moonlight. She stared into the night sky, wondering why she was imagining her mother's voice—and then she saw Krane: shimmering blue in the moonlight, heading straight for her. "Tamra! Wait right there!" Her mother's shout reached her, loud, clear, and unmistakably real.

Tamra was spooked—how could her mother possibly have known where to find her? But as she flew Ramon over to Krane, Tamra realized that she was, for once, pleased to see her mother. D'Mara, however, did not seem pleased to see her daughter. "Tamra Lennix," she said angrily. "What do you think you are doing out here alone on that . . . that nasty little streak of dragon dirt. *How dare you?*"

Tamra wheeled Ramon around so he was safely out of the way of Krane's nose spike. She would not put it past her mother to order Krane to stab Ramon right there. "The dragon dirt has a name, Mother," she said coolly. "He is called Ramon. And Ramon has saved you from losing the Silver."

D'Mara laughed. "Ha! Don't talk rubbish, Tamra. He's the idiot who lost us the Silver in the first place. We have it back now, and no thanks to him at all."

Tamra flew Ramon in neat, fast circles around her mother, delighting in the knowledge that Krane was not agile enough to follow. "You don't know anything!" she yelled at D'Mara. "You think you do but you don't. You don't know that your darling adopted son has flown the Silver away, do you? You don't know that your so-called faithful Lennix Grand, your precious Bellacrux, has gone with them, do you? *And* they've taken the Green prisoner with them. Bet you don't know any of *that*!"

"Don't be ridiculous," D'Mara yelled, furious.

Keeping clear of Krane's snout, Tamra wheeled Ramon in close. She looked her mother in the eye and said, "It's true, Ma. Every last word of it is true. I swear it."

D'Mara stared at her daughter with a dawning sense of horror. "Bellacrux?" she said faintly.

"Yeah, Bellacrux, Ma!" Tamra yelled. "Now we know why all the young Raptors were turning against us!"

D'Mara knew her daughter was telling the truth. "Our Bellacrux has stolen the Silver? Our own Bellacrux?" She felt as though someone had stuck a knife into her heart. It was a terrible betrayal.

Krane felt equally devastated. *Oh, Dee*, he sent, *I should have realized. I am so sorry.*

Too late now for regrets, D'Mara sent.

But not too late for revenge, Krane replied.

"Tamra!" D'Mara yelled. "Where have they gone?"

"To the Greens' hideout," Tamra yelled back. "Ramon's so fast, Ma! He's amazing! I'm going to divert Raid Flight Blue. We'll get the traitors, Ma! We'll get them!"

D'Mara laughed. Sometimes Tamra reminded her so much of how she had been as a girl. "Well done, Tamra," she said. "And if Ramon gets you to the flight in time, there's a pardon for him and his old place back in First Flight."

"He'll do it, Ma! I'll see you at the Greens'!" Tamra yelled as she wheeled Ramon away, delighting in how beautifully he moved, and how natural it felt to be with him. Ramon, Tamra realized, made her feel happy.

D'Mara watched them go, flying faster than seemed possible. She sighed. Tamra's delight in Ramon's speed made her remember how she and Krane too had once flown faster than the wind. But sadly, no more. D'Mara turned Krane around and slowly they set off toward the Greens' hideout. Weak though Krane was, neither was prepared to miss the moment they got the Silver back and destroyed their traitorous Grand.

37

Flight Vengeance

Edward had been dozing on Decimus and woke with a start at the sound of his daughter's voice. He stared at Tamra and Ramon in bemusement. What was she doing riding the prisoner Blue?

"Hey, Pa!" Tamra yelled above the *oosh-whoosh-oosh* of the synchronized wingbeats of the flight.

Edward was not pleased. "Tamra, you have no authority to release a prisoner," he shouted.

"But, Pa—"

"I will talk to you later. You may join the flight. Go to the back."

"Pa, I'm not joining the flight!" Tamra yelled. "The flight's joining *me*."

Tamra reminded Edward far too much of D'Mara: He never seemed able to keep the advantage in any confrontation. "Whatever do you mean?" he yelled angrily.

Tamra flew Ramon close beside Decimus, and as he settled into the leisurely pace of Raid Flight Blue, Tamra took great pleasure in telling her father exactly what she meant—and why. Edward's expression became increasingly thunderous, and well before Tamra had finished, Edward Lennix knew he must grant his daughter her wish—with one reservation. They would not bring the whole flight. It was to be family only. There were two reasons, he told Tamra. Firstly, he was unsure if the older Raptors on Raid Flight Blue would willingly take part in the destruction of Bellacrux. Secondly, if any un-Locked Raptor were to be involved in the capture of the Silver, they might try to claim it for their own as "spoils of war." The family must take their Silver back, and they alone must do it. He hoped, Edward said, that Tamra agreed with him?

Tamra was astonished at the respectful tone her father had suddenly adopted toward her. "Absolutely, Pa," she said. "Family only."

"The flight is yours, Tamra," Edward told her. "You shall lead it and name it."

"Flight Vengeance," Tamra said. "Because that is what it's going to get. Vengeance."

The newly formed Flight Vengeance peeled away from Raid Flight Blue and flew rapidly back toward land, the red pinpoint eyes of their firestix glinting in the night. They made their way over the inland marshes, heading fast toward to the Greens' hideout.

Lysander, Bellacrux, and Herlenna were making good progress toward the hideout. The burned remains of forest were behind them and beneath them now was a living canopy of green. In the distance, glinting in the moonlight, they could see a jagged escarpment of rock rising up from the trees.

"Joss, Bellacrux says we're nearly there!" Allie called over to her brother, pointing to the rock ahead.

Joss gave a thumbs-up. *Hey, Lysander*, he sent. *Landing soon.*

Lysander sounded disappointed. *Not yet. This is such fun; let's fly around some more!*

Joss looked at his beautiful silver dragon. The bone ash was long gone, and Lysander shimmered brightly in the light of the full moon. *But Lysander*, he sent, *you shine like a glow bug.*

So what? Lysander returned. *There's no one to see.*

But Lysander was wrong. Concealed in the darkness of the sky, six Lennixes and six Raptors could see him very well indeed. Keeping to the shadows of a bank of cloud that was drifting in from the sea, Flight Vengeance—completed now by D'Mara and Krane—was silently closing in.

As Herlenna, Bellacrux, and Lysander approached the escarpment, Joss began to feel uneasy. The hairs on the back of his neck prickled and he turned around, suddenly knowing what he was about to see. It was exactly what he had feared: Dark in the sky Joss saw the distinctive arrow of a flight of Raptors.

"Allie!" he yelled. "Behind us!" With a feeling of dread, Allie too turned around. *They've found us*, she sent to Bellacrux. *They've found us.*

Rather stiffly, Bellacrux turned her great green head. She saw the distinctive shapes of her old family and gave a disdainful snort. *They turn up like a bad smell*, she sent to Allie. *Don't worry. You and I will see them off.* But deep inside that leathery green skin, Allie detected a tremor of fear. She wrapped her arms around Bellacrux's neck and whispered, "We'll fight them. And we'll win."

But first, Bellacrux sent, *Lysander and Herlenna must be safe. Tell Joss to go to the Greens' hideout with Herlenna.*

Allie was not surprised when Joss flatly refused to go. "No way, Allie! I am not leaving you!" Joss yelled.

Bellacrux did not insist. She'd been a young dragon once, and she too had refused to flee a battle. Herlenna, however, not only had the hatchling to consider; she also knew that with her torn wing she would be a liability in any fight. With emotion choking her dragonsong, she thanked Bellacrux for her life and that of her hatchling, and reluctantly began a slow glide down to the thick cover of the trees far below, where she hoped to be able to travel home unseen.

Bellacrux and Lysander turned to face the oncoming Flight Vengeance.

38

Battle beneath the Stars

Bellacrux had fought many battles in her long life and she had won each and every one. In her youth she had been known by the name Carli had called her: Death Dragon. Although she was now old, Bellacrux was still a force to be reckoned with, and her knowledge of battle strategy was unsurpassed. But Bellacrux knew she was dangerously outnumbered, and while she did not doubt Lysander's courage, he was only a few weeks old—just a baby, in fact. Through narrowed eyes, Bellacrux sized up the oncoming Raptors. She noted they were placing themselves well, and already had the advantage of height. From the speed they were approaching, Bellacrux realized that she did not have the time to take this advantage from them. Quickly, she told Allie to instruct Joss and Lysander to stay close and follow her every move.

Before they knew it, the Raptors were above them: ominous winged shapes dark against the bright sky, moonlight catching their white bellies. And staring down was a forest of evil little red eyes: firestix.

With a quick downward thrust of her powerful wings, Bellacrux embarked upon a flanking movement that took them rapidly out from under Flight Vengeance. She headed upward fast, zigzagging to avoid a barrage of oncoming red streaks as Kaan, in a frenzy, emptied his firestik holster, hurling one after another at them. Shielded by Bellacrux's wide and powerful neck and her huge wings above, Allie glanced back to check that Joss and Lysander were following: The silver glint of Lysander's wings told her all she needed to know and, her heart pounding, she turned around to face their enemies.

Bellacrux had decided to pick off the two outriders at the rear of the Flight: D'Mara on Krane and Mirra on Trixtan. She knew that these were the two weakest links: Krane because he was exhausted, and Trixtan because Mirra was easily flustered. As they drew near and Allie heard the wingbeats and snorts of the Raptors, a tremor of terror shot through her. This was for real now. For a heart-stopping moment her sweaty palms lost their grip and she slipped to one side. *Stay calm*, Allie told herself sternly as she pulled herself up straight again. *Bellacrux knows what she's doing.*

Deciding to pick Trixtan off first, Bellacrux began advancing under the cover of defensive fire—a diffuse stream of fire from the mouth rather than the nostrils, which was designed to provide cover. Mirra panicked and let loose a volley of firestix. "Not the Silver!" D'Mara yelled, too late. Bellacrux took evasive action; she folded her wings back into the plunge position and dropped like a stone, closely followed by Lysander. As they fell through the air, Allie felt the whoosh of a firestik just above her head, as it shot through the gap between Bellacrux's neck and wings. Allie's heart raced. That was close—*way* too close.

A shout from D'Mara followed them down. "Traitor Bellacrux! Give yourself up! Give yourself up and we will let the Silver and the Green go free! Fight us and we will kill you all!"

This time not even Joss believed her.

Tell Joss we don't give up, Bellacrux sent to Allie.

He knows, Allie sent back.

Now the battle began in earnest. Wave after wave of firestix rained down from Flight Vengeance. Bellacrux and Lysander ducked and dived, all the while circling upward, seeking to regain their lost height.

And then a firestik found its mark—on Lysander's left wing tip. Lysander pitched to one side and sent the weapon bouncing off his armored silver scales. The sudden lurch sent Joss sliding out from the rider's dip. Just in time, Joss grabbed hold of the lowest neck crest and hung on, his legs dangling free. *Lysander, help*, Joss sent as he watched the firestik plunging down toward the trees far, far below, terrified that in a moment he would be following it.

Lysander hovered, hoping that Joss would be able to pull himself back up. But as Joss struggled to find a purchase on Lysander's slippery scales, another firestik came zinging down. *Hold tight, Joss!* Lysander sent. He tipped over to one side, allowing the firestik to pass and Joss to tumble back into his seat.

Far above. D'Mara screamed, "I said, *leave the Silver*! It's mine! Kill the Grand. *Kill the Grand!*" Her patience at an end, D'Mara peeled Krane away from Flight Vengeance and came swooping down toward Lysander. Joss saw Krane's sharpened nose tip glinting like a dagger in the moonlight, and his stomach lurched with fear. He felt Lysander's muscles tighten, gearing up for the fight ahead, and Joss took a deep breath to steady himself. *We can do this*, he told himself. *We can do it!*

With D'Mara and Krane now on a level with them, the volley of firestix above stopped. Joss watched Krane approaching with a peculiar sideways flight, like a crab, which puzzled him, until he realized that it was probably designed for a rapid getaway. This heartened Joss: Clearly D'Mara was not as confident as she appeared, and the reason for that must be Krane. A sudden wobble in Krane's flight convinced Joss he was right—now he began to understand that a battle wasn't only about force, it was also about observation and tactics. *Krane is weak*, he sent to Lysander. *All we have to do is tire him out.*

Fun! Lysander sent back. *Let's mess him around!*

Taking Krane completely by surprise, Lysander flew rapidly—and very cheekily—past his nose spike and at once plunged into a dive. This time, Joss was ready. Gripping tightly with his knees, he stayed firmly in the rider's dip even when, in a daringly taunting move, Lysander twisted sharply back on himself and then flew directly over the oncoming Krane, buzzing the top of the Raptor's wings. And as they flew, twisting and turning, Joss realized he could not stop smiling—he and Lysander were flying as one. Lysander's wings were his wings, Lysander's scales were his own skin, and he saw only through Lysander's deep green dragon eyes. He, Joss Moran, was dragon. Pure silver dragon.

A shout from D'Mara brought Joss out of his dragon trance. "Joshua Lennix! You are dead, you traitor. *Dead!*"

As they flew rapidly up and away, Joss turned and yelled at D'Mara, "Yeah! Joshua Lennix is dead! And Joss Moran is alive!" Joss and Lysander flew rapidly upward, zigzagging as they went like a flash of silver lightning and sending the weary Krane into confusion. As they ascended, Krane dropped farther behind until the last vestiges of strength left his wings and D'Mara was forced to admit that her personal fight for the Silver was over. Trying to hide her despair, she whispered to her Lock, "Krane, my love, you can do no more. Glide down to the forest while you still can and we will rest."

Krane was too exhausted to reply. Desolate with the knowledge that he had failed the only creature he had ever loved, he spread his wings into a broad canopy and began a slow, miserable descent. As they went, D'Mara looked up at the tiny flash of silver climbing astonishingly high up into the night sky, and her eyes filled with tears of frustration. Would she never get her Silver?

Joss watched Krane drop slowly away toward the trees and laughed. *One down, five to go*, he sent to Lysander.

Five pieces of trouble, Lysander sent back soberly. *Big trouble. Look up, Joss.*

Joss looked up, and his heart sank. There, some fifty feet above them, were the five remaining Raptors. And right in the middle of them were Allie and Bellacrux—trapped. One Raptor—a Yellow, which Joss knew must be Declan—flew above, one—a long, sinuous Red—flew below, and three more: Decimus, a Green, and a small, agile Blue circled in tight formation. It was a highly effective maneuver perfected by Edward, and he called it "the Noose."

What can we do? Lysander sent to Joss.

Watch and wait, Joss sent. *When we see a gap, we move up fast.*

Trapped in the center of the Noose, Bellacrux was furious with herself for getting caught. She knew all about Edward's famous Noose and yet she had flown straight into it. She had tried to break out, but whichever way she went, her escape was cut off by a burst of fire or a well-judged firestik. She had sent out three long and powerful firebursts, which had temporarily loosened the Noose, but now it was closing in once more, and with every second that passed Bellacrux had less flying room. She knew it would not be long before she found her wingbeat halted by Raptor fire or a well-placed talon and her flight stalled in midair. And then they would mortally wound her and watch as she and Allie fell helplessly to the ground. That, she knew, was the part Edward looked forward to: "the Long Drop," as he called it.

Allie was clutching Bellacrux's neck crest so tight that her knuckles were white. She was terrified; it was horribly clear that the Lennixes were closing in for the kill. She watched as Edward and Decimus swooped tauntingly past, edging dangerously close to Bellacrux's right wing. She felt the hot breath of Decimus as he flew by and saw the cruel smile on Edward's face. She knew Edward was savoring every moment of her terror and she hated him for it.

Little Lock, the fight's not lost until it's lost, Bellacrux sent to Allie. But Allie had a horrible feeling that the fight was indeed lost. They were trapped with nowhere to go but down in flames.

Keep watching, Bellacrux sent. *Watch their every movement. We wait for our chance. Then we take it.* Allie ducked as Trixtan came winging past, Mirra screaming insults as she went. Behind them came a small, fast Blue with Tamra's taunts already blending with Mirra's.

But Bellacrux was looking up. Above them she watched the white belly of a yellow Raptor and saw it, slowly but surely, moving upward until there was just enough space for her to get through. Allie felt her Lock take a deep firebreath and, then, suddenly blazing out a wide spume of defensive flames, they were soaring up so fast that they sent Mirra and Trixtan tumbling backward in their downdraft. Up, up Bellacrux went, winging past Declan and Timoleon, who to Allie's amazement, did nothing. Timoleon just beat time with his wings, holding his place to one side of the Noose, while Declan watched them go. It was, Allie was sure, deliberate. Bellacrux, however, was taking no chances. She continued her rapid ascent, lashing her tail back and forth to keep any pursuers at bay. Far below Allie heard Edward Lennix's roar of fury, but above she saw to her joy an empty sky, with just the full moon and a bright sprinkling of stars. There was not a Raptor belly in sight.

It was now that Valkea saw her chance. Ignoring Edward's angry shouts—he wanted to regroup the Noose and set off in pursuit—Valkea broke ranks and shot up past Declan and Timoleon in a rapid ascent, heading after Bellacrux and Allie. As she drew near to the thrashing tail, Valkea let loose a long, focused spume of fire. It caught the tip of Bellacrux's tail but did little damage, for the tail-thrash doused the flames and the burn alerted Bellacrux to her pursuer. At once, she wheeled around to face her attacker, and when she saw it was Valkea, Bellacrux opened her wings to their fullest expanse and reared up so that Allie was thrown backward against the old Green's bony shoulders. And then Bellacrux let out a tremendous roar of rage that echoed down to the Raptors below and sent goose bumps running down Edward's spine. He had forgotten how terrifying their Grand in her fury could be. Valkea, however, appeared unimpressed.

Bellacrux loathed Valkea. Delighting in her chance to show the Red exactly what she thought of her, Bellacrux sent a long, thin stream of brilliant orange flame straight into Valkea's face. The Red wheeled backward and the flames shot down the soft and vulnerable front of her neck, sending Kaan shrieking in terror as they flickered over the top of his head and scorched his hair. Valkea screamed in pain. She launched herself into a rapid spiraling dive, a classic movement designed to extinguish flames, which it did, but not before a long line of scales had been shriveled to a crisp by the blast. As Valkea leveled out, Kaan began sobbing with fear. "Let's go home now. Oh, please, please, let's go home . . ."

Valkea paid Kaan no attention. In agony from the burn, she thrashed her neck to and fro, trying to cool the burn, while Kaan subsided into soft mewing moans. Edward and Decimus shot by, heading up to Bellacrux. *Kill her*, Valkea thought. *Kill her and I will be your Grand.*

Far above, Bellacrux watched the oncoming Decimus with relish. Her talons had been itching to fight that arrogant bully for years. Her nostrils twitched and her fire stomach growled—she was ready for him. Allie wished she could share Bellacrux's battle-fury but right then all she felt was scared, and the sight of Decimus roaring upward, his scaly lips drawn back in a battle snarl, terrified her. But Allie was not going to let her Lock down. She squared her shoulders, took a deep breath, and focused all her attention on Bellacrux. Whatever her Lock needed from her, she would have. They would fight as a team, together.

Decimus had now reached their height and was, to Allie's relief, circling at a distance, his great red wings lazily moving up and down as if he was in no hurry to make a move. In between wingbeats, Allie could see Edward Lennix in the riders' dip, resplendent in his leather riding suit with his red silk sash streaming out in the night air like a torrent of blood, and she knew he and Decimus were planning how to kill her and Bellacrux.

Her mouth was dry, her hands clammy. She wished she were braver. And then, from Bellacrux came a message: *But you are brave, my little Lock, and steady too. Remember, brave and steady wins the fight.*

And now it began. Bellacrux started circling, mirroring Decimus's every move. She matched the rhythm of his wingbeats, their style and pace, lulling him into a false sense of security. Allie felt Bellacrux draw in a firebreath, she felt her Lock's muscles tense, and suddenly, Bellacrux shot forward, taking Decimus completely by surprise. A great burst of fire came streaming from Bellacrux's nostrils, and she hurtled past, sending the flames curling over Decimus's left wing. It did little damage—it was the insult that hurt. A combined roar of fury came from Decimus and Edward, and as the Raptor wheeled around and began to draw in his own firebreath, Allie heard Edward yelling, "Go for the eyes, go for the eyes! *Kill, kill, kill!*"

Decimus needed no telling. Gulping air down to his fire stomach as he went, he set himself on course for Bellacrux, honing in on her head. Coolly, Bellacrux hovered while she too took a firebreath, but hers was long, slow, and deep, designed to create a huge reservoir of fire. With her fire brewing, Bellacrux bided her time, waiting for her moment. She knew enough of Lennix strategy to know what would come next, and she was ready for it.

Decimus came roaring in, a brief, bright firestream blazing. Bellacrux did not falter. As the Raptor's firestream died, Decimus did what she expected: He reared up, then with his back legs and talons, he flew above her, raking down at her eyes. Bellacrux now began her fireburst. It hit Decimus on his belly, but he paid no attention—he had a job to do and Raptors were trained to withstand the initial bursts of fire. But Bellacrux's fire just kept on coming and soon Allie smelled the acrid stink of burning dragon flesh. Fire still streaming, Bellcrux dropped down, took a sharp turn, and came quickly up beneath Decimus's belly, and in a classic move, she rammed into it with her snout. Hard. The force of the collision hitting the burned flesh paralyzed Decimus's diaphragm and sent him reeling away, gasping desperately for breath he could not catch.

As his Lock fell, making horrendous rasping noises, Edward sent his last firestik winging across to Bellacrux. It grazed the furthest tip of her right wing and stuck there, swinging like a long, red-tipped needle. Allie watched in horror as Bellacrux's most distal wing finger began to smoulder. *Pull it out, little Lock. Pull it out*, came Bellacrux's surprisingly calm request. Tipping over to the left to maintain her balance, Bellacrux carefully drew her wing in close to her body. The firestik hung from its red tip and Allie could see tiny flames flickering around the wound it had made, and she knew that at any moment the whole wing could ignite. Balancing precariously, Allie stood up in the riders' dip and reached up for the firestik that dangled tantalizingly just above her head, just out of reach. She tried again, stretching as high as she could; the tips of her fingers grazed the end of the firestik but she could not shift it. Allie could feel the pain in Bellacrux's next send: *Pull it out, little Lock. Pull it out. Quickly.* And so Allie jumped. Her feet lost all contact with her Lock and for a terrifying few seconds, she was alone in the air, hundreds of feet above the ground. Allie grabbed the firestik, threw it as far away as she could, and slammed back into the riders' dip. She felt a great sigh of relief come from her Lock and the message: *Just in time, my brave little Lock, just in time.* Allie could not reply. She sat, shaking, and watched the firestik overtake Decimus and Edward and go tumbling toward the forest far below.

Decimus was falling fast. As he dropped past Declan and Timoleon, Edward yelled, "Declan! Get up there. Get that traitor. Firestix, boy, firestix!"

Declan looked up at their old Grand silhouetted against the moon, gently fanning her outstretched wings. She looked magnificent. And there, perched in the rider's dip, almost hidden so that all he could see were the soles of her boots, was the kid who had been brave enough to Lock with the Lennix Grand and get away with it—unlike the last one. Declan thought of all the killing and misery he had seen, how he had grown to hate it, and he suddenly knew he did not want to be part of it for a moment longer. If Bellacrux, their wise old Grand who was someone he had always looked up to, had decided to leave, then why should he stay? His father's harsh voice interrupted his thoughts. "Do it, Declan! Do it now!"

Okay, Declan thought. *I will. I will do it. Now.*

Watched approvingly by his father, Declan flew Timoleon rapidly up toward Bellacrux and Allie. *Tim, I'm leaving,* he sent to his Lock. *I'm not being a Lennix a moment longer. Are you with me?*

With you always until the end, Timoleon sent in return.

Declan hugged his Lock. *Just you and me. We'll be free. Together.*

Declan was now drawing close to Bellacrux and he knew that Bellacrux would see him as the enemy. He must be careful. As he approached he saw Bellacrux open her mouth for another firebreath. "Don't fire!" he called out. "Please. I have something for you."

Bellacrux regarded Declan with wise eyes. She knew he was the best of the Lennix bunch—although that was not saying much—and even though he had a firestik in his hand, she decided to trust him. Warily, she watched Declan bring Timoleon alongside.

"Harlarla te faa," Declan said in dragonsong: *I wish you well.*

Bellacrux nodded, accepting the greeting. She watched Declan lean out and push his firestik holster into Allie's hands. "Take it," he said. "Do what you have to. I'm out of here. Tell Joss good luck from me. Maybe we'll meet again one day." And with that Timoleon wheeled away, and in a moment Declan was heading away from the flight, away from his family, and flying toward the rest of his life.

Far below, as his injured Lock fought for every breath, Edward stared up at Declan in disbelief. *What was the boy doing, handing over his weapon to the enemy and flying away like a coward? It was desertion, no less.* And then the realization hit Edward. Declan had indeed deserted, but not just the battle. It was worse than that: He had deserted his family. "Declan!" Edward screamed out. "Declan! Come back here right now!" But Declan did not even turn his head, and Edward knew his eldest son was lost to him. He hammered his fists in despair on Decimus's hard old neck and pushed back sobs of rage.

Suddenly, Tamra and Ramon appeared at his side. The young Blue was hovering eagerly; he looked fresh and full of energy in a way that made Edward feel old and exhausted. "What is it, Tamra?" Edward asked wearily.

"We'll get him, Pa," she shouted. "Me and Ramon. No one deserts my flight. No one!"

"Leave him, Tamra. He's dead to us now," Edward said. "Get up there and kill the traitor Grand. You're our only hope."

But Tamra's fury with Declan overrode everything. "This is my flight," she said. "And I decide what to do with it. I'm getting Declan." With that, Tamra and Ramon peeled away from Flight Vengeance, and Edward watched his favorite daughter head off on her own personal mission of vengeance. As he watched the lively Blue rapidly disappear into the night, Edward leaned forward and placed his arms around Decimus's neck. He could feel his Lock's muscles straining to pull air down to his aching lungs. "Take it easy, Decimus," he murmured. "Take your time. We've got plenty of it. We're not done yet."

39

A Kill

Tamra and Ramon flew fast in pursuit of Declan, and it did not take long before they were in firestik range. Declan, his mind still buzzing with the enormity of what he had done, was unaware of being followed. Ramon was a highly efficient flyer. He was not only fast but almost silent: No energy was wasted in telltale creaking of wings, or noisy breaths. As they drew closer, Tamra eyed up her unsuspecting target and with a grim smile she steadied her right arm, took aim, and threw. The firestik flew swiftly through the darkness, a red arc in the sky, and found its target.

Timoleon's tail exploded into flames.

Declan, shocked out of his thoughts, wheeled around and saw disaster facing him and his Lock. "Tim, Tim!" he shouted as the smell of burning dragon flesh filled his nose and Timoleon let out a great roar of agony.

Tamra screamed in horror. The moment the firestik left her hand she had regretted it. But it was too late, and now Declan's Lock was on fire, falling into his death dive, taking Declan with him.

"Declan, Declan, I didn't mean it!" Tamra yelled, and set Ramon diving down after her brother. Fast and fearless, Ramon dropped like a stone, and soon he was side by side with Timoleon, tumbling down with him, as the flames worked their way along the tail, consuming all in their path.

"Declan!" Tamra yelled. "We'll get underneath and you jump down. Got that?"

Declan shot Tamra a look of utter loathing. Any doubts he might have had about leaving his family were gone. His vile, murderous sister had killed his Lock, his dearest Tim, a gentle creature temperamentally unsuited to be a Raptor, the only creature in the world whom Declan had been able to truly love. His eyes blurred with tears, Declan glanced back and saw that Timoleon's wings were on fire. He looked up into the dragon's eyes and saw they were clouded and dull. His own true Tim was gone.

"Jump, Declan! Jump!" came Tamra's shout from below.

"Farrelara me soll, sa nar Mifra a te," Declan murmured: *Farewell, my soul friend; may the spirit of the air be with you always.* And then he swung himself out of the rider's dip, and as Tamra and Ramon glided beneath him, Declan looked down at the canopy of trees hundreds of feet below, gulped at the thought of the dizzying drop, and let himself fall.

Declan landed on Ramon's shoulders, just in front of his wings. He slithered down into the rider's dip just behind Tamra, and with tears streaming, he watched the ball of flames that had once been his Lock spiraling slowly down toward the darkness of the Forest. Then he leaned forward and spoke to Tamra with cold fury. "You fly away from here. Right now. You're killing no one else tonight, Tamra. And if you try, I'll kill you first. I swear it. Understand?"

The hatred in her brother's voice sent cold shivers through Tamra. "Yes," she whispered. "Yes, I understand." Slowly, reluctantly, Tamra flew Ramon away.

In the distance, Edward watched the departure of Tamra and Declan with disbelief. What was going on with his children? He'd given his daughter her first flight, allowed her to name it, and now she had shot down his eldest son in mid-battle and was taking him away. It was a double desertion of his two best children. Edward's opinion of his offspring was unclouded by any paternal sentimentality: He knew he was now left with the dross. But they would have to do. "Kaan, Mirra," he called out. "The family honor lies with you!"

Kaan pretended not to hear—he didn't like the sound of that at all. But Valkea heard well enough. And with the burn on her neck subsiding into a bearable pain, she began to make her plans.

40

The Last Throw

Herlenna had found it impossible to leave her friends. She had retired some distance away, and was hovering in the shadows of the treetops, watching the battle with fear in her heart. As the sky above lit up with firebursts and battle roars, Herlenna had done her best to send calming thoughts to Bellacrux and Lysander. It was not much, but it was all she could do. And now Herlenna was watching in horror as what had once been Timoleon was slowly falling through the sky, spiraling down in a ball of flame.

"Farrelara me soll, sa nar Mifra a te," she whispered as she forced herself to watch and bear witness to Timoleon's death dive. The death of any dragon, Raptor or no, was a great sadness to a sensitive Green like Herlenna.

A sudden scrabbling from the increasingly bored hatchling distracted Herlenna. She turned around to quiet it and as she fussed, trying to get it to lie back in the rider's dip, she felt a sudden fierce heat above. Herlenna shot out of the way, but she was a moment too late. The charred bones of Timoleon's tail caught in her torn wing, there was a snap like a pistol shot, and suddenly her wing was hanging down, useless. Herlenna screamed.

Far above, Lysander heard it. Without a second thought, he put his nose toward the ground, folded his wings back, and launched into a dive, hurtling to the rescue. "Lysander!" Joss yelled, clinging on to his Lock's neck. "What are you *doing*?"

With the rush of the wind in his ears, Joss caught just one word of Lysander's reply: *Herlenna*.

It felt to Joss that the plunge went on forever. The treetops seemed to be rushing upward to meet him, and he began to fear that Lysander was out of control. But just as the trees were so close that Joss was sure he could have counted each and every leaf, Lysander dropped his wings down, lifted his nose, and at last Joss felt the uplift of air beneath them. As he caught his breath in relief, there was a violent crashing of breaking branches and a burst of fire rose up from below. Timoleon had reached his final destination—a bed of ashes on the forest floor.

In the light of the fire, they now saw Herlenna, one wing hanging limp, coasting toward a small clearing in the forest. Lysander drew alongside her, offering support, but Herlenna's only thought was to keep the hatchling safe from the imminent crash landing.

"Praya. Picola tirra-te," Herlenna told Lysander in dragon-song. *I pray you, take the little one.*

"Yarilla lo," Lysander replied. *Of course I will.*

Using all her energy, Herlenna gave a sudden twist and dislodged the fidgety hatchling. It went flying through the air, squeaking in panic, its little stubby wings frantically flapping, slowing the creature down just enough for Lysander to grab it gently in his mouth. He turned his head to give the struggling infant to Joss, but as Joss reached out to grab the slippery little creature, it flipped its tail, leapt from his grasp, and shot up into the air. Lysander, forced to choose between helping Herlenna or the hatchling, chose the hatchling. He cruised in beneath it and waited. At the awesome sight of the sleek silver dragon below, the hatchling promptly forgot how to fly. It went into a sudden shrieking nosedive; Lysander caught it neatly in his right wing and rolled the wriggling creature down to Joss. Joss reached out, grabbed a leg and lost it, grabbed the other leg, and at last hauled the prickly, protesting infant onto his lap. Then he carefully folded in its wings and wrapped his arm around its sharp little claws.

With the hatchling finally safe, the last of Herlenna's strength suddenly left her. She keeled over to one side, and with a crashing and cracking of branches, she disappeared through the canopy of trees like a drowning swimmer beneath the waves. Lysander and Joss heard a deep thud, and then all was silent.

Lysander and Joss looked down at the great gash in the forest and saw to their horror that Herlenna had landed on Timoleon's pyre. The flames flared up and they heard the crackling as the fire took hold. A heavy feeling of sadness came over them both—two dragons were lost and gone forever. Joss hugged the hatchling tight and whispered, "We'll take care of you, little one." Slowly, Lysander flew away from the glow, heading back up to join Bellacrux, bearing bad news and a new life.

The remains of Flight Vengeance were flying slowly away, but Valkea hung back, reluctant to leave. The sight of the traitorous Grand serene in her victory was too much for the ambitious young Red to bear. She decided to take a last shot at Bellacrux.

As Lysander slowly ascended, Joss too was watching the magnificent silhouette of Bellacrux flying across the moon. He thought of his sister riding high with her Lock and he smiled. Against all the odds, they had defeated the Lennixes, and now they had a bright future ahead, with the prospect of freedom and safety in the legendary Lost Lands. And then he saw Valkea: flying like an arrow, sharp and straight, heading up toward Bellacrux, straight for her underbelly. And blissfully unaware, Bellacrux and Allie were flying serenely on.

"Allie! Watch out!" Joss yelled, his voice carrying up through the still night air. Allie looked down and saw Valkea almost immediately below. *Bellacrux*, she sent. *Go right.* Bellacrux wheeled away just in time and, outmaneuvered, Valkea went shooting up past them, and as she went past, Allie heard Kaan's screams. She watched Valkea halt some distance above and hover while she decided on her next move.

This time, Allie, thought, things were different. This time *she* was the one with the firepower. Allie was surprised to find she actually welcomed the chance to fight. She took a deep breath and prepared herself for battle. She took a firestik from Declan's holster—which she had slung over her back—and carefully took aim at the white underbelly above. But throwing a firestik was not as easy as it looked, and it traveled wide and then, to Allie's horror, began to drop back toward her and Bellacrux. Bellacrux was prepared. She wheeled quickly to one side and Allie watched the firestik arcing down toward the forest. A flash of silver below told her Lysander was on his way. Allie smiled. They would defeat Valkea together.

Stay steady, Allie, Bellacrux now sent. *Valkea will be diving any minute now. Wait until she's close. Don't take your eyes off her for a moment. I'll tell you when to throw.*

Okay, Allie sent, and began to extricate another firestik. A flash of silver at her side told her that Joss and Lysander had arrived. It was now that Valkea took her chance; she launched into a daring dive, heading straight down, presenting the smallest area of target. Had it not been for Kaan's screams, the dive would have been silent, so streamlined was Valkea. Determined not to miss a second time, Allie let go of her Lock's neck crest so that she could hold her firestik steady in two hands and waited for the word from Bellacrux.

But suddenly Bellacrux, seeing the trajectory Valkea was taking, wheeled to the right, catching Allie unawares. Allie slipped from the rider's dip, skidded down the rough scales of Bellacrux's flanks, frantically scrabbling to catch a hold, and then, heart-stoppingly, there was nothing left to grab but the thin night air. Allie gave a short, sharp shriek. And fell.

"Allie!" screamed Joss, his stomach in his throat. Lysander launched into his dive and, closely followed by a horrified Bellacrux, Lysander swooped beneath Allie. She landed on his tail with a bump and then found herself sliding rapidly backward on the slippery, shiny scales. At the end of the tail the barb stopped her, and while Allie hung on with all her strength Lysander lifted his tail and Allie slid slowly down toward his back. Joss longed to help her, but he was trapped in the rider's dip with the hatchling. He twisted around to see his sister gingerly crawling along the serrated ridges of Lysander's spine, slipping and sliding as she went.

Immediately above them now was Bellacrux, who was hovering, shielding them from Valkea with her open wings. However, Bellacrux was also presenting an easy target. At the very moment Allie dropped into the rider's dip behind Joss and the hatchling, Valkea came roaring in. But Bellacrux was ready. She sent a long stream of fire straight for Valkea's burned neck. Bellacrux knew that targeting an injury in this way was playing dirty, but she no longer cared. Bellacrux knew very well that Valkea would not hesitate to do the same. Roaring with rage at her own weakness and at being thwarted yet again, Valkea wheeled away and climbed to gain a little height, taking care to keep well out of firebreath range. And there she waited for the agonizing burning in her neck to become bearable once more.

With Valkea gone, the two remaining Lennix Raptors— Trixtan and Decimus—moved into position. Trixtan hovered uncertainly a safe distance above Bellacrux, waiting for Mirra to decide what to do. Mirra, however, had no idea *what* to do. She glanced up to her father for guidance. He was circling some distance above on Decimus, and all Mirra could see was Decimus's muscled white belly and the soles of her father's red boots.

Suddenly, Edward delivered the longed-for guidance. He leaned over and yelled down, "Get out of my way, idiot girl!" But the wind took his words away.

"What?" Mirra shouted back. "What did you say?"

Edward was exasperated. *Why didn't his stupid daughter move, for dragon's sake? What was she doing, sitting in the way of the target? Was she a total idiot?* Edward swore loudly but Mirra heard nothing. She was looking down at the small silver dragon below and had just noticed it had two kids and a hatchling on it. Laden and slow, it was a perfect target, but even so, Mirra was scared to go for it. What would her mother say if she injured the precious Silver? And so Mirra dithered, and far above her, Edward and Decimus seethed.

But there was no dithering for Allie. Deciding that Trixtan made the perfect target, Allie pulled two firestix from her holster.

She handed one to Joss—who took it with glee—and pointed upward at Trixtan's skinny white underbelly. And then together they took aim and threw upward at the target. To Allie's amazement, both firestix found their mark. One hit the trident tattoo full on and bounced off, but the other lodged between the segments, and at once flames began to pour from the fat beneath Trixtan's leathery skin. With a great bellow of pain, the Raptor shot upward, but seconds later, as the fire began to burrow deep into the dragon's belly, Trixtan came down again, falling past Lysander, flames streaming out behind him. As he plummeted by, Allie and Joss saw Mirra huddled in the riders' dip, her mouth open wide in a silent scream.

Far above, Edward Lennix sighed—his family was utterly useless. He was tempted to let Mirra reap the results of her stupidity but the thought of what D'Mara would say stopped him. Reluctantly he and Decimus went into a dive and hurtled down after Trixtan.

From the sidelines, Kaan watched the last two members of his family plummet toward the ground and became overwhelmed with great hiccuping sobs of self-pity. His hair was singed to a frazzle, and however much he screamed for Valkea to stop fighting, she took no notice. He was terrified of Bellacrux and even more terrified of Valkea. It was a total nightmare and he just wanted to *go home*. But Kaan knew that wasn't going to happen anytime soon. Valkea would do exactly what she wanted and he dreaded what it would be. He hung on to Valkea's spiky crest and shut his eyes tight. He felt Valkea tip forward, he felt her wings go back as, with an earsplitting screech, she launched into a vertiginous dive. Where she was going, Kaan had no idea. He didn't care and he didn't want to know.

Valkea was going after Lysander.

Bellacrux saw at once what Valkea was doing. She too dropped into a dive, heading after Valkea as she flew like an arrow of doom towards Lysander and Bellacrux's precious Lock. But Valkea was young and fast and Bellacrux was old and slow. As Valkea closed in on her target, Bellacrux knew she could not catch her, and the old Lennix Grand sent out a scream of warning to her Lock.

"Lysander!" Allie yelled. "Watch out!"

Lysander tried to flip out of the way, but with two riders and a hatchling he was slow. In a moment, Valkea was within firing distance; she let loose a burst of flame, aiming to torch his riders, but just in time Lysander put up his wings so they acted as a fire shield. The flames rolled off his wingtips like water from a duck, but Valkea was not discouraged. She saw how encumbered Lysander was, and she knew her quarry was no longer the quick-silver he had been. Now was her chance to get him.

Joss and Allie saw her coming in above them, back legs down, talons extended, ready to snatch them from Lysander's back and send them hurtling down to the forest below. They knew that Lysander was not going fast enough to escape. Lysander knew it too. He went rolling backwards away from the terrible talons, while Allie and Joss clung onto his neck and the hatchling dug its claws in.

Bellacrux was watching in horror when she saw a blindingly brilliant flash of silver light and then, suddenly, Lysander and his riders were gone. Bellacrux stared at the empty space in confusion for a moment and then she understood. A great roar of relief and triumph went echoing up into the night sky.

Far below, Bellacrux saw Valkea pull out from her dive, then stop and look up in confusion at the space where Lysander should have been. Bellacrux sent down a warning burst of fire and at that Kaan's shrieking began once more. The old Lennix Grand smiled to herself as she watched a despondent Valkea slowly head off after the defeated remnants of clan Lennix, her rider's piercing screams jangling her delicate ears.

As Valkea and Kaan flew away into the night, peace returned to the moonlit skies. Bellacrux hovered beside the empty space where her Lock had vanished. She would wait beside the Portal for her last and best Lock to return, and she would guard it with her life.

Somewhere in the space between two worlds, Lysander, Joss, Allie, and the hatchling plunged through the Portal's tunnel of light, twisting and turning at a terrifying speed. Allie thought she was in her death dive. "No!" she screamed out. "No. *Please, no!*"

41

Going Home

No . . . please, no, Sirin murmured to herself. *Please, this can't be true. It can't.* But Sirin knew that no amount of pleading could change anything. She had been ushered silently into Intensive Care and from then on she had felt as though she were in a dream—walking along the shiny floor, her shoes squeaking, dim red lights reflected in the glass, the weird hush and feeling scared because everyone was so very quiet. And then seeing Mum in the bed, with all the tubes gone, so still and pale, looking like she was asleep but she wasn't because *Mum wasn't there anymore.*

Sirin was outside the hospital with Mandy, waiting for their taxi, and it was two in the morning, much later than Mum would ever have allowed her to be out. Sirin stared up at the moon, checking that it was still there. It rode high in the sky, small and bright and perfectly round. The moon was still there but Mum was gone. How could that happen? Mum and the moon were forever, weren't they? Sirin began to shiver and Mandy put her own jacket around Sirin's shoulders.

"I wish that taxi would get a move on," Mandy muttered. "Just because we're south of the river don't mean we don't need taxis."

Sirin didn't want to get into a taxi. She didn't want to zoom away fast in the back of a car full of ads and videos and people talking. She wanted to walk slowly away from Mum and be with the moon. "Why don't we walk?" she said.

"Because it's not nice after midnight, sweetheart," Mandy told her. "There are gangs and stuff. Best get a taxi."

They waited for ten more long minutes and then Sirin said, "I don't want to be here anymore. Please let's walk."

Mandy sighed. She was cold without her coat: A brisk walk would do them both good, and it seemed to be a quiet night. "Okeydokey," she said. "We'll put our best foot forward, shall we?"

They set off along the wide road that took them away from the hospital. A few cars rushed past, and every time Mandy turned to see if it was a taxi, but it wasn't. They took the turn down a street of terraced houses, their windows dark as their inhabitants, each cocooned in their safe little world, sleeping the night away. All the time Sirin stared up at the moon, while she clutched the dragonstone for comfort. It felt warm and soothing and it made her feel as though somehow Mum had left the hospital with her and they were walking together toward the moon.

At the end of the street, Sirin and Mandy had to go down an alleyway between two lines of garages; this was the part that Mandy did not like. She hurried along between the garages, not noticing that Sirin, glad to be free of Mandy's well-meaning bustle, was lagging behind. Suddenly the moon came out from behind a cloud and a shaft of brilliant moonlight slanted down. Sirin stopped. She took out the dragonstone and held it in her palm, watching it shimmer. "This is for you, Mum," she whispered. "Just for you."

Assuming Sirin was following, Mandy was hurrying ahead. She had just reached the open space beyond the garages where a cluster of trash cans were gathered, when a sudden shout of "No!" made her turn around, and Mandy saw to her horror that Sirin was way back at the end of the alley surrounded by three hooded figures. In the moonlight Mandy saw the flash of a blade. "Sirin!" she yelled, but as she raced back down the alley, another hooded figure stepped out of the shadows and barred her way. "Leave it, missus," the girl said.

Mandy looked down and saw the point of a jagged knife pressing into her all too thin cardigan. Mandy's voice came out in a high-pitched squeak. "But we're coming back from the hospital, and . . ."

"Shut it," snapped the girl. "The kid's on our patch. She ain't in our gang so she's paying her toll, right?"

"Troll?" asked Mandy, too scared to make sense of anything.

"Don't get funny with me, you old bag," the girl said. Mandy bristled—she considered that she was far too young to be called an old bag—but the pressure of the knifepoint reminded her to keep quiet. Instead, Mandy kept her eyes steadily on Sirin and prayed she would give the gang whatever they wanted.

Sirin, however, would not. They wanted the dragonstone and they weren't getting it. She shoved it back into her pocket but it didn't stay there for long. One girl put her arm around her neck, half choking her; the other pulled Sirin's arms behind her back while the third shoved her hand deep into Sirin's pocket. Sirin felt the girl grab the stone and pull it out. "No!" Sirin yelled. "No, it's my mum's! Give it back!"

"Ooh, Mummy-wummy will be cross with 'oo, will she?" the girl mocked.

Close to tears, Sirin shook her head.

The girl let go of her armlock and pulled out a knife, drawing the tip of the blade across Sirin's stomach. "We know who you are, kid. You and your little friend owe us big-time. Any more fuss and you get this. Right?"

A movement in the sky caught Sirin's eye and she looked up. Above the garage roofs she saw . . . Sirin gasped. *No, it was not possible* . . . But it had to be possible, because there it was. Shining brighter than the moon, hovering above the garage roofs, wings outstretched, there was a *silver dragon*. As Sirin stared, eyes wide with amazement, the dragon's steady gaze met hers, its brilliant emerald eyes sparkling with green fire.

Time slowed for Sirin. Nothing seemed real anymore. *Mum was dead. There was a gang of girls with knives. And now, there was a silver dragon.* But amid the unreality Sirin was suddenly sure of one thing: that this was the most important moment of her life. A tremendous feeling of power ran through her. With a kick on her captor's shins, she wrenched herself free. She swung around and snatched back the dragonstone and then she was off, racing down the alleyway, hurtling past Mandy, running for her life and for her whole wonderful future: No one was going to mess her around anymore. She ran faster than she ever had and behind her came the gang in full cry, their blades out, glinting in the moonlight.

Lysander was hovering above the garages. He didn't know why he'd flown down to this place, but what he did know was that there was someone in trouble who needed him. *Hey, Joss, we should help her*, he sent.

Joss agreed. "They're as bad as Tamra and Mirra," he said, watching the gang hurtle after the girl, their knives flashing in the moonlight. "Come on, Lysander, let's get her out of there."

Lysander dropped down into a dark open space that smelled of rotting food. He settled lightly on the ground, balancing on the tips of his talons, ready to fly upward at a moment's notice. Seconds later the girl came racing out of the alleyway.

"Hey!" Allie yelled. "Over here."

Sirin needed no telling where to go. The silver dragon was all she could see, all she could think about. And as Sirin ran toward the dragon, she knew that somehow Mum had sent him to her. It was Mum's way of saying that she would be all right and that Mum was looking out for her, just as she had promised she would. And then Sirin was scrambling up the dragon's smooth silver scales, pulled upward by welcoming hands and squashing herself into a tiny space between two kids. Sirin saw the gang halt, open-mouthed, at the end of the alley. Sirin felt the power of the dragon's wings as they came down, and a moment later she was in the air, looking down at the gang and at Mandy. She watched them stare, dumbfounded as she flew away. *On a silver dragon.*

Far below, Mandy watched in a daze as her very first emergency placement rose up into the sky astride a dragon. Suddenly the realization came to her that her career as a foster parent was over before it had begun. Shocked into action, she hurtled out of the alley screaming, "Sirin! Get down off that thing at once. Get down!"

Mandy did not stand a chance. Helplessly, she stood and watched the dragon rise up, its wingbeats sending the old bags of chips and candy wrappers tumbleweeding across the tarmac. Dimly, Mandy became aware that the gang had joined her. One of them took hold of her arm as if they were suddenly best friends. "What is *that*?" the girl whispered, pointing up to the sky.

Mandy felt a wave of exasperation sweep over her. It had been a very trying evening and she had not a scrap of patience left. Irritably, she shook the girl's hand off her arm. "It's a silver dragon," she said. "*Obviously.*"

"Is it yours?" asked the girl, in awe of Mandy's coolness.

Mandy did not like to lie. but just this once she decided to make an exception. "Yes, it is," she said snappily, and in her agitated mind the dragon and the taxi-that-never-came merged into one. "I called it ages ago. I really don't know what's taken it so long."

"Bleedin' Nora," the girl said. "You're effing crazy, you are."

Silently they all watched the silver dragon rise slowly but steadily above the rooftops. They watched as the shimmering silver shape grew ever smaller until a cloud drifted across the moon and they could see it no more.

Another world away, there was someone else who was not having much luck with transportation either: Tamra. Tamra had just been dumped by Declan on a cold and windy hilltop just above the ancient stone circle and was watching her brother fly away with Ramon, to where she did not know, except that it would not be Fortress Lennix. Tears streamed down Tamra's face, but not because her brother was leaving her. The tears were because too late, Tamra had realized that she loved Ramon more than any-thing or anyone she ever had in her whole life. She wished with all her heart that she had Locked with him when she could have, instead of holding out for the powerful but cold Valkea. And now, as the beautiful speck of blue disappeared into the gray predawn sky, Tamra understood that love made you feel happier than power. She sat down on the dew-laden grass and one by one, she watched the stars disappear.

Sometime later, Tamra saw the rest of her family appear in the sky, flying slowly out of the darkness. She jumped up and waved and saw her mother's pale, cold face looking down at her. For a moment Tamra thought they were going to leave her to walk home, but suddenly she saw Valkea peel away from the formation and head toward her.

"Ma said to get you," Kaan told her. "Dunno why."

Tamra did not deign to reply. She climbed up behind Kaan and felt the power beneath her as Valkea lifted up into the sky. Valkea didn't make her feel happy like Ramon did, but power still felt good. As Tamra rejoined the bedraggled remains of her failed Flight Vengeance she saw that Trixtan was gone too, and her sister was sitting with her father, sobbing. Decimus didn't sound too good either—he had a revolting, rattling wheeze.

And so the dismal remains of Flight Vengeance limped home-ward. As they drew near the Black Mountains, Tamra made her move. She leaned forward and hissed in Kaan's ear. "Hey, Kaan. I've Locked you out."

"Huh?" said Kaan.

"Valkea's mine now. Just so you know."

Kaan turned around and stared at Tamra. "What do you mean?"

"I mean we've Locked. Me and Valkea."

"But you can't!" Kaan protested. "Valkea's *my* Lock."

Tamra laughed. "You never Locked with her, Kaan. You just pretended."

"That's not true!"

"It so *is* true. You're a fake, Kaan. You couldn't Lock with a cockroach if it ran up and bit you."

"I could too!"

"Yeah, well, maybe you could manage a cockroach. If the cockroach was desperate," Tamra conceded.

Kaan realized the cockroach argument was not one he wanted to win, and he said no more. He stared at the back of Valkea's powerful neck, the sharpened crests along its spine glistening a deep red in the moonlight, and he felt the immense power of the dragon beneath him as her body moved forward with each downward thrust of her massive wings, and Kaan realized that underneath the anger at his sister and the shame of losing his dragon, what he really felt was that a weight had been lifted from him.

And in another world, in another place, Sirin felt as if all Mum's dragon stories had come true. They were now so high above the city that all the sounds and lights had faded, to be replaced by the silence of the cold, damp cloud that enveloped them in stillness. Deep inside the cloud, with only the gently rhythmic *swish-oosh-swish-oosh* of the silver dragon's steadily beating wings, Sirin at last relaxed and allowed herself to stop thinking and just *be*.

The boy in front of her turned around and smiled. "Hi, I'm Joss!" he said.

"I'm Sirin," Sirin answered. Suddenly something sharp dug into her back and the girl behind her said, "I'm sorry, but it seems to want to sit with you. I'm Allie, by the way."

Sirin turned around and saw to her surprise that Allie had in her arms a tiny, wriggling green dragon. "Oh." Sirin broke into her first real smile for weeks. "Oh, it's so *cute*."

"And snappy," Allie told her. "Watch its teeth. They're sharp. And its claws." Allie passed the tiny creature to Sirin, who had to let go of Joss in order to take it. She clung on tighter with her knees and hoped for the best. "Oh, she's so lovely," Sirin said, as the dragon settled quietly onto her lap.

"We don't know if it's a boy or girl yet," Allie told her. "Or what its name might be."

"Sammi," Sirin murmured. "She says she's called Sammi." Sirin smiled. She had the strangest feeling that from now on, she and the tiny dragon were going to be together. Forever.

ABOUT THE AUTHOR

Angie Sage is the internationally bestselling author of the Magyk series starring Septimus Heap, which was translated into twenty-eight languages and sold more than five million copies worldwide. She lives in the United Kingdom.